PRAISE FOR BELLE NASH AND THE BATH SOUFFLÉ

'A real romp of a book – full of surprises!'
Alexander McCall Smith

*'Funny, clever, silly in the right way, and
strangely moving in its unexpected ending.
I love the alt-Regency Bath universe Keeling has built.'*

Jeanette Winterson

'A triumph!'
Michael Holman

*'By turns incisive, outlandish and hilarious! ...
There's a brilliance in The Gay Street Chronicles,
half-modern, half-Dickensian.'*
Matthew Parris

*'Bravo! A rollicking tale of corruption, intrigue and
romance. A racy read!'*
Peter Tatchell

'An unputdownable Regency frolic!'
Jane Ridley

WITH THANKS TO OUR SPONSORS

Alastair Wilson
Anthony McGarel-Groves
Henry Doubleday
Maggie Bawden
Michael Ross
Susan Thornton
Tamsin Webb-Sykes

ABOUT THE AUTHOR

William Keeling is a former foreign correspondent of the *Financial Times* who exposed a multi-billion-dollar corruption scandal in Nigeria that led to his summary deportation. He eventually left journalism for chocolate, becoming co-owner of the historic chocolate company Prestat, but is still plotting his return to the true home of jollof rice. Like his late uncle (referred to in this book), he has a creative mind. He lives and writes in Somerset. *Belle Nash and the Bath Soufflé* is the first in his series, *The Gay Street Chronicles*.

THE GAY STREET CHRONICLES

Belle Nash
and
the Bath Soufflé

William Keeling Esq.

1
BroadsheetBooks

Published 2022 in Great Britain by BroadsheetBooks
Part of EnvelopeBooks: www.envelopebooks.co.uk
A New Premises venture in association with Booklaunch

BroadsheetBooks
12 Wellfield Avenue
London N10 2EA

Cover design by Stephen Games | Booklaunch

A CIP catalogue record for this title is available from the
British Library

ISBN 9781915023025

Edited and designed by Booklaunch for BroadsheetBooks
BroadsheetBooks 1
www.broadsheetbooks.org
www.gaystreetchronicles.co.uk

Life is mostly froth and bubble,
Two things stand like stone.
Kindness in another's trouble,
Courage in your own.

Adam Lindsay Gordon
1833–1870

For my dear friend
Julian Richard

I'll protect you from the hooded claw,
Keep the vampires from your door ...

Frankie Goes To Hollywood
1984

FOREWORD

It was seven years ago that I received a letter from a solicitor informing me of my death. Like any sane person, I pinched myself, squealed in pain, then re-read the letter. It was not I who was dead but my uncle and namesake Dr W.B. Keeling, a relative of whom, to my shame, I had scant knowledge.

The solicitor explained that whilst my uncle had left most of his estate to charity, he had left an instruction to pass on to his closest living relative a Queen Anne silver toast rack and a small trunk of undisclosed contents. Now, with my own father deceased, I was that fortunate relative and the solicitor suggested that I therefore journey to Bath to collect my inheritance.

As an avid eater of toast but one who lacked a silver toast rack, I took up the invitation. I bid a temporary farewell to my Border Terriers and committed to a weekend trip down memory lane – albeit my uncle's memory lane – by visiting Bath.

His home – a townhouse in Gay Street – had evidently not seen a decorator's brush for half a century. Through the dust of ages, however, the family ties became clear. In a faded photograph on the grand piano, I recognised Uncle William standing next to my father as a young man. The family resemblance was striking.

In other pictures, Uncle William was seen in the company of a gentleman of his own age. There was a photograph of the two men wearing RAF uniforms and smoking cigarettes on a Second World War airstrip. In the decade after the war, they were pictured again holding hands in front of the Duomo in Florence and in a snowy scene on skis with Mont Blanc in the background. I was intrigued.

Alone in the house, I delved further into my uncle's world, opening wardrobes and finding the most wonderful tailored suits and bespoke shoes. In the dining room, the wine glasses were crystal, the cutlery silver with bone-handled knives. There I found the silver toast rack and, in the study, the trunk, the contents of which would change my life by opening my eyes to the lives of others.

The trunk enclosed a few personal effects, some of which established that Uncle William had been a history teacher at a boys' school in Bath. More importantly, there were numerous letters, diaries and records from the nineteenth century and a host of muddled manuscripts written by my uncle, reflecting his enthusiasm for Bath's rich history.

I departed Bath with the trunk and over the past few years have tested my dogs' patience with many an evening spent reconstructing my uncle's work. Much of his writing concerned a colourful character ignored by other historians, a man who once lived in a neighbouring house to that of my uncle: Mr Bellerophon Nash (1796–1864), commonly known as Belle.

According to my uncle's research, Belle Nash was a flamboyant public figure: in the year of the story that follows (1831) he was a city councillor and unashamed of his bachelor status. This was in an era when sexual relations between men were a criminal offence, although Belle Nash was afforded some protection through his family name. The famous Beau Nash, very probably his grandfather, was the Master of Ceremonies who had made Bath the social hub of England a century earlier.

My uncle's research uncovered Belle Nash's close friendship with Mrs Gaia Champion (1795–1873). In modern parlance, Gaia Champion was a feminist outlier and she and Belle Nash supported each other's determination to cut a swathe through the conventions of Bath society.

2

But my uncle did more than simply collect the records from the era. Instead, endowed with a creative mind, he sought to bring Belle Nash and his friends to life, for inside the trunk were hundreds of pages of typed manuscripts visualising their lives. At what point Uncle William wrote *The Gay Street Chronicles* is not certain. No attempt was made in his lifetime to publish them and, sadly, not all have survived. On a later visit to his house, I found more than a few pages lining a cat's litter-tray. Such was the nature of the man and of the teacher.

What remains I have tried to reconstruct and now publish. I am sure that you, fair reader, will find errors and false assumptions – huge ones. Rather than make corrections, I, a mere compiler of my uncle's efforts, have provided a few notes at the end of each chapter, confident in the knowledge that my uncle has not needed my help to resurrect an era long gone and revivify one of its most remarkable characters: Belle Nash, bachelor extraordinaire of Gay Street.

PART FROTH

CHAPTER I

A birthday party awaits

P ACKING AWAY A dead man's clothes is never a joyous task, the worse when the man concerned was the husband whom you loved. But a year had passed since Hercules Champion had died and his widow Gaia felt in her heart that the time had come to recognise the past tense and say goodbye if not to the memory of the man then to his garments.

The decision was made in the knowledge that this is what her husband Hercules — rationalist, lawyer and businessman — would have desired. Abiding by her late companion's will one last time was small comfort, though Gaia Champion too was unsentimental in nature. To delay the task would only have been to sustain unnaturally Hercules's presence in the house.

She did, however, feel anger at his death. Hercules and the happiness they had shared had been cruelly taken from her by cholera. The epidemic in England had been indiscriminate, felling rich and poor, saints and sinners, alike.

'The Church would have us believe that there is a benevolent God,' Gaia said to her young maid Mary as she passed over a shirt to be packed away. 'But in that case, either God is as indolent as the men He created or in full-blown retreat from the Devil below.'

The maid was an uncomplicated girl, better suited to lighter topics.

'Are you saying that there is no God?' asked Mary in a troubled voice. She had been taught by her parents never to question the ways of the Almighty, let alone His existence.

'That's not what I'm suggesting,' replied Gaia, who realised the concept of atheism might be a step too far for Mary. 'I simply wish that He wasn't male. A female God would never have allowed cholera to take hold and would know how to put the Devil in his place.'

Mary gave the notion some thought. She knew Gaia held forthright opinions, in particular that women were disadvantaged by men in the affairs of the home and of the State. Of the Divine, too, it now appeared.

'She'd have to lose that beard, though, wouldn't She?' the maid said.

'She most certainly would. We can't have a female God looking as if She'd been away at sea for seven years.'

Mary was always shocked by Gaia's willingness to challenge convention but never surprised. After Hercules Champion's death, it had been anticipated that the size of the household would be reduced, with a smaller, more modest abode better suiting a widowed status.

Gaia, however, adored the grandeur and elegance of Somerset Place, which ranked among Bath's finest crescents, and the house deserved a full complement of staff. Thankfully, maintaining one was well within her income.

Moreover, she enjoyed the company of Mary, and John Pritchard, her butler, as well as Mme Galette, the cook – and it was not her style to discard her loyal staff on the flimsy grounds of social expectation.

Returning to the chest of drawers, Gaia lifted out the last of the shirts, white cotton but with a dark red stain across its chest. At first, she wondered why Hercules had kept it, then recalled the occasion of their tenth wedding anniversary and the party they had thrown at the Assembly Rooms. Wine had been drunk and not a little spilt. It had been a memorable event for the best of reasons.

8

As, she hoped, the evening ahead – a birthday dinner she was holding for her closest friend – would prove to be.

'Oh, Hercules, I miss you so,' she said, momentarily hugging the shirt to her bosom. Raising it further to her face, she breathed deeply, identifying the smell of his cologne.

MEANWHILE, BELLEROPHON 'BELLE' Nash, the grandson of Bath's most famous Master of Ceremonies, Beau Nash, was busy tying his cravat in his bedchamber. His home, a townhouse on Gay Street by the corner of Queen Square, had an elevated elegance that matched the man. His task of dressing for the party, however, had been complicated by his companion, Gerhardt Kant, monopolising the bedchamber's full-length mirror.

'Do you *für mich* love have?' said Gerhardt, staring at his beauty and untroubled by the unbeauty of his words.

The nephew of the late Prussian philosopher Immanuel Kant of Königsberg had hit upon the question that for millennia has troubled humans more than any other, although not one that bothered his new 'cousin' just at that moment.

'I wish you'd finish with the mirror, Gerhardt.'

Tying a cravat blind was nigh-on impossible and Belle cared about such things. On any ordinary day he would have taken pride in dressing well; for Gaia Champion to hold a party in his honour deserved special attention.

'I asked, if you for me love have, *oder* ... ?' repeated Gerhardt in what would have been perfectly fluent German had he not been at pains to translate his question into perfectly clumsy English. He gazed at himself dreamily in the mirror, before being distracted by his genetic predisposition to philosophical speculation. 'I see in the *Spiegel* a *Spiegelbild* but how know I it me is? *Heiaha*! So funny.'

Gerhardt's ramblings broke the near silence of a still evening.

From the bedchamber window, there was a majestic view of the city looking eastwards to the River Avon.

'You and your *Spiegel*, Gerhardt: you are a flibbertigibbet,' Belle protested. 'Like young Narcissus, your reflection is your truest love. I shall have to start this knot again.'

Gerhardt did not care. Overwhelmed by his own image, he reached down to caress his hips and marvel at his yellow knee-breeches made of knitted silk.

'Look at *meinen* body. Is it not a beautiful body, *hein*? But what is beauty, *ja*?'

It had been eight months since Belle had travelled to Berlin to add to his prized collection of *Königliche* porcelain. He had, instead, returned with a 'second cousin once removed' ten years his younger, whom he had met in the gardens of the late King Frederick the Great's Sanssouci Palace.

At the time, Belle thought their meeting serendipitous, as there was a symmetry to their lives. King Frederick, though married, had been a bachelor at heart. He had liked parties and there had been no greater party organiser than Belle's ancestor Beau, whose services had been sought in Potsdam. And when not frolicking among the topiary, the monarch had had an intellectual bent and been a patron of Immanuel Kant's.

Belle and Gerhardt had met on the terraces of the palace, walking on opposite sides of one of the long lines of trellised vines. Looking through the vine leaves, Belle had glimpsed a man of delicate features and elfin charm in effusive conversation with himself, and had pushed aside a trailing vine, heavy with over-ripe fruit, to make his acquaintance.

'My,' he had said, 'what a lovely bunch of grapes.'

'*Na ja*,' Gerhardt had replied, reaching out to fondle the fruit. 'You are right. Juicy *und* purple. *Und* they do not suffer as man-kind suffers. I could these grapes some jealousy feel – but they are not as lovely as I. Correct? "As lovely as I", not "as lovely as me"?'

'Both,' Belle had said and, sensing a mutual self-interest, they had explored the garden's greenhouses together where oranges, melons, peaches and bananas grew in thick abundance. An hour in each other's company had turned into days, days to weeks and weeks to seasons as Gerhardt returned with Belle to England.

It was fair to say, however, that their relationship was not entirely tranquil. While Belle largely enjoyed the younger man's company, it had been awkward explaining to others how he shared a relative with Immanuel Kant.

Living with Gerhardt also introduced him to an unwelcome new constant.

'Belle, you love me, *nicht wahr?*' Gerhardt asked again, viewing himself at different angles in the mirror, his eyes sparkling with obsessive energy.

Belle sighed.

'Gerhardt, you beautiful creature, you're becoming a bore. I have to put up with the company of city councillors all day, not to mention the vile beast in the magistrate's court. Guildhall is ghastly enough; please don't add to my woes at home.'

'So, you love me not. *Keine Liebe.* I knew this.'

Belle's second attempt at tying the cravat was nearing completion.

'I said nothing of the sort, and I won't pander to your nonsense. We have a party to attend, and Gaia will not want us to be late.'

'So *interessant* a name: Gaia. Such a name have I hitherto heard not.'

'Her parents clearly had ambitions for her. As did mine for me; it is no small burden being named after the slayer of the Chimera. No matter. We all have to live with the consequences of our parents' whims. Now hurry up and put on your wig.'

Gerhardt, however, as was his wont, continued to gaze at himself.

11

Gaia handed her husband's wine-stained shirt to Mary, who placed it alongside the others in a battered trunk that had been pulled down from the attic. The two women had been clearing the room for three hours and the task was complete.

'My husband did like a drink,' commented Gaia.

'He did, Ma'am. That was always the way with our Mr Champion.'

As she closed the chest of drawers, Gaia turned to peer at the stained shirt one last time.

'I wanted to turn that shirt into rags, but he wouldn't hand it over. And this is where he hid it,' she reminisced. 'Oh well, one shouldn't become maudlin about a stained shirt. A pauper will be grateful for it.'

'Are you sure, Ma'am?' asked the maid, uncertain whether to shut the lid of the trunk.

Gaia was firm. Love, loyalty and friendship she embraced but she abhorred sentimentality.

'It's hardly the Shroud of Turin, Mary. I'd rather it clothe an unfortunate in the workhouse than have it feed the moths here. When you're done, call one of the footmen to take the trunk away. Then go to the bedchamber and lay out my clothes for dinner.'

Mary nodded, but with some reluctance. She did not always agree with her mistress. If it had been *her* husband who had died, Mary would have kept the shirt for eternity, along with a lock of his hair. And while the maid had great respect for Gaia, she would certainly have waited the customary two years of mourning before touching his garments.

'Are you thinking of any particular dress, Ma'am? The black silk ... ?'

Gaia raised her hand. She had something else in mind.

'No, Mary. I have decided that the period of mourning for Mr Champion is over. It may have been just twelve months, but I care not for the strictures of *Cassell's* and nor would he. He would have wanted laughter in the house, not tears. Unless I marry and am widowed again, never more will I suffer crêpe against my skin. Dinner tonight is in honour of my dear friend Councillor Nash. It is the occasion of his thirty-fifth birthday, so something with gaiety and colour will be in order.'

As ever, Mary was shocked by her mistress's flouting of social rules but also delighted. A broad smile broke across her face. She, too, had tired of black and grey and longed for her mistress to return to the colourful end of the wardrobe.

'A party, Ma'am?' declared Mary. 'With Councillor Nash?! I had heard rumours but had not believed it!'

Gaia raised a hand again.

'Not a party as such, but an evening for celebration. Councillor Nash has been working all hours in Guildhall preparing for the forthcoming visit of Princess Victoria, who will open our city's new park. He needs an evening of light relief from his fellow councillors, so let us choose a dress with a touch of spring in it to match the season. But not too colourful. I have no wish to compete with Councillor Nash for flamboyance, let alone with Herr Kant.'

Mary's mind was already working through the options. She knew Councillor Nash liked to dress up and that his Prussian relative had a reputation for sartorial excess. It would be a challenge to find Gaia an outfit that was colourful but sober. Not insurmountable, however, such was the extent of her mistress's wardrobe.

'What about jewellery, Ma'am?' she asked.

Gaia hesitated. Out of practice for a year, she had forgotten how complicated getting dressed for a party could be.

'Let me think. Lady Passmore of Tewkesbury Manor is among the guests and I would not wish to compete with her pink diamonds. I suggest we stick to pearls this evening.'

With her spirits raised, Mary patted down the shirts into their new resting place and closed the lid of the trunk. The thought of once again having Gaia's full wardrobe available filled her with excitement and she quietly blessed her mistress for forgoing a second year of mourning.

'I hope you don't mind my enquiring, Ma'am, but who else is attending the dinner?' Mary asked.

Until Hercules Champion's death, the house at Somerset Place had been renowned for dinner parties that routinely seated twenty guests. Gaia had enjoyed playing host and her skill had benefited her husband's interests as a lawyer. Tonight, however, would be less lavish.

'It will be a modest affair,' explained Gaia. 'Mrs Pomeroy of Lansdown Hill and Miss Prim of Gay Street are the other guests, so there will be six of us. Mme Galette is at work in the kitchen preparing Councillor Nash's favourite dishes: cheese soufflé followed by rib of beef. I believe she also plans a steamed sponge pudding for dessert.'

Mary's feet could not help but shuffle in excitement.

'A soufflé, Ma'am! I do so love a soufflé. There's always such a rush to get it upstairs to the dining room before it sinks and ...'

'Now Mary,' interjected Gaia, 'we seem to be finished here, so go to the bedchamber and lay out my clothes. Off you go.'

Mary did a little curtsy and hurried from the room, closing the door behind her, leaving Gaia standing alone.

W HILE TARDY ARRIVAL at a dinner party is undeniably impolite, it is more painful to those of higher social standing to arrive earlier than those below them in rank. Lady Passmore of Tewkesbury Manor considered herself to be of the most elevated order and while her magnificent chaise and four carriage always reached its destination well before the allotted hour, she then remained within it, studying from behind a curtain the arrival of the other guests. That way, she could choose the correct moment to make her entrance.

This evening, as ever, she was accompanied by Mrs Pomeroy, a friend of many years' standing. Both ladies were in their fifth decade, Lady Passmore a little taller and thinner, Mrs Pomeroy somewhat shorter and very much broader, thanks in no small measure to her partiality to slices of cake and to additional slices of cake. If the phrase 'a moment on the lips, a lifetime on the hips' had been coined with a person in mind, Mrs Pomeroy would have been that person.

There was once a time when Lady Passmore required Mrs Pomeroy to disembark and make a separate, earlier entrance, for Mrs Pomeroy was a plain Mrs while Lady Passmore of Tewkesbury Manor was Lady Passmore of Tewkesbury Manor. Mrs Pomeroy, however, had ten years earlier rebelled, pointing out the absurdity of pretending not to know of Her Ladyship's whereabouts while being fully aware that her friend was within earshot of the party. So it was that the two women could be found this evening in a carriage parked under a large oak tree in Somerset Place about thirty yards from Gaia's house at No. 24.

'You are far better placed than I am, Mrs Pomeroy,' said Lady Passmore, shuffling on the velvet seat and checking her hair. 'Do you see any motion from your window?'

'It seems very quiet, Lady Passmore of Tewkesbury Manor,' replied Mrs Pomeroy, reaching into her handbag for her lorgnette, an instrument more often used to amplify the size, though not the sound, of the latest and most fashionable tenors at Bath's musical gatherings. 'I see light in the drawing room, but no activity. Do we know how many guests are expected?'

Lady Passmore reached into her own handbag and opened a small notebook. She had done her research.

'I understand that this is a very small dinner party. Indeed, it seems cavalier to be having a dinner party at all, barely one year after Hercules Champion's passing, but we must stand by Mrs Champion regardless of her eccentricities.' Finding her page of notes, she confirmed, 'In addition to ourselves, there will be Councillor Nash and his peculiar cousin, of a decidedly distant nature: Herr Kant. And Miss Prim.'

'Miss Prim! How lovely. And I rather like Herr Kant,' countered Mrs Pomeroy, who kept the lorgnette trained on the front door. 'He has a fine mind.'

Lady Passmore was not in the habit of being contradicted.

'He may have, or he may not have. I have told you before, Mrs Pomeroy, to avoid the dangers of intelligent conversation.'

Mrs Pomeroy turned to protest but Lady Passmore stopped her.

'Keep looking, woman. Watch the front door. Has no one entered? We do not wish to be earlier than society demands.'

Mrs Pomeroy returned to her duties and saw in the late evening light the outline of two women rounding the corner by Lansdown Crescent.

'I believe Miss Prim is arriving, accompanied by another person of female appearance.'

'That's very early of her,' said Lady Passmore.

'Not as early as us,' thought Mrs Pomeroy.

'And impossible,' said Lady Passmore, checking her notes. 'Miss Prim should be alone.'

Mrs Pomeroy quickly provided clarification.

'The second person is her cook, Mrs Mulligatawny. She appears to be carrying Miss Prim's bag. How thoughtful.'

Lady Passmore chose to remain confused.

'Why would a cook carry a bag? If a bag is to be carried, her maid Millicent should be doing it.'

Mrs Pomeroy knew Miss Prim and her household well enough to hazard a guess.

'Millicent has a man friend and it's a large bag, so I suspect Miss Prim has brought her knitting. She rarely goes anywhere without her knitting.'

16

Lady Passmore was unimpressed.

'But to a dinner party? I shall have words with Miss Prim on the matter. Still, if that is her, we can be certain that Councillor Nash and Herr Kant have yet to arrive. No one is ever earlier to dinner than Miss Prim. Now all we need to do is wait for the men.'

Mrs Pomeroy's face fell. She had tired of her duties and was beginning to get a cricked neck.

'Or we could go in,' she ventured, in a display of bravado. 'I expect Mrs Champion has ordered up Champagne. She always does for a party.'

Lady Passmore was having none of it.

'Go in?! Go ahead if you insist on deserting me, Mrs Pomeroy, but I shall stay. I cannot make an entrance until all the guests have arrived. But tell no one I am here.'

Mrs Pomeroy was thrown into confusion. She had no desire to return to the dark days of pretence, but she disliked delay when all the fun was to be had indoors.

'It was merely a suggestion, Lady Passmore of Tewkesbury Manor. And there is no disgrace in entering before the guest of honour.'

What Mrs Pomeroy said was true. This evening's party undeniably belonged to Belle Nash, but Lady Passmore automatically considered herself to be the guest of honour at any event.

'You have taken leave of your senses,' she pronounced.

'But the party is for Councillor Nash!'

'Which I do not deny. What you have forgotten, however, is that Councillor Nash will be accompanied by Herr Kant and I, my dear, will not repeat the error of the Duke of Wellington by turning up before the Prussians.'

With that, the two ladies hunkered down for a further thirty minutes as the Champagne was readied for opening at 24 Somerset Place and Belle gave Gerhardt a last helping hand in Gay Street.

T HE WIG, GERHARDT.'

Gerhardt threw his hands in the air.

'*Mein Gott*, the wig. I have the wig to prepare forgotten. Why reminded you not me?'

Gerhardt's failure to take responsibility infuriated Belle.

'Because, unlike you, I have moved on from the eighteenth century and don't care to wear a wig. You really must speed up. It is not acceptable in England to be late to one's own birthday party.'

If Belle thought he could hurry Gerhardt he was sorely mistaken. An unusually large, voluptuous wig was removed from a box and liberally covered in a cloud of Cyprus powder scented with clove and rose oil.

A process that might have taken thirty seconds now stretched to fifteen minutes. Belle opted to lie on the bed and read a book. Organising a royal visit to Bath was a lot easier than helping Gerhardt to dress. After a chapter of *Ivanhoe*, his companion had finally donned the wig.

'*Gut*. This is now fine,' said Gerhardt.

'Well done,' replied Belle, swinging his legs off the bed and thinking for an instant they might be ready to depart. 'So, are you set to go?'

'What do you think?'

Belle smiled.

'You look beautiful, of course,' he said.

Gerhardt studied himself in the mirror anew.

'*Natürlich*. I always perfect look. I am perfection. I am the *Konzept* of perfection.'

'Apart from one thing,' Belle noted. 'You're not wearing any shoes. And now you've got that ridiculous wig on your head, you can't bend down to put them on.'

Gerhardt stared at his stockinged feet in dismay. Having behaved like a petulant peacock for the past hour, he needed help.

'Schnoodle doodle, *das ist* crazy. You must it for me do, Belle. Help me *meine* shoes to on put.'

'You'll have to ask more politely than that to get my help. And more idiosyncratically.'

'Are you mad? I have already *zwei* hours getting dressed spent!'

Belle placed a hand on his companion's shoulder in an effort to calm him.

'Manners, Gerhardt. Say please and I may just do it.'

His Prussian companion stared at him in astonishment, teetering on the edge of rage. Then, remembering that it was Belle's birthday, he acquiesced.

'So, tonight am I the *Arschkriecher* to be. OK, very well: *bitte* Belle, please me with *meinen* shoes to help.'

'I'd be delighted,' said Belle, dropping to his knees.

'*Und* while you are down there,' Gerhardt added, running his fingers through his companion's hair. 'Happy *Geburtstag*, dear friend.'

GAIA HAD STOOD in her late husband's dressing room alone. Alone: a solitary word, like 'widow', that clings to and defines the bereaved.

With the closing of the door and the departure of jolly Mary, her spirits had fallen. For all the talk of the end of mourning, the maid's absence had left a shadow. Gaia had found herself staring at the closed door.

'When someone dies, there is always silence,' she thought. 'How I wish it would end and happiness return.'

She walked to the window that looked over the Royal City of Bath. It was a splendid view. She wondered how many times Hercules had stood in that very spot taking pleasure from the beautiful buildings of honeyed stone. Here on top of Sion Hill, she could see the roofs of Royal Crescent and, to their left, the outline of Bath Abbey, on whose edifice sculpted angels climbed to heaven. She recalled Hercules joking that the angels were God's wingèd spies, reporting back on the behaviour of England's gentry.

Taking the waters, indeed! England's finest come to Bath to gamble, drink and whore! As its citizens, how do we put up with it?

Thus would Hercules proclaim. And Gaia remembered her answer:

We rise above it — together. The corrupt councillors and deceitful merchants will forever exploit Bath's citizens and visitors alike. We put up with it, Hercules, because we have each other.

'But with you gone ... ,' she now added to herself.

Standing where her husband had stood ten thousand times, she moved her face closer to the window and for a moment imagined raindrops outside. But the evening was clear, and they were not raindrops she saw but tears reflected in the glass. Tears cascading down her cheeks.

'Hercules, how could you have left me?' she said, weeping openly. 'Look at what's happened. Thirty-six years of age and I have nothing. I never gave you children, but we were together and now I am left without husband or purpose in life. Come home, Hercules. I want you to come home.'

She leant on the sill for support, blinded for a moment by loss.

At that moment, Mary knocked on her door.

'The first guest, Ma'am, has arrived early,' she said. 'Miss Prim. With her knitting. And the footman says Lady Passmore's carriage has been seen waiting in its usual place. The Champagne has been opened, so we had better hurry and get you dressed for the dinner.'

Drawing air into her lungs, Gaia recovered her composure. She was not a person to be easily defeated. Far from it. And, as is so often the case, out of the depths of misery, resilience grows. When she looked up, the reflection in the glass was the handsome face of a woman of granite determination.

'The silence of death is bad enough,' she said sternly to herself. 'I'll be damned to let melancholy occupy my husband's place. What you need, Gaia, is a plan of action. It's time to get on with life. There are friends to care for. And a future to be faced.'

With those words, she dried her cheeks, turned and, with a firm stride, left the room.

NOTES

- Cholera arrived from Bengal, via the Baltic, in October 1831 and Princess Victoria opened the Royal Victoria Park in Bath in 1830, so my uncle is a little awry with his dates. The fondness of royalty for Bath underpins my late uncle's reference to it as a Royal City.

- The rules of social etiquette for mourning were provided by publications such as *Cassell's* but *Cassell's* was not established until 1848 and so, again, my uncle was unreliable in his reporting. Two years was the common period of mourning for a spouse, during which ladies would wear dresses made from matt black paramatta silk trimmed with rough black crêpe.

- I have found no evidence to support my uncle's assertion that Frederick the Great and Beau Nash were acquainted but he is correct in asserting that Frederick was a 'bachelor' at heart. Aged 18 and having entered the army, Frederick attempted to elope with handsome Lt. Hans Hermann von Katte. The elopement failed and Frederick was made to watch the beheading of his lover (ordered by his father, an enraged Frederick William I).

21

CHAPTER II

A soufflé fails to rise

'COUNCILLOR NASH!' said Pritchard, the butler, announcing the latest guest to No. 24 Somerset Place to an otherwise empty hall. 'And might I be so bold as to offer you my own most felicitious felicitations on this most momentous evening?'

Belle Nash spread his arms and laughed, delighted to have arrived not too late. 'You may, John, you may!' he said, removing a pair of fine cotton gloves – elegant but barely capable of fending off even the slightest evening chill. 'You know my second cousin once removed, Herr Kant?'

Gerhardt Kant stepped forward, the breeze from Lansdown Crescent sending a cloud of Cyprus powder aloft from his bobbling wig.

'Welcome to Somerset Place, Herr Kant,' Pritchard continued. 'And do take care to mind your head as you step inside. Though the house was designed on a grand scale, allowance may not have been made for a wig of such generous proportions as yours.'

Gerhardt ducked as he stepped through the doorway.

'How true,' Belle agreed. 'A small mind cannot conceive of a large wig, as my sagacious grandfather Beau Nash once said.'

'*Sicher* was he a wise man,' agreed Gerhardt, righting himself as he entered the hall.

'Indeed, Sir,' Pritchard nodded. 'Now, if I may be so venturesome as to show you upstairs to where Mrs Champion awaits you in the drawing room. She is presently in conversation with Miss Prim.'

Belle, who had seen Lady Passmore's chaise and four a short

distance away and Mrs Pomeroy's face at its window, recognised an opportunity for mischief. 'Only Miss Prim, John? Are Lady Passmore and Mrs Pomeroy not yet arrived?'

Pritchard replied with a grin. 'Almost, Sir, but not quite. Their carriage was spotted in the vicinity some time ago but they have yet to make the final advance.'

Belle laughed again. He could sense it would be an excellent evening.

'Tremendous. In which case, Gerhardt, let us ascend the stairs and join dear Gaia and the delightful Miss Prim. John, would you lead?'

The three men moved forward through the spacious hallway and climbed the broad stairs to the drawing room. Built late in the previous century, the house had high ceilings embellished with decorative cornices and rosettes, from which hung fine glass chandeliers.

Belle had thought that with only five guests, Gaia might have approached the evening with a degree of modesty. Instead, the drawing room looked fit to impress five hundred, such were the displays of spring flowers and the lamps and candles that lit up the silk-covered walls and oil paintings. The room glistened with light and colour, and the fragrance of flowers filled the air.

Belle gasped with pleasure and Gerhardt's wig emitted small puffs of joy.

'Councillor Belle Nash and Herr Gerhardt Kant,' announced Pritchard.

Gaia, who had been listening to Phyllis Prim describe the challenges of knitting with a four-ply yarn, broke into a huge smile.

'The birthday boy is here,' she declared, crossing the room and kissing him on both cheeks. She turned to shake Gerhardt's hand warmly. 'And what a delight that you join us tonight, Herr Kant. Let me introduce you to Miss Prim. You are neighbours in Gay Street, are you not?'

23

Indeed, they had met more than once, although it would be fair to say that eternal friendship had not yet sprung from their meetings. Miss Prim, physically slight and frail, had spent the first forty years of her life failing to overcome a nervous disposition. Her family had sent her to Bath with a modest stipend, partly in the hope of the waters improving her condition but mostly to free the family home, Brandon Hall, from her twittering presence and faints.

Miss Prim had a long list of people who frightened her. At the top of it were tradesmen. Foreigners were close behind, which meant that she looked upon Gerhardt with suspicion and a little fear, an emotional state not helped by the sight of his enormous wig lurching towards her.

'Miss Prim, *mein plaisir*,' said Gerhardt, employing three languages to effect his simple, civil greeting.

'Oh,' replied Miss Prim nervously, holding out a hand and bracing herself for the possibility of a faint.

Of all the guests, Belle cared for Miss Prim the most and he quickly stepped in to save the day. He took her outstretched hand and held it gently.

'Dear Miss Prim, I cannot think of a nicer way to spend my birthday than with you. Let me lead you away from Gerhardt and Mrs Champion, so we can while away the hours until the artificially belated arrival of Lady Passmore and Mrs Pomeroy.'

'A fine idea,' replied Miss Prim as she took Belle's hand. 'Do excuse us, Herr Kant. If you can.'

As they settled down on one of the broad settees, Belle could see that Miss Prim remained nervous.

'I do hope my dear cousin did not alarm you in any way. The problem with having foreign relatives is that they have surprising ways. He means no obvious harm.'

'Oh! He had no intention to frighten, I'm sure,' said Miss Prim. 'It's just his wig ...'

'... which looks uncommonly like a flying sheep,' Belle joked, prompting Miss Prim to nod vigorously in agreement and causing Belle to realise that she was in earnest. 'Are you afeared of sheep, Ma'am?'

Miss Prim had an admission to make.

'I shouldn't be, Councillor Nash. I use their wool for knitting after all. But sometimes I dream they may be angry with me. I get scared the sheep may want it back.'

'Oh dear.'

'And my uncle was found drowned in the Middle Lake at Brandon Hall. With a sheep. There never was an explanation.'

'Indeed?' he proffered.

'But I do like lamb cutlet with broccoli that Mrs Mulligatawny cooks each Tuesday.'

Not for the first time, Belle found himself lost in Miss Prim's mental maze. Her last comment, however, did spark a thought.

'On the subject of food, I wonder what the excellent Mme Galette is cooking up tonight. She has a capacity for culinary perfection that is unique to the French.'

Their conversation was at that moment interrupted by Pritchard offering them each a glass of Champagne.

'I don't know if I should,' said Miss Prim. 'I have had one glass this evening already.'

Belle slapped her gently on the hand.

'Of course you should. It's my birthday,' he said, and took both glasses. Then, making use of the butler's presence, he added, 'Any idea what culinary joys await us, John?'

Pritchard prided himself on being well informed.

'I believe Mme Galette is planning a cheese soufflé, Sir, followed smartly by rib of beef. For dessert ...'

His voice carried across the room and caused their hostess immediate consternation.

'John!' cried Gaia, breaking off from Gerhardt, with whom she had been discussing the system of English currency. 'The secrets of the evening's repast are not a topic for general conversation.'

The butler stood to attention. Embarrassed to have spoken prematurely, his face changed to a violent red.

'I am all apologies, Ma'am. Without a dinner party to oversee over the last sad year, I fear I forgot myself. I should have bethought me and I bethought me not.'

Gaia waved the matter aside.

'At least the pudding will be a surprise. And I do believe that that's the front doorbell ringing,' she said to the sound of tinkling in the hallway. 'At last, the final guests are here.'

Pritchard bowed and made his exit to welcome the new guests. As soon as he had left, Belle clapped his hands in delight. He, for one, was thrilled with the butler's indiscretion.

'Cheese soufflé. Praise and praise again to the goddess Edesia! My absolute favourite. I adore soufflés. Can't get enough of them. I used to demand a soufflé for every meal when I was a child. And rib of beef! No one cooks a soufflé or a rib like Mme Galette. Oh, how exciting!'

Gaia could but smile. Belle's love of life's bounties was always a pleasure to behold.

'It's true one never forgets one's childhood favourites,' she noted, using the comment to open up the conversation. 'What food did you enjoy as a child, Miss Prim?'

The spinster was gingerly sipping her Champagne.

'Stewed plums,' she replied. 'Fresh plums made me sad.'

Gaia decided not to enquire further.

'Speaking for myself, I adored raspberry jelly when I was a young girl. What about you, Herr Kant?' Gaia asked, tactfully bringing the whole room into the conversation.

'I a young girl never was,' said Gerhardt.

'I guessed,' smiled Gaia, 'but what was your favourite food?'

'*Königsberger Klopse*,' he replied, raising a finger to his lips as

26

he considered the question. 'Boiled meatballs in caper sauce. *Wunderbar.*'

Gaia did her best to maintain her smile.

'Prussian cooking at its finest,' said Belle, who wagered, rightly, that gentle sarcasm would slip below Gerhardt's lofty gaze.

The opportunity for further comment was removed by the appearance of Pritchard with the new guests. Everyone turned to greet them.

'Mrs Pomeroy and Lady Passmore,' announced Pritchard, still red-faced from his earlier indiscretion and distracted by the faux pas of revealing the menu to Belle.

At the indignity of being announced second, Lady Passmore's back stiffened and she took a firm hold of Mrs Pomeroy's arm. Neither of them moved as the rest of the room looked on in silence. All eyes turned to Pritchard, whose face now turned to deathly white as he realised his error.

'Of Tewkesbury Manor!' he added. 'And the other way round.'

There was a collective sigh of relief as Lady Passmore now consented to make her entrance. Gaia walked quickly across the room to greet the guests.

'Lady Passmore of Tewkesbury Manor and dear Mrs Pomeroy, how wonderful to see you. I hope the journey by carriage did not take too long.'

'Precisely the right amount of time,' said Lady Passmore.

'But longer than it might,' added Mrs Pomeroy, a little tartly.

Gaia accompanied them to the centre of the drawing room. 'You know Miss Prim, of course, and Belle the birthday boy. And Herr Gerhardt Kant from Prussia you will have met before.'

Gerhardt stepped forward to shake the ladies' hands.

'Your Ladyship,' said Gerhardt, bowing.

'Indeed,' said Lady Passmore.

'Mrs Pomeroy, *mein plaisir*,' Gerhardt repeated.

'*Enchantée*,' said Mrs Pomeroy.

27

The dinner guests began to discuss topics of no importance, as fashion demanded on such occasions, and Pritchard served more Champagne before directing a footman to the kitchen to make sure that Mme Galette had put the soufflé in the oven.

'What beautiful diamonds, Lady Passmore of Tewkesbury Manor,' commented Belle, who had long admired the grande dame for her jewels, her carriage and her ability to put the fear of Jupiter into all around her.

'How kind of you to notice, Councillor Nash,' said Her Ladyship, whose earrings, necklace and brooch sparkled wildly, each in its own lavish silver setting. 'My husband, Admiral Lord Passmore of Tewkesbury Manor, sent them to me from Jaipur.'

'The benefits of world travel,' said Belle, who in all the years of knowing Lady Passmore had never met her husband.

A few paces away, Mrs Pomeroy and Gerhardt were also finding shared ground.

'I must say, Herr Kant, that you are blessed to have Councillor Nash as a cousin — and to think that we had no idea until you arrived that he had European relatives.'

Having endured more than an hour in the carriage, she was not going to honour Lady Passmore's injunctions about avoiding intelligent conversation.

'Councillor Nash is frightfully smart, of course. His knowledge of history and the classics is unsurpassed in Bath. I first met him in a tearoom and he knew the entire history of the Battenburg dynasty.'

'*Ja*. The House of Hesse-Darmstadt. *Eine* important *deutsche* family.'

'Almost as important as your own family, Herr Kant. We've all heard of your late uncle Immanuel, of course.'

Gerhardt, wearied by society's fascination with his uncle, took her comment as an opportunity to provide his own slant on life.

'It is true that he is famous, Mrs Pomeroy, but what *mein* uncle wrote is not even half the story. *Ja*, he explored our thought — *unser Denken...*'

'Did he now?'

'... but not our suffering — *unser Leiden, verstehen sie?*'

Mrs Pomeroy's brow furrowed, for she did not *verstehen* what Gerhardt meant at all.

'Not entirely. But I don't have a great mind like yourself.'

Gerhardt attempted an explanation.

'It is easy, Mrs Pomeroy. Take Fräulein Prim. I overheard her saying that she suffers — *seidet* — from a fear of sheep.'

'Miss Prim is frightened of most things,' Mrs Pomeroy noted. 'That's why she knits.'

Gerhardt was excited by the answer.

'We must ask "why?". From where has this irrational fear *vor* the woolly *Schafen* arisen? Such a question was not by *mein* uncle asked but this will be the purpose of *mein* life: to *verstehen* the suffering of the mind. How think you, Mrs Pomeroy?'

Her brow was sufficiently furrowed to plant potatoes. Fortunately, ever alert to a guest's plight, Gaia came to the rescue.

'I'm sure Mrs Pomeroy is delighted that you have a purpose in life, Herr Kant. Everyone and everything should have a purpose. Which rather makes me wonder why on Earth dinner hasn't been called. Please excuse me while I interrogate John.'

Gaia looked around but the butler was nowhere to be seen. This was an unusual state of affairs and one that did not bode well. Dinner for six people should have been within the competence of her staff of eight to organise. It seemed she had misjudged them. She went from the drawing room to the landing, from where she could hear raised voices below. She hurried down the stairs.

'Mary, is that you?' she called. 'What is happening?'

'Oh, Ma'am, it's a catastrophe, that's what. I never seen Mme Galette in such a bate. Even Mr Pritchard don't know what to do. It's all gone wrong in the kitchen.'

29

'What has, girl? You're making fearfully little sense.'

'The soufflé, Ma'am. Mme Galette, she been whisking like crazy until her arm near dropped off but it won't rise. It just won't. What are we to do?'

Gaia took stock of the news. The problem, she surmised, was twofold: firstly, the planned opening course had failed; secondly, this being her first social occasion for a year, there was little in the larder with which to create an alternative. However, one thing sprang to mind that would keep Belle happy. Eggs. He loved eggs and there were probably enough to satisfy him.

'We'll talk about the soufflé later. If it has sunk, it has sunk. Listen to me carefully, Mary. Tell Mme Galette to do baked eggs with cream in ramekins. Put some parsley on top. Councillor Nash adores eggs and he'll be perfectly happy. I want them on the table in ten minutes. Go on! Hurry down to the kitchen or the beef will be overcooked as well.'

She turned back towards the drawing room as Mary scurried away. Now it was Gaia's turn to have a furrowed brow. Mme Galette had made soufflés so many times that she could do them blindfold with one hand tied behind her back – if someone else could hold the whisking bowl. She was French, after all. How could her soufflé fail, tonight of all nights?

NOTES

- My uncle had a much-thumbed 1869 edition of *The Book of Household Management* by Mrs Beeton. The great lady made the following General Observation on Soufflés: they 'demand, for their successful manufacture, an experienced cook. They are the prettiest but most difficult of all entremets. The most essential thing to ensure success is to secure the best ingredients from an honest tradesman.'

CHAPTER III

When is a glove not a glove?

T HE DINING ROOM looked as magnificent as ever, the table resplendent with a white embroidered cloth adorned with candelabra and silver bowls of fresh fruit. It had been a lonely room this past year, as if in hibernation. At last, warmth in the form of human conversation had returned and with it the room's purpose.

'The baked eggs were sublime and the beef exquisite. Mme Galette has lost none of her touch,' declared Belle Nash, wiping his lips with a napkin as two footmen cleared the plates away. 'Thank you.'

The beef had indeed been cooked to perfection along with the *pommes de terre rôties* in rosemary, the Savoy cabbage, parsnip fingers, *roulade de poivron* and buttered carrots. The gravy had been a little garlicky but nothing to diminish the quality of the meat.

'Most gracious of you,' responded Gaia Champion light-heartedly, delighted that the dinner was back on track. 'In truth, I have no idea why the soufflé failed to rise, but I can assure you that it will be the subject of the fiercest investigation.'

'What questions will you ask?' said Mrs Pomeroy, who had been deeply disappointed at the demise of the first course. 'What causes a soufflé not to rise?'

It was not a subject that anyone's upbringing had prepared them for. Emboldened by claret, however, Lady Passmore seized the opportunity to put Mrs Pomeroy in her place.

'Insufficient hot air. Really, Mrs Pomeroy, you ask the silliest things.'

Mrs Pomeroy blushed, while others at the table wisely left Her Ladyship's statement unchallenged. The topic of the soufflé, however, had yet to run its course. Belle felt the need to make an apology of his own.

'I wouldn't have known we were to be served a soufflé if I hadn't pestered John. I believe its failure was a direct consequence of my rudeness, so I am to blame, not Mme Galette.'

His generosity was understood and appreciated by all but one. On the opposite side of the table, a wig wobbled and Gerhardt Kant, who had enjoyed the Champagne, the white Burgundy and the claret, sprang to life. To the Prussian mind, driven by reason and fuelled by logic, Belle's statement required a response.

'*Ja wirklich*?' Gerhardt said, fascinated. 'You think that a personal act of rudeness in a room upstairs – in the *Obergeschoss* – can affect the cooking of a soufflé in a kitchen downstairs – in the *Erdgeschoss*? Different acts, the mental *und* the physical, by different people, you *und* the cook, but connected through time *und* space?'

Belle forced a smile amidst the sea of confusion.

'I'm not sure that's exactly the point I was making,' he said to his companion. 'Although if it was, let's hope the pudding on which we will shortly feast has not been similarly injured.'

There was polite laughter around the table but, again, Gerhardt looked intense. As seriously as the English take their humour, so the Prussians take their philosophy.

'You think I am the humbug talking, Belle, but imagine if you are right: it would transform our *Verstehen* of the world.'

Belle's smile weakened. While he knew his Locke from his Hume, he could not imagine the other ladies sharing an interest. In this he was mistaken, for wine when drunk in sufficient quantities makes philosophers of us all. It was Mrs Pomeroy who spoke first.

32

'I agree with Herr Kant. Councillor Nash, you may have come up with something really clever. Herr Kant was explaining to me before dinner about how his new philosophy departs from that of his late uncle.'

Lady Passmore was quick to recognise signs of disobedience in the ranks.

'Mrs Pomeroy, I warned you earlier about intelligent conversation.'

'But I found it most interesting,' insisted Mrs Pomeroy, now in defiant mood.

Lady Passmore redirected her attack.

'Well maybe Herr Kant would explain to me the principles of his uncle's clever prattlings so that I, too, can form an opinion.'

Neither Belle nor Gaia could see much good emerging from the conversation, but Belle rarely imposed his will on his companion and Gaia disliked policing her guests' discussions. Gerhardt leant forward to lock horns with Lady Passmore.

'It would be my privilege, *liebe geehrte Frau*. But how to begin? *Ja*, I have an idea. I would like to ask Miss Prim what she is knitting at the moment.'

Phyllis Prim was startled at this unwanted enquiry.

'Oh, let me think. A pair of gloves for my cook, Mrs Mulligatawny. She is from India and finds the weather here most inclement. I have them in my bag, if you wish to see them.'

Everyone watched as Miss Prim reached into her bag and retrieved a finished glove, then a second that consisted of a lone finger connected to two balls of soft pink wool.

'*Bitte*, if I may, *ja*?' said Gerhardt, taking the finished glove from Miss Prim's hand. '*Und* what see you here, Miss Prim?'

'I'm sorry?'

'*Was ... sehen ... Sie .. hier*?' he repeated in German, slowly and more loudly, as if that would help in a strange way.

Everyone stared at the glove and Miss Prim giggled nervously.

'A glove, of course, Herr Kant. What a funny question.'

But Gerhardt was not joking. He raised the glove high in the air as if it were an exhibit in court.

'I am explaining. Please consider this *Handschuh* – I say 'hand-shoe'; you say 'glove'. This saying is funny for *die Engländer*, this 'hand-shoe', *nein?* So, you have experienced what the hand-shoe is like. You have touched the wool, you have your fingers felt, as you shuffle them into the hand-shoe. Your mind, *ja*, has experienced these sensations *und* then in order them put. But how?

'By supplying what we shall "the *Konzept*" call. *Ja*! The concept that this a hand-shoe is. Your mind has acted in time *und* in space, *und dann*, like magic, you understand the experience that is the hand-shoe. But maybe it is not a hand-shoe, after all! *Heiaha!*'

Gerhardt handed the glove back to Miss Prim, who hurriedly returned it to the safety of her bag. They all spent a few seconds considering the philosophical insight that had been provided.

It was Lady Passmore who spoke first.

'From what I understand, Herr Kant, you are suggesting that Miss Prim may not actually have been knitting gloves at all.'

'*Das ist* correct. But if you consider it a 'glove', as you say, then it is. But only because you consider it so.'

Mrs Pomeroy was confused.

'But what else might it have been?'

Gerhardt shrugged.

'The udder of a cow, perhaps,' he said, adding '*das Euter einer Kuh*', to provide more declarative emphasis.

'An udder!' the rest of the table exclaimed in unison.

While Miss Prim was not alone in looking shocked, she took the statement personally and felt the need to defend her knitting.

'But I haven't been knitting udders. I've been knitting gloves. Mrs Champion, please tell me that I haven't been knitting udders.'

Gaia, who was widely read, was happy to reassure Miss Prim by putting Gerhardt's philosophy into perspective.

34

'Don't take what Herr Kant says too seriously, Miss Prim. What he has explained is only that the world is an endless series of experiences that our minds put into order and from which we draw conclusions. We have all experienced the characteristics of a glove, so we may reasonably conjecture that the glove you have knitted is – a glove!'

'But it *is* a glove,' Lady Passmore huffed. 'I'm sure you'd agree, Councillor Nash.'

Belle had been waiting for the conversation to come round to him and, now that it had, he attempted to draw an amicable end to the proceedings.

'I have no doubt that what we had before us was a glove and, if I may be so bold as to affirm, a particularly lovely example of a glove. Miss Prim, as we know, is not only one of Bath's most prolific knitters but also its finest. Her tea cosies, of which I own a few, are perfect examples of the craft.'

Miss Prim's distress turned to instant happiness at the compliment. A faint would not now be necessary.

'And on the subject of the inestimable Immanuel Kant,' Belle continued, 'I am forever struck by the fantastical nature of modern European scholarship. I agree with you, Lady Passmore of Tewkesbury Manor, that tremendous effort is expended by fine minds on proving that a dog is a dog and not a cat.'

Lady Passmore smiled, her point vindicated.

'But I also support Mrs Pomeroy's contention that we should sometimes engage in intelligent conversation,' Belle continued, undaunted, 'and Immanuel Kant was a brilliant man. I remain intrigued by his early proposition that the Earth, the moon, the sun, the planets and all the stars began as a single giant cloud of gas. That, to my mind, is a worthy idea.'

'He proposed that we're all made of hot air?' Lady Passmore objected, suddenly roused.

'Just like a soufflé!' noted Mrs Pomeroy.

'Exactly,' said Belle. 'The world, like philosophy, is a great big soufflé. And, I would posit, as inconsequential as a soufflé, too. Which is an excellent reason for us to look forward to a fine pudding!'

It was a point well made and left all parties satisfied. But Belle had spoken too soon.

'Or not, as the case may be,' commented Gaia, for she had caught sight of the cook, Mme Galette, standing by the door with her head bowed. 'Is there something wrong, Mme Galette? Please not another failure, I pray.'

Mme Galette was a decent woman and a fine cook. She was content that her place was in the kitchen and it was not her custom to interrupt the meals she had cooked. In this instance, however, she had journeyed upstairs to explain personally a distressing sequence of events. She was visibly shaken.

Speaking in her finest Parisian accent, she said, '*Oh Madame*, something most terrible 'as 'appened. I 'ave never seen anything like eet. I was cooking *un pudding à l'éponge cuit à la vapeur*, but *l'éponge* is more like – how you say it *en Angleterre*? Like a ... , like a ... '

'Like a milkmaid's kiss?' suggested Belle warily.

'*Pas du tout, Monsieur*! Like a doorstop. It makes perhaps a year that I cooked *pour un diner*, but for *un soufflé* not to rise itself and for *l'éponge* to turn out *comme une brique* ... ?! I am lost for words.' And she burst into tears.

At the sight of her cook's distress, Gaia rose, crossed the room, led Mme Galette to a chair and sat beside her.

'There must be a simple explanation,' Gaia said. 'We all know you are a most wonderful cook. You learned your craft under Monsieur Antoine Beauvilliers in the kitchens of La Grande Taverne de Londres, no less.'

But Mme Galette was inconsolable. She cared for every single meal, and for the inaugural dinner party of the year to be ruined, one given for Belle's birthday and the first since the death of Mr Champion, seemed to her not just a calamity but a personal failing and a repudiation of her entire life's work.

'I am finished. My reputation — *elle est ruinée*! Monsieur Beauvilliers would never take me back now. I was 'is prize pupil. It is impossible to understand. *Amposseebl!* I have used *zese* recipes *deux cents fois. Les oeufs, le lait, la crème, zey* were all fresh. I sent Florence to buy flour *cet après-midi* after she found a weevil. I wanted to go myself, but we were out of the time and ... and ...'

Mme Galette hesitated. Something had occurred to her.

'What is it, Mme Galette?' asked Gaia.

The cook wiped her eyes. She had found a possible explanation for the night's culinary woes.

'I sent Florence to Helmsworth's Stores but now I wonder if *la fille idiote* went to Porter's instead. I do not trust Porter but she has a cousin who work there sometime. *Ze* prices are less but, *oh mon Dieu! Le qualité! Day-plo-rabl!* Per'aps it *ees* the flour. *Quand j'y réfléchis encore,* it had of *ze mal* texture: *eet* make *ze* sauce go *solide*.'

The mention of Porter's prompted Belle to speak up.

'You're right, Mme Galette. There's gossip in Guildhall about Hezekiah Porter, and none of it good. He is Dolos incarnate, the god of trickery and guile — master of cunning and deceit. His shop has an errant set of scales, by all accounts.'

Everyone, including Mme Galette, looked at him in surprise.

'Heavens, Belle. Do you do your own shopping?' asked Gaia.

Belle laughed.

'Apart from buying pies from Mrs Crust's Pie Shop and purchasing my own tea and claret, and hams and guinea fowl, and caraway seeds and saffron and ground ginger, and chestnuts and mushrooms and artichokes and pineapples, and cheeses and chocolate and comfits, I am not yet so reduced! But as a city councillor I catch whispers. From what I hear, Porter should have been prosecuted ten times over, but he has a friend in Obadiah Wood, our detestable city magistrate. It wouldn't surprise me if Porter has been selling mealy flour.'

The others took their time to digest this information; Miss Prim, who by nature distrusted general stores, started looking queasy.

'Shocking,' agreed Mrs Pomeroy. 'Truly shocking.'

'Disgraceful,' said Lady Passmore. 'But are you sure that Magistrate Wood is protecting Mr Porter? I have never liked the man, but even so ...'

Belle rose from the table and crossed to one of the room's large windows. The city's newly installed gaslights flickered outside. Belle did not make accusations lightly but the city magistrate was one of several men walking the corridors of Bath's Guildhall whom he could not abide. He considered Wood to be a man driven by prejudice, greed and intolerance.

'Our magistrate enjoys power. There's no surprise that he employs Special Constable Dimm as his henchman. Get on the wrong side of those two and you'll soon find yourself in the clink, guilty or not.'

'You are suggesting that the magistrate acts outside the law?' asked Gaia.

'Outside the law?' Belle queried. 'For Wood, there is no law – except his own.' And then he paused. He had begun to feel queasy.

'I have no firm evidence, but he is a large, unwholesome man with a big appetite. Mme Galette may shun Porter's, but I suspect that Wood frequents the shop often. Perhaps it wasn't my rudeness that caused the soufflé not to rise after all.'

All eyes focussed on Belle as he stretched out an arm and pointed through the window to the city below.

He continued, 'I fear my birthday fayre has been blighted by corruption. There's something rotten in the Royal City of Bath and it has ended up on our dinner table.'

It was a bold, challenging statement and one that spurred his friends into action.

Mrs Pomeroy said, 'Something must be done about it. As we speak, soufflés could be collapsing in houses across the city.'

Gaia agreed. Having exhausted her tolerance for black crêpe after a year, she saw no reason to remain passive while men like Porter and Wood wrecked people's dinners.

'I concur. The matter requires Bath's citizens to take action, and none are better placed than we. We must avenge our spoiled dinner!'

This prompted further declarations of support.

'I agree,' replied Mrs Pomeroy. 'We must rise to the defence of hot air.'

'Hear, hear,' triumphed Lady Passmore. 'The fight will have the full support of Tewkesbury Manor.'

'Oo, yes!' squealed Miss Prim. 'I could knit a protest muffler.'

The righteousness of the cause was sufficient to create pan-European unity.

'I understood not a word of the French Frau, but that the soufflé must be saved, that agree I with,' declared Gerhardt, rising to his feet, powder bursting from his wig like smoke from a line of muskets.

'Then we are as one,' said Gaia, enthused that after a year of passivity there was something she could do. 'We should gather evidence. What I learned from working with Hercules was the importance of building a case. I suggest that we each conduct separate investigations and then share the results. Act quickly and we can prevent an epidemic of sunken soufflés. Belle, after our initial efforts, might we reconvene for tea at your house this Saturday afternoon?'

Although his stomach protested at the mention of more food, Belle adored giving tea parties for the ladies and the proposal met with his immediate approval.

'An excellent idea. Together we will rid Bath of corruption and enjoy a cup of tea in Gay Street. Hurrah!'

'Hurrah!' the others all shouted, rising to their feet.

Unfortunately, this sudden movement had a deleterious impact on their stomachs. Belle was not the only one to be suffering. Something they had all eaten had been stirred back to life.

One by one, they grasped their bellies and then fell back into their chairs, overcome by nausea. As if struck by a biblical plague, Lady Passmore's perpetually straight back suddenly bent. In desperation, Miss Prim reached out for the comfort of her knitting. Beside her, Gerhardt's wig sagged in empathy with his stomach, while even Mrs Pomeroy felt that she had eaten too much.

'The birthday gravy,' gasped Belle, correctly identifying the culprit.

'Yes, indeed, the gravy,' spluttered Gaia. 'Mme Galette, we need six bowls and in double-quick time. There's not a second to waste.'

NOTES

- Antoine B. Beauvilliers (1754–1817) was a pioneering French chef who opened, in about 1786, Paris's first fine-dining restaurant, La Grande Taverne de Londres (an ironic name, given the general French disdain for English cuisine), replete with trained waiters, fine linen and a wine cellar.

CHAPTER IV

Mrs Crust tells a tale

I T MIGHT SEEM absurd that something as inconsequential as a soufflé should rouse society's passions, let alone that a single soufflé's failure to rise could have repercussions enough to affect the course of people's lives. A soufflé, light and fluffy as a lover's promise, should not have the force to cause waves. The tiniest ripple, perhaps, but not the tidal wave now in the making.

More likely, it is a reflection on the greater fragility of the human condition that a soufflé should have such substance, a matter Immanuel Kant might have put in his pipe-of-reason and smoked. So, let us follow the course of the failed soufflé from the moment of its being discarded by its creator, Mme Galette.

Gaia Champion and her guests had thankfully survived to live another day, but not so the soufflé.

'*Vas-t'en*,' the cook had said upon throwing its remains into a bin. 'You're *une chose horrible*.'

Ever a thrifty woman, Mme Galette had the habit of gathering wasted food and vegetable peelings for livestock. No such animals had their home in Somerset Place, but a cart passed by each morning to take the scraps to farms in nearby villages such as Charlcombe. The cart was owned by a Mr Cudworth, who made deliveries of cattle-feed before sunrise and then spent the first hours of daylight collecting household scraps to feed chickens.

One might have expected, therefore, the soufflé to travel north-east of Somerset Place, which was Mr Cudworth's usual route, but with the sun slowly rising in the sky, the cart instead trundled south towards the city centre. There had been a public gathering the previous day and Mr Cudworth knew from experience that there were pickings to be had.

The old horse had experienced in its lifetime a wide and varied range of noxious waste, but even he let out a neigh of disgust as the soufflé was tipped from Mme Galette's bin into the cart. The crows that followed the cart in search of carrion also looked doubtful. One bird pecked at the rubbery mess of baked egg and flour and promptly dropped dead. The rest took heed and sloped off.

The cart worked its way along Lansdown Crescent, past the house where the elderly William Beckford resided following the collapse of Fonthill Abbey, his poorly constructed Gothic fantasy. If Beckford had glanced through the shutters at the cart, he might have pondered how the durable solidity of Mme Galette's soufflé could have saved his abbey and his fortune.

The horse moved onto Lansdown Hill Road, which leads into the heart of Bath, providing us with the opportunity, were we to hold our noses against the stench, to catch a lift for a brief tour of the city. To the left and right, the slopes were filled with houses built during the previous century by architects who took their inspiration from the Palladian tradition of Venice and were nearly all called John. The exception was Robert Adam who, having designed Pulteney Bridge, picked up his compass and ran.

Halfway down the slope the horse and stinky soufflé crossed into Old Bond Street and a neighbourhood of Tudor wood-beamed buildings that in turn bordered a maze of Jacobean alleys. As a visitor to the city, if you successfully navigated the maze you would find at its centre Bath Abbey, beside which are the famous Roman hot springs.

It is in this, the oldest quarter of Bath, that the best and the worst of the city's traders were to be found (including, at night, the brothel-keeper Molly Jenkins and her goddesses).

On the plus side, the tearoom of Sally Lunn in North Parade

Passage was a pleasure to behold, its famous light buns a joy when smothered in soft butter and strawberry jam and washed down with a cup of Indian tea. The incautious visitor, however, might easily (and to their misfortune) enter the rival tearoom close by on Abbey Green owned by its namesake Shirley Haytit, a woman notorious – and not for the best of reasons – for rock cake.

Also, on Abbey Green, a small, cobbled triangle dominated by a large oak tree at its centre, were the excellent Mrs Crust's Pie Shop and the deplorable Porter's, the trouble-making general store whose flour was suspected of ruining the soufflé and the digestive tracts of Gaia's guests.

So, as the horse pulled the dreadful soufflé past the store's grey door, let us jump off the cart, release our noses and take a closer look at Abbey Green, for this is where the gathering storm was to be centred.

Mrs Crust represented the best of Abbey Green, a sturdy, middle-aged, West Country lady who knew how to bake a proper pie. She used only the finest ingredients: Cornish chickens for their plump thighs and breasts; Devon Red Ruby cows for their marbled meat; and Tamworth pigs because ... well, because she loved the way they looked with their ginger straw hair.

For her fruit pies, she bought apples and pears from the orchards in Combe Down and summer berries from the allotments in Smallcombe. She trusted her suppliers and her customers trusted her.

She would bake before dawn and, half an hour before the shop was due to open, would fill the shelves with cold pies from the pantry and fresh hot pies as required. Meat pies would go to the counter and fruit pies to the window. Removing her apron, she would brush her hair and dab a little orange blossom water about her neck so that she smelt lovely for her customers. It really was no wonder that Mrs Crust's Pie Shop was the pie emporium of choice for all pie lovers.

43

The same could not be said for tea lovers of Mrs Haytit's tearoom on the other side of the green, an establishment that aspired to mediocrity and failed even to deliver that. Whereas Mrs Crust carried the scent of oranges about her, Mrs Haytit's sallow skin smelt of gin. And that was first thing in the morning.

One should never disparage a lady without good reason, but it is fair to say that the low esteem in which Mrs Haytit was held was well deserved. Cast an eye about her tearoom and you would find the cloths soiled, the crockery cracked and the larder infested with vermin. But worse than her unconcern for cleanliness was the depravity of the food she served.

Mrs Haytit was not naturally a woman to put in an early shift, except for the attraction of the spirit bottle. She would stagger into her tearoom at the same time as Mrs Crust was placing her pies in the window. By then, her two hopeless pastry cooks were already at work. They were not blessed with the greatest culinary skills. On any given day their pastry could be as soggy as a peat bog or as hard as a dry-stone wall.

'These apple turnovers are disgusting!' Mrs Haytit would habitually scream. 'They're vile! You're all worse than useless in this kitchen. I'd prefer to eat a wolfhound's vomit than have this rubbish on my plate. Now put 'em out on the counter while I get myself ready to serve the cussed customers!'

What Mrs Haytit did not do was question why her food was so horrid. She did not care that the cooks barely knew how to make a drop scone or that the stale eggs and rancid butter she purchased were a certain recipe for failure.

In that regard, it should come as no surprise that the willing supplier of her rank ingredients was none other than Porter's, the final merchant of interest on Abbey Green.

Gaia's cook, Mme Galette, had been accurate in her description of the store. Hezekiah Porter offered low prices but at a cost to the customer in quality and health. Mr Porter had started his career working for the store's previous owner, a decent man named Thomas Fulbright, as the lad taking deliveries. In return for Fulbright's trust, Hezekiah Porter pilfered goods and sold them on.

When the business failed and Fulbright was declared bankrupt, Mr Porter took on the store's lease with his ill-gotten gains and changed the name to his own. Needing now to alter his *modus operandi*, he stopped stealing from the storeroom and set about fleecing his customers by selling poor-quality goods and using false weights to measure them out. For years he had profited from his sharp practices, although they had not gone unnoticed by others such as Mme Galette and a certain pie-maker on the other side of Abbey Green.

L IKE MOST RESIDENTS of Bath, Mrs Crust enjoyed a good chat. She also had a sixth sense in knowing her neighbours' business. Taken together, it was no surprise that she should be the first port of call for Belle Nash who, having recovered from the birthday gravy, was eager to take part in the investigation of the failed soufflé.

His morning walk to his office in Guildhall took him past Abbey Green, and he'd usually stop to buy a slice of pie and chat for a few minutes with Mrs C. This morning, after a jovial exchange of greetings and a compliment on the excellence of her pastries, he casually switched the subject to Hezekiah Porter.

Belle was a grandmaster at getting people to divulge their closest secrets, but none of his skills was required on Mrs Crust, who now unleashed a torrent of gossip, all of it unsubstantiated. It took ten minutes before he was able to interrupt.

'Is all of that so, Mrs Crust?' Belle gasped at last. 'So, he's been cheating all those customers for thirty years? And his wife, before she left him?'

Mrs Crust nodded busily, her cheeks puffed out like puff pastry.

'I swear on my rolling pin, I do, Councillor Nash. The man was born a rogue and will die one too.'

Belle did his best to look shocked.

'It's a grotesque tale. He should be taken to court. Shall I inform the Honourable Magistrate Wood?'

Mrs Crust spluttered in derision.

'Magistrate Wood, you say! He and Hezekiah Porter are as one man: two sides of the same coin and thick as thieves, mark my words. The magistrate is in that shop near every day, collecting his provisions. I see him, Councillor Nash, I do. Just last evening he took a side of ham away and Porter's don't even sell ham. I'd wager my daily takings he don't pay for nothing.'

That confirmed one rumour Belle had heard in Guildhall, that Mr Porter paid in kind for the magistrate's protection. Not wanting to show his hand any further at this stage, he decided it was time to move on.

'Well, it's been a pleasure chatting with you as ever, Mrs Crust. Most instructive. And thank you, once more, for the delicious pie.'

She finished wrapping the slice as he handed over a coin to conclude their business. But she was reluctant to see him go without a further exchange of words.

'The decent people of Bath are tired of corruption,' she whispered. 'It's about time somebody put it right.'

Belle smiled a politician's smile as he took the slice of pie and prepared to leave. Complaints about corruption were commonplace.

'You won't get any help from my fellow councillors, I fear, Mrs Crust. They're all too busy looking after their own interests to care about the interests of others.'

Mrs Crust laughed. She liked Belle and didn't care one jot for the lewd innuendos that he and his fellow bachelors attracted. She considered him a decent man, a good customer and that rarest of creatures: an honest councillor.

She came around the counter to open the door for him.

'What we need is a few women running this city. But that's never going to happen, is it?'

Belle did not reply, although the statement lodged like a seed in the fertile earth of his mind – a mind that was soon thinking further on the scoundrel Hezekiah Porter.

Like all who are born in the British Isles, Belle made frequent reference to the weather when analysing life's challenges. Mr Porter was transparently a rascal, but the detail of his malfeasance remained hidden from view: the man was, Belle decided, like a bank of fog on what was otherwise a clear day.

It made him wonder what his competing friends would discover: the four ladies and, if he could tear himself away from the mirror, Gerhardt Kant. He wondered also about Magistrate Wood who, gnawing on a side of ham, might prove a considerable obstacle to any progress. It would be cursed luck if their task of saving the soufflé was stymied by a corrupt gourmand.

With slice of pie in hand, Belle crossed Abbey Church Yard, the site of the old Roman forum, eighteen hundred years in the past.

'It was ever thus,' he muttered. 'Rogues, damned rogues and magistrates. Not to mention city councillors, of course.'

A minute later and he was climbing the steps to enter the administrative centre of Bath. Guildhall was an imposing and functional, rather than a beautiful, building. On the ground floor were the court and offices, above them the Council Chamber and the inevitable Banqueting Hall, for one can never be short of a banqueting hall in Bath.

'Good morning, Councillor Nash. You look sprightly today,' declared the doorman, who was paid to say such things. 'Is that a piece of Mrs Crust's pie?'

'Good morning, Bullard. Yes, it is. And you're not having any of it. Am I the first of the vipers to arrive?'

The doorman smiled at Belle's description of his fellow city officials.

'Not quite, but almost, Sir. Chairman Camshaft turned up half an hour ago to do something important but had sadly forgotten what it was by the time he arrived.'

This was not an unusual event for Ernest Camshaft, the nonagenarian chairman, whose sight and mind had been failing for decades now.

'At least he found his way to Guildhall rather than disturbing the Mineral Water Hospital again,' said Belle, recalling an earlier incident.

'It's true his eyesight leaves much to be desired,' laughed the doorman. 'As does his memory. He never remembers my name these days.'

Belle gave the doorman a sympathetic pat on the shoulder.

'Don't take offence, Bullard. It's when we can't remember our own names that we need to start worrying.'

NOTES

- The immensely wealthy William Beckford, supposedly the wealthiest commoner in England, spent much of his vast fortune adding a mock-Gothic abbey – Fonthill Abbey – to his Wiltshire home. Unfortunately, its poorly constructed ninety-metre-high tower, made from an early form of West Country concrete, had a habit of collapsing.
- Uncle William is somewhat amiss in suggesting that all Bath's notable architects were named John. In addition to all the Johns (John Wood the Elder, John Wood the Younger, John Pinch the Elder, John Pinch the Younger, John Eveleigh and John Palmer), there were also a couple christened Thomas (Attwood and Baldwin).

CHAPTER V

An opportunity arises

THOUGH SMALL, BELLE Nash's Guildhall office had the attraction of morning sunlight and a window looking onto Pulteney Bridge. Atop the hill in the distance, he could see Sham Castle, a reminder that all is not as it seems in life.

Belle reached for a quill and paper to make notes for the day ahead. There was much to be organised for the impending visit of Princess Victoria. He began writing down a list of 'do not forget' items: ribbon; scissors; umbrellas in case of rain ... . By such lists are empires run.

Then, as he sat tickling his chin with the quill, thinking what else he needed to add, he looked up and saw the City Corporation's ancient chairman, Ernest Camshaft, at the door.

Camshaft was an unmistakable figure, a small man bent and buckled by age. What hair remained formed a horseshoe around an otherwise bald scalp; loose skin mottled by liver spots hung in great flaps like purses beneath his failing eyes. He was a living example of the extreme consequences of old age on the human body. And the mind.

'Compliments of the morning, Chairman,' said Belle, who in light of the doorman's comments wondered whether the chairman would know who he was. 'Fine weather we're having.'

'Eh? Who are you?'

It was a response that answered the query.

'Belle Nash, Sir: one of your councillors. And you're standing in my office.'

49

Camshaft peered towards him.

'Belle Nash, you say. I knew your father Beau,' he said, missing out a couple of generations. 'What am I doing here?'

Belle put down the quill and drummed his fingers gently on his desk.

'I fancy you came to see me. Just a suggestion.'

Camshaft looked up into a corner of the ceiling as if whatever he was meant to be doing could be found there.

'Did I now? Forgotten what it was. Frightfully boring, old age. Are you old?'

Belle took pity. He stood up and went over to the chairman, taking him by the elbow.

'Older than I was, Sir. Thirty-five yesterday. Come in and rest awhile. Have a seat.'

It was an offer gratefully received.

'May I? Most handsome of you.'

'Your most obedient servant,' said Belle, deciding there might be a political opportunity to be had. It was not often the chairman came to his office. 'Perhaps you wanted to know what's going on in my world.'

'Perhaps I did. What is going on in your world, Sir?'

Belle pulled up a second chair so he could sit beside the old man.

'To speak truly, Sir, I have been fielding complaints about Magistrate Obadiah Wood. The word is, he's in league with a rogue called Porter who runs a grocer's store close to the abbey.'

'Wouldn't surprise me, Sir. Never liked Wood. Too gross to be trusted. The jowl of corruption and all that. What else have you been up to?'

It was a typical Ernest Camshaft response. Being told about a problem and confronting it were two different things. His decades-long leadership of the City Corporation had been characterised by docile inactivity, which suited the bevy of corrupt officials heartily.

'Organising the visit of Princess Victoria. You appointed me. Her Royal Highness is opening the park beside Royal Crescent.'

The visit was easily the biggest event of the year, but news of it took the chairman by surprise.

'Is she, by Jove?! Tremendous. To think that I knew her father, King George I.'

Belle could but laugh at the claim.

'My dear Chairman, even you aren't old enough to have known George I. George II, maybe. And he wasn't her father.'

The old man shrugged his shoulders. True and false memories had long since melded into one in his head and the confusion did not worry him one jot.

'Dash it all, Sir: is that so? Anyway, his name was George and he wore a crown. What are you putting on for the dear child?'

Belle was happy to share the detail of his endeavours.

'The normal meeting of Bath's worthies, including you, Sir. And I have arranged for a recital by the Abbey School for Boys' Choir. The music master, Mr Arthur Quigley, will conduct.'

The chairman recognised the name and dug deep to put a face to it. A memory from his own youth emerged.

'Young Arthur Quigley. Hasn't he gone potty?'

The statement was half true. At within ten years of Camshaft's age, Quigley was hardly young. He had, however, gallantly failed to teach Belle the violin and had gone quite mad, although the two were unconnected.

'Eccentric, certainly,' agreed Belle, who felt protective towards Mr Quigley. 'He likes to wear a tea cosy for a hat. But he's not so young. He's well into his eighties.'

Camshaft nodded.

'That's the chap. I remember him as a child. Pretty thing. Grew up to be a bachelor, I recall. You're a bachelor, aren't you?'

The directness and unexpected nature of the question surprised Belle.

51

'Yes,' he admitted cautiously.

'Nothing wrong with being a bachelor. Thought of being one myself before I met my wife. And after. Against the law, of course; death by hanging and all that. Load of nonsense. If we hung all the bachelors in Bath, we'd lose half its population of men and all its organists, heh?!'

He patted Belle on the knee.

'A good number of both, certainly, Sir,' Belle agreed, uncertain as to where the conversation was heading.

'Including my great-grandson, which ...' Ernest Camshaft stopped mid-sentence. He had remembered something. 'Heavens above!'

The old man stood up. Belle stood too.

'That's why I came here this morning!'

'You've lost me, Sir.'

'To talk to someone about the boy, of course. A fey lad if ever I've met one. He lodges outside Bath and spends his days cluttering up my library reading poetry when what he needs is employment. Do you have a clerk?'

Belle had a social conscience and – being without a permanent clerk – was in a position to help. He was also not averse to fey lads. He held back, however, as a thought crossed his mind. It would be remiss of him not to seek advantage from the situation.

'Before I say yes, Chairman, there's a small matter that is troubling me. Would you honour me with your advice?'

Belle detected a glimmer of understanding in Camshaft's eyes.

'I'm at your service, young Nash.'

'How does one get rid of a magistrate?'

Camshaft sat back down.

'Damn difficult. You have to prove wrongdoing. Not worth trying, in my opinion. The judiciary's a wretched bunch. Tend to stick together. Job for life. Shocking, really.'

Belle tried a different angle.

'How about getting a new one elected?'

Camshaft paused but only briefly. On such technical points, his mind was clear.

'First, the incumbent has to die. Then the Magistrate Selection Committee elects a new one.'

Belle nodded.

'And who is on the committee, Sir?'

Camshaft racked his brain.

'Been a long while since it met. Let me think. I chair the committee and Councillor Pollard is a member.'

'Jacob Pollard?' winced Belle with disgust.

He considered Pollard to be the worst of men. A bachelor at heart but twisted by hypocrisy into marrying, Pollard presented himself to the world as a worthy Methodist and preached against loose morals. In the moonlit hours, however, he would leave his wife at home and frequent the towpath of the Kennet & Avon Canal, where he was well known among the narrowboat lads who liked to earn a few shillings on the side. In Belle's opinion, hypocrites such as Pollard brought nothing but misery to the world.

'Yes. And Ashcroft!' continued Camshaft. 'There you are. Still got my wits about me.'

Or not, thought Belle, on hearing the name of Ashcroft.

'Charlie Ashcroft, Sir? He fell off his horse and broke his neck years ago.'

'Really? No one bothered to tell me. Or if they did, I've forgotten. I suppose we'd better elect a new member, then.'

Belle paused. An opportunity had opened up.

'And how is that done?' he asked cautiously.

Fortunately, the chairman had the answer to hand.

'It requires a quorum – and a quorum for a committee with only two surviving members is one. As committee chairman with the casting vote, that's me. I get to choose the new member. Quite right too. Why? Are you looking for a job?'

BELLE WAS NOT the only person getting on with their day. In Somerset Place, Gaia Champion had woken in brighter spirits than she had experienced for several months. Though she doubted her capacity to be stimulated by an investigation into the soufflé, she had enjoyed the company of friends the previous evening despite the calamitous food. It seemed ridiculous that she had waited an entire year before deciding to entertain.

'Why society should enforce misery on the bereaved is quite beyond me,' she thought, finishing off her breakfast of toast and marmalade in the parlour. 'And now that I no longer have Hercules to help in his work, I must find something to occupy my mind.'

She had fallen in love with Hercules in part because of his respect for her mind. She recalled how, when they were courting, he had shown her papers from his legal practice. They related to a brewery that had belonged to a late client. The widow was under pressure to sell the enterprise to her brother-in-law.

'Her future income is dependent on the monies of the sale,' Hercules had explained, 'and I fear a swindle is afoot. The profits of the brewery have declined precipitously since my client's death and my colleagues are at pains to understand why. Before I delve into the matter myself, I thought you might give it your attention.'

Within a few hours Gaia had found the answer.

'In the past twelve months, the brewery has purchased twice the volume of barley for the same output of beer. The books are either understating the inventory of beer or overstating the purchase of barley. That means either that the general manager is falsifying the books or that he is in league with the barleyman, or with the local tap houses, and the brother-in-law must be a fellow conspirator. Either way, the poor widow is being wronged and her rights must be protected.'

Hercules had been delighted but not surprised.

'Gaia, you are a shining star!' he had declared. 'I suspected that the brother-in-law was behind the plot. Now that you have drawn aside the veil, either he must pay the true price for the brewery plus a penalty for his crime or I will ensure that he and others are brought before a court.'

Hercules had continued to share his work with Gaia, and this had formed the basis of a happy and prosperous marriage. It was no great wonder that he had quickly become the preferred lawyer for Bath's widows. His firm had grown, albeit with the most important partner of all, Gaia, invisible to the eye.

It was with regrettable irony that the one widow whose interests Gaia had been unable to protect had been herself. With Hercules's death, her work had ended. Reluctantly, she had returned to the role ordained by men for women in society and the widows of Bath had lost their unacknowledged champion.

'At least from today I have banished black,' she said to herself, finishing her tea and rising from her chair. 'And I have a small task to entertain me.'

She rang a handbell on the table and the butler, who had been waiting outside the room, entered.

'You can fold away the table, John. To your knowledge, are Mme Galette and Florence in the kitchen?'

'I believe they are, Ma'am.'

'Good,' she replied, putting down her napkin. 'Then I shall proceed downstairs.'

She could sense the butler watching her as she left the room. There was tension in the air following the previous night's events. The household knew she would be investigating and they awaited the consequences.

Gaia could have called Mme Galette and Florence to her study for a meeting but she preferred not to appear haughty. Instead, she would visit the scene of the crime. It was her right, as mistress of the house, and she was likely to learn more besides.

In the hallway, she opened a hidden door in the panelling and descended to the basement. At the bottom of the stairs, she turned towards the kitchen. She found Mme Galette slicing vegetables and Florence on her knees, scrubbing the floor.

'Good morning, Mme Galette. Good morning, Florence,' Gaia said, announcing her presence.

Florence scrambled to her feet, keeping her eyes down as she dried her hands on her pinny. Mme Galette laid down her knife.

'*Bonjour Madame*,' replied the cook.

Florence had already endured a sleepless night. Now, with her head bowed, she burst into tears while simultaneously attempting an unsolicited explanation.

'I'm so terribly sorry, Ma'am, truly I am. Mme Galette told me to go to Helmsworth for the flour and I should have obeyed her, I know, but I hadn't seen my cousin Sally for a week – she works at Porter's on occasion – so I went to say hello and before I knew ...'

Gaia raised a hand.

'Florence, hush! And wipe away those tears. You're a grown woman and this is not the time to cry.'

The maid dried her face with a sleeve.

'Yes, Ma'am.'

Gaia continued, 'It is customary in an investigation that questions precede answers. Only in that way can an enquiry be conducted in a proper manner. I have determined that a full light shall be shone upon the sorry matter of the soufflé.'

'Yes, Ma'am,' the maid repeated. 'I understand.'

Gaia breathed in deeply, allowing all parties time to regain their composure.

'Having ascertained that you disobeyed Mme Galette, Florence, I wish to know exactly the type of flour you bought at Porter's which resulted in such a miserable soufflé.'

NOTES
- Sham Castle is a folly built in 1762 by the businessman Ralph Allen, who wanted to improve the view of Bathwick Hill from

his drawing room by adding a touch of medievalism to the hill beyond. Needing only the appearance of a castle, he built a castellated screen wall with four towers but nothing behind. It now graces the practice range of Bath Golf Club.

CHAPTER VI

A gathering of spies

WHEN PURCHASING HER magnificent chaise and four, Lady Passmore of Tewkesbury Manor had spent many an hour considering the decoration of its interior. Most carriages had leather seats, but Lady Passmore did not wish her carriage to be like others. Instead, she had ordered red velvet on the grounds that it was softer on the derrière.

To accompany the velvet, she decreed that the interior be lined with Italian red floral silk and red English Axminster carpet. The most challenging decision had been the curtains. After much deliberation, she had chosen Indian silk, red again but edged with gold brocade. Tied back to admit light, the privacy of the occupants remained satisfied by embroidered cotton net curtains from France.

It was not an inconspicuous carriage, nor one that naturally melded into a background. Nevertheless, it was the vehicle of choice for Lady Passmore and Mrs Pomeroy to conduct their investigation into the errant ways of Hezekiah Porter. Having committed themselves to the task the previous night, they, like Belle Nash, wanted to be ahead of their companions in the game. Parked indiscreetly beside Mrs Crust's Pie Shop, life inside the carriage was evidenced by the twitching of the net curtains between which hovered a lorgnette.

Standing behind the counter, Mrs Crust asked her assistant, 'How long has Lady Passmore's carriage been there?'

'An hour by my reckoning,' the girl answered, 'and still no

one's got out. The coachman's on show like a prize poodle, all dressed up in his fine clothes.'

'Go and see what they're up to,' ordered Mrs Crust, who could no longer bear not knowing. 'Apart from anything else, they're blocking our view of the green and the green's view of us. We might be losing a sale.'

The girl put on her bonnet and went outside. She looked up at the coachman.

'Upon my word, 'tis chilly for the time of year,' she started. 'Mrs Crust was wondering if you'd consider a slice of her fruit pie. We'll give you a special price and it's still warm from the oven.'

The coachman gave the girl a look of genuine regret.

'Not allowed to eat on duty, Miss,' he replied sadly. 'Not even something as lovely as a piece of Mrs Crust's fruit pie.'

'On duty? You been here the past hour doing nothing else but block our view. What's going on?'

'Can't tell you,' he replied in a hushed voice. 'Been sworn to secrecy by Her Ladyship.'

The girl put her hands on her hips. She was not used to people turning down an offer of pie.

'You're not being very secretive. This carriage is taking up half the green and you're sitting on top of it.'

The coachman frowned. What he wanted to say was, 'Tell that to Her Ladyship inside.' What he actually said was, 'You're doing no good bringing attention to the fact, Miss. When I'm off duty, I'll come by for a slice of pie, but for now please leave us be.'

Sensing that she would get no more out of him and thinking better of offering a slice of pie to the occupants of the carriage, the girl beat a retreat into the shop to give Mrs Crust an account of what had happened.

In fact, after an hour of intense undercover surveillance, Mrs Pomeroy was working up an appetite and, in the absence of cake, a piece of apple pie would have gone down nicely. She had wisely

59

insisted on bringing a small stool on which she was now perched and could see directly out of the window. Behind her, Lady Passmore reclined in regal comfort with her notebook on her lap and pencil in hand.

'I must say, Mrs Pomeroy, it has been a thrilling morning. I cannot recall another occasion when I've learned so much in an hour. To think that the Duke and Duchess of Cavendish's housekeeper shops at Porter's and not at Helmsworth! I would never have guessed. It's not as if they are short of a penny. Or, perhaps, they are.'

Mrs Pomeroy kept stock-still, eyes fixed to the lorgnette.

'I agree, Lady Passmore of Tewkesbury Manor. I was equally shocked to see Mrs Whitworth do her own shopping. No wonder she was wearing a veil. The shame of it!'

'But what, if anything, have we learned about the terrible Mr Porter?' asked Lady Passmore. 'That's what Mrs Champion would be asking us. And I want to find out before Miss Prim and the others get in on the act.'

Mrs Pomeroy paused to give the question some thought.

'It seems that this Mr Porter is able to seduce even decent people by charging them less than Helmsworth. I had not appreciated until today what an uncaring society we live in.'

Lady Passmore concurred.

'For once, you are correct, Mrs Pomeroy. In that regard, spying on Mr Porter has been most unsettling. In our short time here, we have lifted the lid off a terrible truth: that people we hold in the highest regard are not as we see them.'

She stopped as Mrs Pomeroy raised a hand, a pre-agreed signal to ready the pencil.

'Miss Applegate is approaching.'

Lady Passmore's pencil hovered expectantly.

'The same Miss Applegate who does the flowers at St Michael's Without?'

Mrs Pomeroy nodded.

Lady Passmore made a note of Miss Applegate's name and the time of her entering the shop.

'Never did like that woman. Painfully self-righteous. Now we know her sordid secret. Whoever next, I wonder?'

The street was quiet for five minutes, with no greater event to record than the departure of Miss Applegate with a brown cauliflower and a pair of drooping leeks.

'My back is starting to hurt,' complained Mrs Pomeroy.

Lady Passmore, relaxing into her red velvet seat, was not a woman who countenanced weakness in others.

'No one said this was going to be easy. Saving the soufflé will take guile and endurance. And nothing will be solved until we ascertain how Hezekiah Porter perpetrates his dreadful crimes.'

Mrs Pomeroy's hand shot up again. Lady Passmore fell quiet in anticipation.

'Damnation!' said Mrs Pomeroy sharply.

Her Ladyship stared at the back of her companion's head.

'Damnation because ... ?'

'We are not alone.'

Lady Passmore slapped down her notebook in impatience. It really was too much when subordinates failed to follow the drill.

'Mrs Pomeroy, I require detail, not drama!'

Mrs Pomeroy broke from her watch and turned inside. If Lady Passmore wanted detail, then she could have it.

'It's Miss Prim,' she explained. 'Phyllis Prim is here.'

This was important news; competition had arrived. Lady Passmore shifted across the seat to a position where she was above Mrs Pomeroy on the stool. Very gently, she parted the net curtain so she could see outside.

'This is our territory. How dare she intrude?'

'She doesn't know that. Shall I descend and tell her to come back later?'

Mrs Pomeroy had made a fair point, but Lady Passmore decided otherwise.

'Too risky. We would give ourselves away.'

They both looked through the gap in the net curtains as Miss Prim, her knitting bag in hand, passed the door of Porter's shop. She turned her head briefly to look inside but did not break stride.

'Amateur,' said Lady Passmore, withdrawing to her seat.

Mrs Pomeroy wiped her brow with a lace handkerchief and returned the lorgnette to her eyes. In an instant, her hand rose again.

'Miss Prim hasn't gone far. She has entered Haytit's tearoom and has taken a table by the window. From what I can see, she has removed a large shawl from her knitting bag and ... well, that is possibly the most peculiar piece of knitting I have ever seen.'

Lady Passmore was once again frustrated.

'What is? Really, Mrs Pomeroy, your reporting is as good as useless. Don't tell me it's the protest muffler she mentioned last night.'

'No, she's knitting a large pink shawl,' elaborated Mrs Pomeroy.

'Nothing peculiar about that.'

'With two holes in its centre.'

This piece of additional information hurriedly brought Lady Passmore back to the window. She swiftly took possession of the lorgnette.

'Clever girl,' she said. 'We underestimated her.'

'How do you mean?'

Lady Passmore gave herself a moment for further consideration but decided there was, indeed, only one possible conclusion.

'Miss Prim is spying on Porter's just as we are but using the shawl as camouflage. She is hiding behind her knitting but keeping a watch through the holes. Take a look.'

Mrs Pomeroy was about to obey when, at that moment, the

morning took another turn. In the far corner of Abbey Green appeared Gerhardt Kant, the last of the dinner guests to take up the challenge of investigating Hezekiah Porter. All had remained loyal to the pledge but each had approached the task differently.

Unaware of the tactics of the others, and having eschewed a disguise, Gerhardt recognised the carriage on the other side of the green and waved at the two women inside.

'*Guten Morgen*, Lady Passmore of Tewkesbury Manor,' he shouted across the green. '*Und* Mrs Pomeroy!'

'The fool,' snapped Lady Passmore. 'Now everyone will know we're here.'

Gerhardt would have waved at Miss Prim as well but her attempt at camouflage kept her hidden from him. On seeing the Prussian, her natural fear of foreigners had led her to retreat into deep cover by placing the entire shawl over her head. Only her eyes remained visible through the holes.

Having waved merrily at the carriage, Gerhardt set about his own more direct plan of action. He stood outside Porter's for a few seconds to study the shop, then stepped forward to enter.

'He's going in,' said a stunned Mrs Pomeroy.

'What a brazen Prussian,' remarked Lady Passmore. 'Entering the lion's den.'

'Ooh,' twittered Miss Prim in Haytit's tearoom, in a mixture of fear and excitement. She began to shake, the large shawl over her head quivering like a giant pink blancmange, inadvertently transforming herself into the most appetising thing seen in the window of Haytit's for years.

P ORTER'S HAD A stale, musky and slightly rancid smell like that of a gravedigger's shirt, and the visual appeal of a morgue. Half-dead vegetables and tired fruit waited for their demise in wooden boxes. On the shelves, bags of sugar, salt and flour were lined up like so many discarded gravestones. A single lamp cast a dull light over the rear counter on which were placed the scales. Gerhardt cast his eyes around and thought how no shop like this would be allowed in the *Deutschordenstaat*. Only in England would anyone countenance a place like Porter's, let alone dignify it with their custom.

Gerhardt picked up a sad bunch of carrots and inspected them.

'*Typische* English limpness,' he said disparagingly. '*Ach, für deutsche Stärke.*'

A man approached from behind him, his clothes the colour of jute, his hair and skin grey. Skilled at passing unnoticed, he came to within a foot of his new customer.

'Was it carrots you were looking for, Sir?' he asked in a weasel voice.

Gerhardt turned around, surprised by the man's proximity.

'*Nein*,' he said, taking a step back.

'We normally sell them by the bunch, rather than individually. It's cheaper that way, which is what our customers want.'

Gerhardt blinked in amazement. He picked up another bunch.

'These your customers want? But they are miserable, *vilted* things!'

Hezekiah Porter took the carrots from Gerhardt, returning them to their box.

'They are wilted, Sir, because they come from Wiltshire. It is the local variety and we wouldn't stock them if our customers didn't demand them. Now if it's not the Wiltshire wilteds that you want, what are you after?'

Gerhardt had not expected to be put on the spot. Or to be so easily intimidated.

'I am newly here in this Royal City of Bath. *Und* I am liking to see the sights.'

It was not an answer that satisfied Mr Porter, who had never met a customer like Gerhardt, nor Gerhardt's infelicity with language.

'You decided just to "pop in", as it were? Or was Porter's specifically recommended to you? We supply some of the very best households in the city.'

Gerhardt squirmed. He was regretting entering the shop but decided he had to work a little harder.

'Your store is in the whole of *mein Heimatstadt* Königsberg famous. I was passing *vorbei und* decided that I a closer look must take.'

More mystified than flattered, Mr Porter took a step forward.

'And where are you staying in the city, Sir, if you don't mind my asking?'

Gerhardt took a step back.

'In Gay Street,' he replied. 'You surely know it.'

'Charming spot, Sir. And what brings you into the city centre so unfashionably early in the morning?'

Mr Porter's dark eyes stared intensely into Gerhardt's own. The young Prussian struggled to make up an answer.

'The air.'

'You're tired of the air on Gay Street? You prefer the stale air of the city centre?'

Gerhardt had to do better.

'*Und* sugar!' he declared. 'Now I am remembering! I am wanting *ein* pound sugar to buy.'

Mr Porter removed a bag from the shelf, placed it on the counter and returned to Gerhardt.

'A pound of sugar, Sir. But we have a special price if you buy two. Or perhaps a tin of Jeremiah Colman's mustard at half-price.'

The multi-layered offer disorientated Gerhardt who, under his powder, felt a sweat breaking out. Mr Porter's complex approach to retail pricing was confusing him.

'*Nein, danke.*'

'Are you sure, Sir?' Mr Porter said, as if providing a lifeline to a dying man. 'We have an excellent offer on radishes this week.'

'Radishes? *Ach*, *Radieschen*,' Gerhardt replied, escaping for safety into his native tongue. '*Nein*, for *die Radieschen* have I no love. The sugar only, *bitte*.'

Mr Porter shook his head in disappointment.

'You won't get the best deal by just buying sugar, Sir. But if that's what you want, then it's thruppence.'

Gerhardt heaved a sigh of relief. At last, a price to complete the purchase, although he had no idea whether it was a fair price or not. To make matters worse, he had a poor understanding of English currency. He removed his purse and peered into it, looking lost.

'Can I help you, Sir?' said Mr Porter, moving his head closer. Reaching into the purse and removing a shiny shilling, he said, 'There we are, that's what we want. Thruppence exactly. A good day to you, Sir.'

Mr Porter, however, had overplayed his hand. Though not a master of the currency, Gerhardt still recognised a shilling from a thruppenny bit and realised that a theft had been committed.

'I want a receipt,' he demanded, filled with Prussian pride.

'A receipt, Sir?'

'I demand a receipt. A *Kassenbon*. *Eine Quittung*. *Ein* pound sugar *für* three pence. In Königsberg, we are always the receipt demanding.'

Reluctantly, Mr Porter went behind the counter and brought out a receipt book. He dusted it off and wrote down the details of the purchase before tearing out the slip.

'There, Sir. One pound of sugar for three pence.'

Gerhardt took the receipt, considered asking for his change, then thought better of it. On balance, the theft of ninepence at this point was money well spent. With the receipt and the sugar in hand, he left the building.

NOTES

- The old English currency, abolished with the UK's entry into the European Economic Community in 1971, had pounds, shillings and pence, now called old pence. There were twelve old pence (12d) to a shilling and twenty shillings (20s or 240 old pence) to the pound. The penny itself could be subdivided into two halfpennies (always known as ha'pennies and pronounced *hayp'nies*) or four farthings. The system made good sense when items such as eggs were bought by the dozen, as they still are. Goods were, therefore, never bought in tens.
- There are over sixty churches in Bath, two of which are named St Michael's Without and St Michael's Within. The former is built just outside the city's original walls, the latter inside.

CHAPTER VII

Of Paradise Lost and Frankenstein

GAIA CHAMPION SAT in her study, awake but with her eyes and mind closed. It was a very different state of being from the days when she had advised her husband on how best to protect Bath's widows. His death had brought her a year's isolation and entrapment in loneliness, as demanded by polite society.

Dressed in black, immobile in her chair, she had questioned the cruelty of a world that had taken from her not only a husband but also the ability to use her mind. She had counted the weeks and wondered at how the very thing that had given her purpose – her work – had vanished with Hercules's death. With him at her side, she had visualised her future spreading out as a twin progress; without him, that future had turned in on itself, the days heaped like concentric circles, each a repeat of the last.

When Hercules was alive, she had given her dependency on him little thought. They were equals in marriage and it was on that basis that their relationship was founded. Only with his death had she realised that their equality was a fiction. Had she been the one struck down by cholera, Hercules would have mourned her passing but his work – his purpose in life outside marriage – would have continued. How very different it was to be a woman.

She realised that the semblance of equality that she had achieved in marriage had been that of the man to give, not the woman to take. It had been gifted to her by Hercules as an act of love: equality as an act of charity. How blind she had been. It was not

Hercules's fault or intention, but she had never been his equal, merely the recipient of his patronage.

'It is unjust,' she said to herself. 'Simply unjust. Equality should be a fact, not gifted, nor transient. And if it is neither, how, then, might it be achieved?'

It was her first full day of discarding black. Like dinner the night before, it had seemed a significant step, a declaration that she would re-engage with society, even if society decreed otherwise. She had begun the day energised from questioning Mme Galette and Florence on the issue of the soufflé. An hour later, however, she found herself back in her study, alone in her chair.

She was succumbing once more, the sense of entrapment returning, her thoughts all prefaced by the same four words: when Hercules was alive ...

The circle that bound her was broken by a knock on the door and the appearance of Mary, her maid.

'Oh, Mary. I was lost in thought and none of it good. You have done me a service by coming in. What concerns you?'

'A young man, Ma'am. He's brought you a note from Guildhall. He says he is Councillor Nash's clerk.'

This raised Gaia's interest.

'A clerk? Councillor Nash has no clerk! Let me see.'

Mary handed over an envelope and Gaia pulled out a slip of paper. She recognised Belle's handwriting.

My dear Gaia,

I have been given as a clerk Chairman Camshaft's great-grandson, one Lucius Lush. He is thin but enthusiastic. I don't know what to do with him, so I have sent him on an errand to deliver the note you now read.

Would you be so generous as to feed him and send him back to me, with a note of your own, confirming that I may attend Somerset Place this evening to discuss events with you?

69

With all my heart,
Belle
P.S. A wonderful dinner last night! I am ever your servant.

Gaia laughed, partly at the idea that Belle required permission to visit her home. As her closest friend and confidante, the door was always open.

'The young man is waiting downstairs?' she asked.

'Yes, Ma'am.'

'Excellent. I will write a note for him to take back to Councillor Nash. But before he returns to Guildhall, Mary, please direct him to the kitchen and ask Mme Galette to give him a sandwich and a glass of milk. I take it that Mme Galette is here.'

'Indeed, Ma'am,' confirmed Mary. 'She is with Miss Prim's cook, Mrs Mulligatawny. They are inspecting the flour that was used to make the soufflé. Mme Galette thought a second pair of eyes would be handy.'

Gaia had crossed to her desk and was already writing a reply to Belle.

'The more help we have, the more progress we will make. Here, Mary, take this note.'

'Yes, Ma'am.'

The maid took the folded note, which had been placed into an envelope, curtseyed and made to leave the room. Then a thought occurred to Gaia. A positive thought.

'Oh, Mary. The clerk, is he a nice young man?'

The maid blushed.

'Yes, Ma'am. Very nice – indeed!'

Gaia smiled.

'We must never forget the importance of making new friends in life. And of looking after those we already have, of course. In which regard, please tell John that Councillor Nash will honour us with a visit this evening.'

70

LUCIUS LUSH HAD become excited at the thought of working as a clerk for, much as he loved poetry, *Paradise Lost* had a diminishing return on its twentieth reading. On entering Guildhall, he had been enthralled. The building was alive with intrigue as men dashed hither and thither with bundles of papers while others held whispered conversations in dark nooks. Sitting serenely in their midst had been the councillor for whom he might now work: the urbane, casual and elegant Belle Nash.

Having shaken his hand, Belle had stepped back and studied Lush. In some ways, he had seen elements of his younger self: slim, a little shorter, skin the colour of milk, chestnut eyes that matched his hair and an engaging smile. Indeed, he had been struck by Lush's beauty – graceful Ovid could have been no fairer – and had been about to congratulate him when the thought of Gerhardt congratulating himself on his beauty every time he looked in the mirror came into his head.

In fear of incipient narcissism, he therefore had said only, 'I am honoured to make your acquaintance, young man. Please sit. You come highly recommended, but I suppose I should interview you first to ensure your suitability. The recommendation was that of your great-grandfather, after all!'

'Thank you, Sir,' Lush had replied. 'That would certainly make sense.'

Returning to his desk, Belle had decided the best approach was to ask Lush's advice on matters of the day.

'So, young Master Lush, when it comes to being introduced to a princess, should the bishop of Bath & Wells rank above or below the chairman of Bath City Corporation?'

The new clerk might as well have been questioned on the properties of helium.

'I fear I couldn't say, Sir. Might it be decreed somewhere? In an Act of Parliament?'

Belle had laughed.

'Parliament passes plenty of laws but none on what matters. These are decisions that we have to make for ourselves. In this case, Chairman Camshaft is our employer and Bishop George Monstrance my godfather – a High Church man with a reputation for unholy tantrums and a love for his cat.'

'Then I suppose it depends on who would take the greater insult. Things happen around Great-Grandfather Ernest that he fails to notice. In such circumstances, I'd opt for the bishop, Sir.'

'A good answer, young philosopher,' Belle had agreed, 'but it also depends on who represents the greater threat. Remind me to lend you a book on the subject. It's written by an Italian who knew a thing or two about difficult bishops and civil rule.'

'Machiavelli, Sir,' Lush had responded immediately. 'Niccolò di Bernardo dei Machiavelli: 3 May 1469 to 21 June 1527. Italian Renaissance diplomat, philosopher and writer, best known for *The Prince* (*Il Principe*), written in 1513. Often called the father of modern political science. Served for many years as a senior official in the Florentine Republic. Wrote comedies, carnival songs and poetry.'

Belle had taken another look at his new clerk. He'd liked the boy at once and had found his merry wit attractive. He had also agreed with the chairman that Lush was a bachelor through and through, although whether the lad appreciated the fact for himself had yet to be revealed.

With the essentials of the interview now complete, Belle had informed Lush of his appointment to the post and had sent him out with the note for Gaia. That way, Belle had surmised, he could get on with the rest of his own day's work unimpeded.

So it was, less than an hour later, that Lush found himself in the kitchens of Somerset Place, eating a chicken sandwich and drinking a glass of milk, his day having taken another turn.

'Very handsome of you, Madam,' he said to Mme Galette. 'The walk up the hill gave me a hunger. And this chicken is delicious.'

'*Oui*, it was a good bird,' Mme Galette replied. 'Mind you, even a *poulet pourri* could not have been worse than *le soufflé* I made *hier soir*.'

'The soufflé?' asked Lush.

'*Le monstre* came out the oven *comme une roche*. It is why I invited *la cuisinière de* Miss Prim for 'er advice. *Je pense que l'idiote* Florence was cheated on the flour. *Donc,* we are making *deux soufflés de plus* from the same recipe, one with fresh flour from Helmsworth, and *ze ozzer* with the sawdust from Porter's. That will tell us whether *eet* is Porter's flour which was responsible for *la catastrophe culinaire*.'

Being politely brought up, Lush cleaned his fingers on a napkin and rose to introduce himself. He had earlier made the acquaintance of Mary and Florence, both Somerset girls, but on approaching the guest cook he noticed she was from climes more distant than even Mme Galette's Paris and correctly deduced India as her birthplace.

'Lucius Lush, Madam. And whom do I have the honour to address?'

Before the lady from Tiruchirappalli in Tamil Nadu could open her mouth to speak, Mme Galette interjected.

'*Elle s'appelle* Mulligatawny,' she explained. 'She is *une dame charmante* and an excellent cuisinière but, *bien súr*, she will not *comprendre* a word you say.'

'Delighted to make your acquaintance, Mrs Mulligatawny,' said Lush, who had never met anyone named after a soup before.

Mrs Mulligatawny raised her eyes to the heavens. Contrary to Mme Galette's assertion, she had a fine grasp of the English language, was an avid reader of novels and could make herself perfectly well understood when anyone gave her the chance. Indeed, given that she could understand even Mme Galette's garbled mix of French and English, it was a source of eternal frustration that only one person in Bath – Mrs Champion – had ever bothered to pronounce her real name, let alone find out what it was: Aagalyadevi Balasubramaniam. Aside from Gaia, everyone named her by the soup she prepared to perfection.

It was not a satisfactory situation and Mrs Mulligatawny – whose given name we feel obliged to fall in with – had committed herself to return an insult with a jibe. Not that her English listeners, let alone the French, ever understood her purpose, so incredibly dense were their brains.

'Carrot to you,' she replied sharply to Lush, before shifting her gaze in Mme Galette's direction. 'And *choufleur* to my friend, Mme Galette.'

I N THE PAST year Belle had made a point of visiting Gaia, if not every day, then several times a week. The company of friends had been essential for her to survive the period of mourning. He believed it would be equally important now that she sought to rebuild her life.

To Belle's mind, the loss of Hercules Champion had been a political calamity for Bath as well as a personal tragedy for Gaia. In Guildhall, the most corrupt councillors had cheered the news that cholera had claimed Hercules because it meant that his wife was now removed from the legal cut and thrust. The widows of Bath and their assets were once again vulnerable and ripe for the plucking.

Although legal opportunities were closed to her, Belle longed to help Gaia find a way to participate in city life once more. He knew how valuable she would be. As a councillor, Belle had some authority, but he could be lazy and lacked Gaia's passion. He also acknowledged that Gaia had the better mind. On the rare occasion when he was faced with a challenge, it was Gaia to whom he would turn for advice. She also had qualities of leadership that he lacked. It was an idiotic society, in his opinion, that denied her the means to use them.

It was six o'clock in the evening and Belle and Gaia were sipping the drams of whisky that Pritchard had brought them. They relaxed, as friends do at the end of a day, the setting sun casting its last light through the windows, a small fire in the grate fending off the chill that still accompanies nights in late March.

Belle explained to Gaia about his appointment to the Magistrate Selection Committee and about his hiring of his new clerk. Gaia congratulated him on both.

'Removing Magistrate Wood would be very welcome,' she agreed. 'It is a pity we must wait until he dies before there is a change.'

'Bath needs a fresh beak on the bench.'

'And a less corrupt one.'

'Even a slightly less corrupt one.'

There was a pause while they both tried to imagine an uncorrupt magistracy.

'Which of Bath's great statesmen could be relied on to prosecute Hezekiah Porter for ruining our soufflé?' Belle wondered. 'That, in a nutshell, Madam, is the problem. That, and Wood's longevity.'

'No easy justice, then, for Mr Porter's victims,' nodded Gaia. 'Not that we should give up the fight.'

They sipped their whiskies. Until the wider group of friends reconvened on the Saturday for Belle's Gay Street tea party, there seemed little more to say on the subject. Instead, Gaia turned to domestic matters.

'Herr Kant — I thought he was on tremendous form last night.'

Belle recognised the compliment as a mild admonishment.

'A little too combative, I fear. He gets easily bored. You'll never guess what he said on the way home.'

At that point, Pritchard entered the room and made a light cough into his white glove, as butlers conventionally do, to announce his presence and that of the Mesdames Galette and

Mulligatawny out in the corridor. Gaia, however, held up a hand to interrupt him for she wanted to hear Belle's story first.

'During your supper, Gerhardt overheard Miss Prim say that she is frightened of sheep,' Belle went on. 'It sparked his interest. He believes he can rid her of "this irrational fear". He wants to undertake an experiment of "the mind" – *ein Experiment des Geistes* – on her.'

Gaia laughed and sipped her whisky.

Belle continued, 'He's been reading that frightening novel *Frankenstein*, by Percy Shelley's widow ... .'

'Mary Wollstonecraft's daughter.'

'Exactly. And in German too! Can you imagine? We must find something to distract him.'

In the corridor, Mrs Mulligatawny's mouth fell open and the blood drained from her face. She and Mme Galette had wanted to show Gaia the results of their own experiments with the two flours, but what Belle had said was no laughing matter. Caring for Miss Prim was already a daily burden, what with the faints and her habit of dropping balls of wool for the cook to trip over. The idea that Herr Kant might do anything to her mistress approaching what Dr Frankenstein had done to his collection of body parts filled her with horror. She had just been reading *Frankenstein* herself and was considering translating it – into Tamil.

NOTES
- Belle compares Lucius Lush to Ovid. According to Ancient Greek legend, Ovid was born an exceptionally handsome boy and, after a dalliance with the water nymph Salmacis, was transformed into Hermaphroditus, the god of effeminate men, from whom the word 'hermaphrodite' derives.
- Mary Wollstonecraft (1759–1797) was a feminist philosopher who wrote novels, treatises and a history of the French Revolution. *A Vindication of the Rights of Woman* (1792), often

regarded as the first feminist treatise, imagined a social order based on reason in which women had equality with men. She married William Godwin (1756–1836), a fellow philosopher and novelist. Wollstonecraft died less than a month after giving birth to their daughter Mary Shelley.

CHAPTER VIII

Of tea and dishwater

I
T WAS ONLY a matter of time, Belle Nash thought, before his elevation to the Magistrate Selection Committee would cause a stir. No matter that the committee had not met for more than a decade and might not do so for another. In his experience, it was often the most inconsequential of events that caused the worst storms.

As a man at home in the England of the first half of the nineteenth century, Belle was a betting man and, besides, a man who divided up his day by cups of tea rather than the striking of the hour. He placed a penny piece on his desk and wagered with himself, therefore, that a response to his appointment to the committee would come as early as the next working day, and he put the time more precisely at around the third cup of tea.

To try and force the wheels of chance, and to give his new clerk something to do, Belle appointed Lucius Lush his personal *chai wallah*, and Lush rose to the challenge magnificently. One cup followed another, and shortly before eleven o'clock Belle had his third cup of tea in hand. He was studying the proposed decoration of a bandstand for the forthcoming royal visit when, as anticipated, a man with a formidably broad frame filled the doorway.

Belle was alerted to the visitor's presence by the sound of Lush's teacup suddenly rattling on its saucer. It was the first time the young man had met one of the bigger beasts of Guildhall.

'Magistrate Wood! You honour me with your presence, Sir,' declared Belle. 'In my doorway. In all your splendour.'

78

Obadiah Wood did not move and time seemed suddenly frozen, with Belle sitting at his desk about to sip his tea, Lush standing by the window about to drop his and the magistrate's ample figure seemingly stuck halfway between his own realm and Belle's.

Some people carry their weight well, retaining their facial features intact above the bulk beneath. The magistrate was not such a one. His flesh swelled over his collar, his features were engulfed by fat, his eyes sunken into their sockets as if cored from a ball of lard.

Recalling Mrs Crust's tale of Wood having left Porter's two days earlier with a side of Wiltshire's finest, Belle was suddenly struck by the thought that a transmogrification had occurred. As Wood stood seemingly wedged in the doorway, Belle imagined him as a giant piece of gammon.

His reverie filled the awkward silence, but left the magistrate stranded.

'Invite me in, you buffoon,' he said at last. 'That's the practice in Guildhall. I can't stand here all day.'

'My apologies, Magistrate Wood. You perceive me to be impolite but I was merely overawed by your vast presence.'

'What?' roared Wood, suspecting an insult.

'I mean, vast in its natural authority, in comparison with which my own pretensions to eminence are thin.'

'Thin?'

'Thin, Sir, as are we all who do not live off the fat of the land,' replied Belle, nimbly backtracking whilst overlaying an insult with an insult. 'My chamber is spartan, but I would be honoured if you would fill it.'

'Fill it?'

Belle laughed, for there was nothing more enjoyable to him than a war of words.

'With your sagacity and charm, Sir. Nothing more.'

79

Wood entered the room and did almost fill it. He was without question a large man. His hips and shoulders were more than a yard in width, while circumnavigating his girth would have satisfied many a morning constitutional.

'Master Lush, a chair and a cup of tea for our learned and honoured guest.'

Lush looked round desperately for a chair that might take the councillor's weight and finally pulled up a sturdy Jacobean carver that had always seemed out of place among Belle's flimsier Regency models, with their splayed legs and curved arms.

The chair audibly groaned, and the arms visibly twisted as Wood applied his weight to it, cantilevering his giant belly down between his legs. He leant forward and confronted Belle across the table, threatening to poke his host in the eye with a finger.

'You're up to something, Nash, and I don't like its smell.'

'Am I up to something, Sir?' Belle said, with a slight smile. 'Were that so, Special Constable "Dimwit" would have me arrested at once and I'd be in your dock. Master Lush, the magistrate's tea, if you'd be so good.'

The magistrate was not in the mood for humour. Lightness of any kind was alien to his nature.

'You should show more respect for our special constable, Nash. And you know full well what I'm talking about. You've been appointed to the committee responsible for choosing the next magistrate. It's a disgrace.'

'So that's what's brought you!' protested Belle, collecting the penny piece off the desk. 'But it's not such a heavy matter that it need concern you, Sir. Chairman Camshaft realised the committee was a member short, that's all.'

It was not an explanation that Wood was prepared to swallow.

'It's marbles that he's short of. You're the most worthless man ever to have been made a councillor and utterly unfit to choose a magistrate.'

Belle smiled. He took such insults as a compliment.

'Magistrate Wood, in insulting me, you do Chairman Camshaft an injustice for I was his choice. As for the chairman, allow me to introduce my new clerk, who has the honour of being his great-grandson.'

Wood twisted his upper body, to the extent that his torso had any lateral mobility, and the chair gave another creak. He fixed Lush with a withering stare, all the while processing this new information. Knowing how the machinery of Guildhall worked, he quickly made the connection between Lush and Belle's appointment to the committee.

'Your tea, Sir,' said Lush, timidly holding out a china cup and saucer.

The magistrate sneered and returned his gaze to Belle.

'Step carefully, Nash. I have little time for you and your limp-wristed ilk.'

Behind the insult, Belle sensed that his visitor was undecided whether or not a political game was afoot, but, by now, his patience was exhausted.

'Me and my elk, did y'say? You are mistaken, Sir. I own no elk. I once had a Border Terrier named Pickles but never an elk. Master Lush, are you aware of my ever having had an ...'

Belle's descent into nonsense had its desired effect. Wood heaved himself to his feet, at the same time wrenching the arms of the carver out of their sockets.

'You're wasting my time, Sir!' Wood roared. 'You're nothing but a preposterous fool.'

He wobbled to the door like a sea cow on rocks and nearly flattened another man who at that moment was attempting to enter. Being of inverse proportions to the magistrate, the newcomer survived by pressing himself against the wall. Belle sighed despondently on recognising the identity of the next visitor. How much better for the world if he had been flattened.

81

'More tea, please, Master Lush,' he said. 'Unless Councillor Jacob Pollard will partake of Magistrate Wood's undrunk cup as we discuss my appointment to this contentious committee.'

FIFTEEN MINUTES LATER Councillor Pollard departed in no more gracious a mood than Magistrate Wood had done before him.

'Goodness,' said Lush. 'What was that all about? They seemed terribly upset about something of no consequence. Or have I misunderstood the committee to which you've been appointed?'

Belle slumped back in his chair, exhausted. He had dealt with both men with aplomb but had found the experience draining, like a pugilist undertaking consecutive fights.

'That, dear boy, is what politics is all about. Threat and fear.'

'That's silly.'

'But true, nevertheless. To them, the world is full of phantom dangers all feeding their anxieties and prejudice.'

'Phantom dangers? Such as?'

Belle did not know how frank he should be. Should he suggest the fear of men ceding control to women; or the fear that love between men might destroy society? Instead, he opted for prevarication.

'It's complicated, Master Lush, especially for one of so tender an age as yourself.'

It was not an answer that satisfied his employee.

'I can handle complicated, Sir. What did Magistrate Wood mean by "your ilk"? I understood the wit of your reply but not his comment. And why was Councillor Pollard ill at ease in our presence?'

The lad was no fool, thought Belle. He had recognised Pollard's inner turmoil even if he did not yet understand the conflict that fed it: the warped anger of the twisted bachelor. But as he was trying to frame an answer, a separate thought occurred, one that followed from his conversation with Gaia Champion the previous evening. Maybe if he introduced Lush to Gerhardt Kant, the clerk could distract Gerhardt from his unusual desire to experiment on their Gay Street neighbour Phyllis Prim by engaging in a healthier pastime.

'Your questions are timely,' he said, reaching for his quill, 'but time is of the essence. There's someone I'd like you to meet. Here's his name and address and I'll write a note for you to take. He's Prussian — not in itself a shortcoming, but he doesn't know how to make tea. Perhaps you could show him how it's done.'

'Are there no other tasks for me? Teaching tea-making to a Prussian seems an indulgence for a rainy day.'

'On the contrary,' said Belle, sealing the note in an envelope with a wax stick and handing it over. 'It is of the highest urgency. Off you go.'

As Lush slipped away, Belle placed his head in his hands to think things through.

'No harm can come from it,' he whispered to himself. 'It will give the boy something to do and get him out of my office. Having someone closer to his own age to talk to will also be good for Gerhardt. And, after consuming five cups of tea before midday, it will rescue my abused bladder from further punishment. Thus is solved that most difficult of issues: what to do with an unoccupied clerk.'

BELLE WAS NOT the only person acting on what they thought was a good idea. For a second day, Miss Prim had placed herself in the window of Shirley Haytit's tearoom to study the premises of the master criminal Hezekiah Porter. The problem Miss Prim faced was maintaining the requirement of being occupied by knitting. She simply knitted too quickly. In the last twenty-four hours she had completed the shawl (with eyeholes), two scarves and three pairs of gloves.

83

The rising pile of finished knitwear had attracted the attention of the dame Haytit. On principle, to have any returning customer was unwelcome because it risked being held to account for the quality of her offering; Miss Prim was even less welcome, for she could survive a whole day on a single cup of tea and half a scone and was now turning the tearoom into a clothes emporium. Eventually, the shop-owner had had enough.

'Why all that knitting, Ma'am, if I might beg to ask? If you're helping the war effort, France was defeated long ago.'

Miss Prim was not a woman to nurse dislikes, but she made an exception for Mrs Haytit, who smelt of liquor and whose unwanted attentions disrupted her ability to monitor Porter's. Not that there had been much to observe. Belle's distant cousin had not returned, and the rival team of Passmore and Pomeroy had managed a mere two-hour stint that morning.

'I am aware that the war is over, thank you. Mme Galette would not be working as cook for Mrs Champion if it were not.'

Mrs Haytit stuck her head forward, presenting a view of her grease-laden, lice-ridden scalp.

'What's that you're knitting there, then? Looks like half a cannonball to me.'

'It's a tea cosy,' Miss Prim explained coolly. 'They're all the rage in polite society.'

'And what do you need that for?'

'For keeping tea warm, of course.'

There was nothing Mrs Haytit liked less than being taken for a fool, the more so on her own premises, and she flew into a rage.

'You wouldn't need to knit a tea cosy if you drank the stuff before it got cold. It's customers like you who make my life a nightmare. Sitting there all day at my best table in the window as if you own the place. Why don't you go back to your drawing room and do your knitting there?'

Miss Prim blanched at the ferocity of the assault.

'I don't understand.'

'Making a tea cosy in my tearoom. Jesus and Mary, whatever next? Won't have a second cup? You're up to something, you are. Spying on Porter's if I'm not mistaken. Don't think I haven't noticed. Now you put your knitting into that bag and take your leave before I kick you out.'

Miss Prim had not anticipated being found out and could feel a faint coming on. She clutched at her collar.

'Right, that's it,' snapped Mrs Haytit, who turned towards the kitchen. 'You two cooks in there, stop chipping the burnt bits off them rock cakes and come out here. There's a customer needs to leave.'

When she turned back, however, Miss Prim was no longer in the chair. Instead, she was spread-eagled unconscious on the floor. Mrs Haytit threw her hands in the air, the veins beside her temples pulsating furiously.

'Mother of God, that's all I need, a customer a-fainted on the floor! I hate customers, I do. Hate them all.'

'Is everything alright, Mrs Haytit?' said one of the cooks.

'No, it's bloody well not. Fetch me a bucket.'

'Throwin' up, is she?' enquired the cook, who was familiar with customers' most common response to what they were served.

'She's not hurled, she's passed out,' Mrs Haytit yelled back, rolling up her sleeves. 'Fill the bucket with bilge water and bring it here. She'll soon wake up with a good soak.'

CHAPTER IX

Experimentation

GERHARDT KANT COULD not imagine life without a mirror. He thanked Belle Nash for providing him with a home, a means of physical interaction and a counterpart for verbal discourse but for true companionship there was nothing quite like a mirror. On first arriving at Gay Street, he had rushed from room to room in a state of nervous excitement. Belle had been thrilled, believing his new companion to be enthralled by the fine proportions of the rooms and his impressive collection of *Königliche* porcelain. Instead, Gerhardt's purpose had been to identify the location of all the mirrors in the house.

His day followed a routine. Before and after dressing, he would study himself in the full-length mirror in the bedchamber. He would then catch his profile in a small oval mirror on the half-landing. In the hallway, at the foot of the stairs, there was a third mirror with a plain oak frame in which he would check that he had survived the descent intact before entering the drawing room. Once inside, a gilded Queen Anne mirror hung between the two large windows that looked onto Gay Street. Most people would by instinct walk to the windows to watch people promenade, but Gerhardt had no interest in the city and stood between the windows to admire the view of himself.

On this particular spring morning, he had descended in high spirits and was engaged in an extended period of self-admiration. With the light streaming in, he focussed on his face, turning his head this way and that, admiring the profile and the quarter-profile, then trying the same look but with his head bent forward or to one side, at an angle. He studied himself wearing a broad smile with his teeth gleaming and his hands held out behind his head in an exclamation of joy. Then he adopted an alternative pose with his mouth closed and lips pursed, fingers across his eyes in mock distress. Finally, he broke the pose and jumped up and down like an Athenian athlete limbering up before a marathon.

'I am beautiful,' he declared to himself in the mirror. 'Even if the rest of the world exists not, I remain beautiful. *Warum?* Perhaps I am a tiny "monad", *ja*, endowed with perception *und* appetite. Certainly, I have an appetite for *Frühstück*. So, maybe *mein* name is Gottfried Leibniz. *Heiaha!*'

Overwhelmed by a joke only he could understand, Gerhardt creased up in laughter. He rocked back and forth, moaning with intellectual pleasure until he fell to the floor with his thin legs kicking in the air. He could have stayed there for hours like a beetle on its back, but the doorbell rang and interrupted his joy. Wiping tears from his face, Gerhardt righted himself and clambered to his feet. The doorbell rang again.

'*Ja, ja, ich komme!* *Ihr* damn *Englisch* are *mit* your *verdammten* doorbells so impatient.'

Belle employed a part-time maid, but she was encouraged to arrive at midday so as not to be embarrassed by unruly morning activity. If the door was to be opened at this hour, it was to be self-service. Gerhardt twisted the handle.

'So, who on this day here in Bath, disturbs *mein* time *und* place?' he said, looking out onto Gay Street. He found himself staring at a fresh-faced, wide-eyed young man whose cheeks were ablaze with colour following an uphill walk from Guildhall. His hair was dishevelled from the morning breeze. Gerhardt's manner changed instantly.

'*Guten Morgen*, most charming young visitor. *Willkommen in der Gay Street.*'

87

'Good morning, Sir,' replied Lucius Lush, for it was he. 'Please excuse me for interrupting your day, but I have a message from Councillor Nash for Herr Kant. Might you be Herr Kant?'

Gerhardt blinked. His fame was growing.

'*A votre service*,' he said, bowing theatrically.

'Then this letter is for you, Sir,' proffered Lush, handing over the sealed message.

Gerhardt took the folded paper and broke the wax. The arrival of the message from Belle was an unexpected pleasure, made more welcome by the good looks and soft graces of the messenger. Guessing that the missive might contain private words, he stepped into the hallway to read it.

Dearest Gerhardt,

Meet my new clerk who goes by the name of Lucius Lush. He is a delightful man, almost a boy, seemingly unaware of his own bachelorhood. Let us pray that his innocence does not turn to bitterness; that the sweet petals of rosy youth do not shrivel and decay.

There is, however, little for him to do at Guildhall today and I thought you and he could entertain each other in conversation or by doing a jigsaw, collecting insects or drying spring flowers.

Master Lush also makes an excellent pot of tea.

Big kisses,

Belle

Gerhardt read the letter not once but twice. He looked up and studied the outline of the messenger, who smiled kindly in return. He immediately dismissed the idea of doing anything as dull as a jigsaw.

Instead, he saw in the clerk the perfect candidate for testing his theories of the mind, better even than Phyllis Prim. At last, Gerhardt could break free of his uncle's yoke and shatter the confines of staid philosophy. The thought filled him with tumescent fervour.

'*Meister* Lush, I presume,' said Gerhardt, returning to the doorway. 'It is a delight your acquaintance to make.'

'Thank you, Sir,' replied Lush, beaming but awkward.

Gerhardt clapped in delight.

'Excellent! What a fine-looking man, if a man you are. So pretty. *Hübscher*, indeed. Come in. Maybe we can share some tea, although there is no maid at this hour to make it.'

Lush grinned. Here was an opportunity to abide by Belle's instructions.

'I can put the kettle on, Sir. Show me any stove and I'll show you how to make tea.'

The offer was met with a wild laugh that bordered on a hysterical giggle.

'So useful! *Und*, *bitte*, call me not "Sir"! I insist that you me Gerhardt call, *und* I will you Lucius call. We must from formality everything strip. It is the curse of *das Englisch* that in the bodies that *Gott* gave them, they do not comfortable feel. With this, I can help you, *ja*. Let us start, Lucius, by we your coat removing. In this house, must you learn both body *und* mind to disrobe.'

With some foreboding, but still trustful of his new employer, Lush entered the house and placed his coat, then himself, in Gerhardt's hands.

T HAT BELLE HAD provided Gerhardt with a young Englishman on whom to experiment was to Miss Prim's good fortune, and good fortune was a commodity she needed after the unpleasant experience of being drenched in bilge water in Shirley Haytit's tearoom.

Abbey Green was only a five-minute walk from her home in Gay Street but Miss Prim's sorry return journey, dragging her bag of sodden knitting behind her, had been an effort, nor had it gone unnoticed, for her figure was bent and spectral and she groaned as she walked. Had Dickens needed a model for a wife of Marley's ghost thirteen years later, this would have been it.

'Oooooah!' cried Miss Prim as she dragged herself across West Street, sending people scurrying into shops and slamming their doors in fear.

'Oooooah!' she moaned again, breaking the silence on Quiet Street and causing two terrified horses to bolt.

No one had come to her rescue. The rector exiting the abbey might have taken pity but he mistook her for one of the vagrants that begged in its shadows. Mrs Crust would have offered her some company, had she seen the bedraggled spinster exit the tearoom, but she had been in the storeroom fetching a venison and ale pie for a customer. All other citizens of Bath espying her soaking countenance recoiled, believing the wet, lank hair and the white, skeletal face to be the symptoms of disease. Such was the state of Christian compassion in this most fashionable of cities. Miss Prim's cause was not helped by the unnerving howls of distress she continued to emit as she stumbled home.

'Oooooah!' she wailed as she traversed the east side of Queen Square, the remnants of water dripping from her hem and slooshing from her boots.

The sight of her home in Gay Street provided only a modicum of solace. Having pulled the doorbell, she shivered as she waited to be let in. Unfortunately, believing her mistress to be occupied for the day, the maid Millicent had gone to meet a footman from No. 8, so Miss Prim had to wait for Mrs Mulligatawny to ascend from the kitchen.

Eventually, the door opened.

'Lorks, Madam, what a state you're in! I've never seen such a thing. And the smell!'

The comment sent tears of anguish flowing down Miss Prim's cheeks and mixing with the foul water that greased her hair.

'Help me, Mrs Mulligatawny.'

'Broccoli, Madam. Take hold of my hand,' said the cook, who did not shy away from her duty of care. 'We must go upstairs immediately, and you must remove those wet clothes. I shall bring hot water to the bedchamber so you can wash. Then I shall fetch the doctor.'

The spinster stretched out a weak arm.

'And a priest. I fear I may die.'

Though belonging to the Church of England, Miss Prim was decidedly Catholic in her spiritual demands and found comfort in being administered Extreme Unction from a vicar at least three times a year. The cook was unconvinced.

'Let's not bother the priest just yet, Madam. First let's wrap you in warm towels and then I can feed you a hot broth that I've been making.'

The mention of the broth perked up Miss Prim.

'What sort of broth, Mrs Mulligatawny?'

'Turnip, Madam,' the cook replied, before correcting herself. 'Chicken. It's a chicken broth. Now up the stairs we go.'

An hour and a half later, Miss Prim could be found propped up in bed, her body and hair washed clean, wearing a newly laundered nightdress and a warm towel around her shoulders. She was sipping from a bowl of broth and was in the awkward territory for the habitual hypochondriac of actually feeling better.

She had been visited by Dr Sturridge, pre-eminent among Bath's physicians (who numbered more than one hundred, such was the demand from the city's visitors for good health). The doctor had examined the patient and was confident that no long-term damage had been done.

Once in the corridor outside the bedchamber, he conferred with Mrs Mulligatawny for corroborating details. The door, however, remained ajar and Miss Prim, who had many weaknesses but none of hearing, could discern each and every word.

'Another fainting episode, I'm afraid, but nothing more serious than that,' diagnosed the doctor. 'It appears that Mrs Haytit from those peculiar tearooms decided to revive Miss Prim by throwing a bucket of water over her.'

'Was that a bad thing?' asked the cook.

Inside the bedchamber, Miss Prim put aside the broth. She was all ears.

'It's a traditional method of revival but not one we recommend any longer. Medicine has moved on in recent years. Personally, I recommend smelling salts. They have the additional benefit of counteracting the noxious miasma that causes cholera. If people would simply inhale smelling salts once a day, we could rid society of disease. I have left a bottle for Miss Prim.'

The lady in question gave a sideways glance at the small flask inscribed Spirit of Hartshorn on her bedside table.

'Are you sure?' queried the cook, who distrusted all doctors. 'When the cholera was at its worst, I always made sure to keep the kitchen clean and to boil the water thoroughly.'

Dr Sturridge laughed and, in the bedchamber, Miss Prim shook her head at the ignorance of the servant class.

'Dear Mrs Mulligatawny: boiled water, whatever next?' admonished the medic. 'Boiled water is fine for tea but quite unnecessary when it comes to health. Disease enters the body through the nose, mark my words. Smelling salts will save the world.'

'Carrots.'

'No harm in them, either. Is there anything else I can do for you or Miss Prim?'

Mrs Mulligatawny hesitated. There was, indeed, something she wanted to raise: a matter that had been worrying her ever since her visit to Somerset Place to advise Mme Galette on the soufflé. Dr Sturridge seemed as sensible a person as any to ask.

'There is. Do you perhaps know Herr Gerhardt Kant? He is a cousin of our neighbour, Councillor Nash.'

The doctor nodded.

'Indeed, I know him. I was at Councillor Nash's house only a fortnight past and Herr Kant was complaining of a chest infection. It was nothing more than the inhalation of wig powder, I am glad to report. I left him with some smelling salts. What of Herr Kant?'

Mrs Mulligatawny swallowed hard.

'Does he have any medical expertise?'

Dr Sturridge laughed again and, inside the bedchamber, Miss Prim tittered.

'None at all. Why? Were you planning for a second opinion on your mistress's condition?'

Mrs Mulligatawny shook her head.

'No, Doctor,' she replied earnestly, unaware that her mistress could hear. 'I overheard from people whose names I cannot share that Herr Kant plans to experiment on my mistress. Like Dr Frankenstein.'

Inside the bedchamber, Miss Prim stopped tittering and ceased worrying about feeling better. Very quickly, she began to feel a whole lot worse. Her eyes widened in horror at the thought of what the mad Prussian who kept a sheep on his head might have in mind. She wondered what Gay Street and the world were coming to. She could not have a cup of tea in a tearoom without being insulted and assaulted. And now, lo and behold: the shocking news that the second cousin (once removed) of her friend and neighbour wished to experiment on her.

'Ooooah!' she wailed. 'Ooooah!'

It was a cry of such distress as to prompt Dr Sturridge's immediate return to the bedchamber and for Mrs Mulligatawny to seek help. In times of crisis, a person of sound mind was required, and there was no one better in Bath in that regard than Gaia Champion.

NOTES

- Gottfried Wilhelm Leibniz (1646–1716) was a Hanoverian polymath and philosopher who developed two, sometimes contradictory, philosophical theories: one a theologically imbued fantasy designed to please his royal paymasters; and a second more austere philosophy based on logical principles. Students of Leibniz tend to be bamboozled as to which part of his thinking fits into which approach. For instance, he theorised that the ultimate elements of the universe are individual centres of force, which he termed monads. He also believed that everything in his experience would remain unchanged even if the rest of the world were annihilated. He never married and, like Gerhardt, wore enormous wigs.

CHAPTER X

Buns with Mr Quigley

MRS CRUST OF Mrs Crust's Pie Shop had not seen Phyllis Prim leave the adjacent tearoom, but she was soon hearing tittle-tattle about 'a strange going on'. Word spreads quickly in Bath, the more so when it concerns a dripping, diseased spectre walking the streets with a bag of sodden knitting. With a constant stream of customers visiting her shop, over the course of the morning she gradually pieced together the picture until ... .

'Oh, my goodness!' Mrs Crust exclaimed in response to yet another account from a customer. 'That can't have been a ghost, it must have been Miss Prim. She has been sitting in the window of Shirley Haytit's tearoom these past two days with her needles and wool, poor mad thing. What I don't understand is how she became so deluged.'

The customer was delighted to be ahead of Mrs Crust when it came to gossip.

'You know, I think it may well have been Miss Prim. She was soaked through from head to toe. And she smelt. The stench — appalling! Worse even than the drains around the abbey.'

Mrs Crust shook her head. What she was hearing was not right on so many levels.

'That's not how she likes to be seen, our Miss Prim. She's always spotless clean when she comes in for her quarter-slice of pie. There's something right peculiar going on, I tell you.' Turning to the girl beside her, she asked, 'Didn't you see nothing earlier today? It happened right across the way.'

Somewhat sheepishly, the girl shook her head. Mrs Crust squared up to her. Her baker's eyes bore down as her baker's hands moved purposefully to her baker's hips.

The assistant replied, 'No, Mrs Crust. Well, not clearly. I might have caught sight of her leaving the tearoom looking a little wet, but I was busy serving and ...'

Mrs Crust's eyes rose to the heavens. There was more offal in one of her pies than there was brain in her assistant.

'So, you did see, and you said nothing about it. What is wrong with you?'

The girl turned puce at being publicly admonished.

'I was putting the customer first, Mrs Crust, like you've always told me.'

It was not an excuse that washed. Not in this instance. Mrs Crust wagged a finger at her.

'Miss Prim's a customer, too, you foolish girl, whether she's inside the shop or outside. Dripping wet through and through, this lady says, and you didn't do nothing to help her? What's worse, we've had to learn what happened second hand and that won't do. It's not how I run this shop.'

'Yes, Mrs Crust. I'm sorry,' apologised the assistant again, having now learned that good gossip in Bath is worth more than a slice of pie, even a pie of the quality of Mrs Crust's.

Mrs Crust turned back to the customer, whose day had already exceeded expectations and was waiting with coin in hand to pay for her purchase.

'What are we to do?' asked Mrs Crust.

'We need to do something,' the customer replied. 'Maybe we should inform a special constable. We can't have the health of the city put at risk again.'

Mrs Crust untied her apron. She had decided that action was required.

'I'm going over to see that creature Haytit right now. Decent people like Miss Prim can't just be soaked in water without good cause. I'm not having it, I'm not. Not at all.'

THE FAMILIAR MORAL that hard work is rewarded has as much substance as the belief that contributing to the church collection during Sunday mass will get you into heaven. Both rely on a large dollop of faith and lashings of hope.

A greater truth in life would be that there's nothing more important than gossiping and listening to gossip. And no mutterings should ever be discounted, whether of friends, enemies or those considered stark crazy.

Every two weeks, Belle Nash arranged to meet his old music master Arthur Quigley for tea and a bun at Sally Lunn's tearoom, sensibly eschewing Mrs Haytit's dubious establishment. Mr Quigley, an advanced octogenarian, was among Bath's most senior bachelors and remained the music master at the Abbey School for Boys. He was a man for whom Belle had great affection.

He recalled the moment when the headmaster had brought the pupils together and explained that Mr Quigley had suffered a bereavement and would not be attending school for a number of weeks. And prior to the teacher's return, how the headmaster had explained that any pupil who sought to make fun of Mr Quigley would be severely flogged.

The purpose of the threat became clear when the tall, thin music master resumed his duties. Though his knowledge of music and his passion to teach remained undimmed, his mind had in other aspects gone quite awry. A pair of odd socks would be complemented by mismatched shoes. Tailored flannel trousers would be rolled up to the knees with a nightdress for a shirt. Most bizarre of all, Mr Quigley had taken to mistaking a tea cosy for a hat, which barely restrained his billowing white hair.

As Belle later discovered, bereavement at the loss of his companion Richard had deeply affected Mr Quigley. Twenty years had

97

passed, and the madness persisted, although it was not a condition to be feared. The citizens of Bath accepted the music master as a kindly man who taught children the wonders of Thomas Tallis while wearing a tea cosy on his head.

Their fortnightly meetings were a highlight of Belle's life. Normally their conversation focussed on mere pleasantries, but today's meeting had a purpose, for once.

'Mr Quigley, we must talk about the concert I've asked you to arrange for Princess Victoria, the one with the Abbey School for Boys' Choir,' said Belle, as the two men sat at their usual table with tea and warm buns. 'The opening of the park is only ten days hence.'

'Ten days, hah?' replied the music master in a voice as vibrant as his appearance. 'It's all in hand. Nothing to worry about at all. Much more important is what I chanced to see this morning. In the middle of Bath, 'pon my word. Near Milsom Street.'

Belle was not in the mood for gossip.

'Mr Quigley, let us remain focused. What programme of songs are you planning?'

'A ghost, Nash! My eyesight is not what it was, but it had the likeness of a woman who had swum back across the River Hades.'

Belle looked fondly at the older man. While appreciating the classical reference, it appeared his condition had worsened and that his madness had escaped the confines of sartorial peculiarity.

'Have another bun.'

His old teacher was not so easily diverted.

'You don't believe me! I tell you I was not alone in seeing the apparition. Ask the good people around us.'

Belle wanted to avoid an embarrassing scene.

'I don't think that's necessary, Mr Quigley. It's not that I don't believe you. I've long believed people will see what they want to see. My beloved second cousin Gerhardt is considered by a mutual friend to have a sheep on his head.'

98

The change of tack worked but not in the way that Belle had intended. At the mention of Gerhardt, Arthur's eyes misted over.

'Delicious Herr Kant, I so enjoyed meeting him here the other week. To be young and in love. It reminds me of a party at Fonthill thirty or so years ago given by that esteemed bachelor William Beckford. Richard and I attended dressed as Queen Elizabeth and her lapdog Mrs Perico. Guess who went as Mrs Perico, woof-woof? Mink collar and snakeskin lead no less!'

Ladies at neighbouring tables turned their heads.

'Mr Quigley, quite enough of that, please. I must insist on returning to the purpose of our meeting today.'

The music master raised a hand in acknowledgement.

'Quite right. The sighting of the undead!'

Belle clenched his fists in desperation. Entrusting Mr Quigley with the task of providing entertainment in the park could yet prove a mistake.

'No, we are here to discuss the concert you are arranging. To be given by the Abbey School boys. For the twelve-year-old Princess Victoria.'

Mr Quigley returned a bemused look.

'Oh, that? I told you. It's all in hand.'

'But is it? We can't risk getting it wrong.'

The bemused look of his musical mentor turned to one of mild indignation that a former pupil should be so distrusting.

'You are aware, Nash, that despite my best efforts you were never adept at music.'

Belle's head dropped.

'That's why I've asked *you*, Sir, to arrange the concert.'

'A sensible and commendable decision,' replied the music master. 'And I have given the occasion much thought. Not for the young princess the lewd and bawdy songs enjoyed in the public house.'

'No? I'm so glad.'

99

'Not at all. Rather, a collection that I have entitled "Songs of Childhood & Innocence".'

Belle broke into a smile. This was just what he wanted to hear.

'Such as?'

Mr Quigley returned the smile but gently shook his head.

'You should know better. You cannot expect a maestro to reveal his secrets in advance. But have no fear. It will be a concert of perfect beauty. *Bellezza perfetta, beauté parfaite, perfekte Schönheit.* Beauty is universal, Nash. It will be an occasion that the princess will remember for the rest of her life.'

And he was right.

WHEN GAIA CHAMPION had been asked by Mrs Mulligatawny to attend to Miss Prim, she had told herself not to panic. Her friend was forever fainting and pronouncing herself at death's door before making a reluctant but full recovery. Nevertheless, as is the way with friends, by the time she arrived in Gay Street, Gaia had imagined the worst. Why else would Aagalyadevi Balasubramaniam have been in such a state unless her mistress's death was imminent?

The cook had outlined to Gaia the incident at Shirley Haytit's tearoom and Dr Sturridge's prescription of smelling salts. She had explained that Miss Prim had been showing signs of a recovery until a sudden relapse had occurred. Dr Sturridge had been at a loss to explain the cause and had further prescribed a soothing syrup of morphine, being his own preferred tipple on the quiet.

Ten minutes after entering the house, Gaia had heard much the same from Miss Prim herself, who was doing her best to look grey and drawn while propped up in a nice warm bed on soft down pillows. From experience, Gaia knew that the best medicine for Miss Prim — far better than smelling salts or morphine — was love and sympathy.

'Miss Prim, if only we could have foreseen what happened!

None of us considered the danger that you were in. I understand Mrs Haytit escorted you from the premises using the foulest of language ...'

'The language of the devil,' confirmed her friend.

'... and the foulest of water.'

Miss Prim recoiled at the memory.

'Oooah!'

Gaia leant forward and dabbed a handkerchief on Miss Prim's forehead, only to find no evidence of a fever.

'Relax,' she said. 'Do your best to forget what happened. And have this cup of tea.'

It was not a suggestion that went down well.

'I shall never drink tea again,' Miss Prim cried, waving the chinaware away with her small right hand.

'Never drink tea again?' gasped Gaia. 'In Bath?'

'Tea was part of the problem. I'd already had a cup, but Mrs Haytit insisted I have another. It was then that the abuse started.'

For a few moments the women fell silent. Gaia had sat herself on the bed, believing that close proximity would provide a source of comfort. It also allowed her to study Miss Prim in detail as she spoke, the way her mouth twitched at its edges and the nervous movement of her eyes. There was, she surmised, a hidden story.

'And why did you cry out after Dr Sturridge attended you? I understand you were enjoying a broth and then ... something occurred.'

Miss Prim brought her hands together and twiddled her thumbs.

'Perhaps ...' she replied weakly.

'Tell me,' said Gaia.

Miss Prim looked at her nervously.

'In confidence?'

'Not a word to anyone,' agreed Gaia, who was always the most loyal and honest of friends.

'Not even to Councillor Nash? You mustn't tell Councillor Nash.'

Such a request came as a surprise. Gaia knew the affection that Miss Prim and Belle shared and had not imagined there might be room for distrust.

'Not even Councillor Nash. I promise.'

And so it was that Miss Prim recounted how she had overheard Mrs Mulligatawny say that Gerhardt Kant planned to conduct Frankenstein experiments on her and how she really, really did not want to be experimented upon by anyone but particularly not by Herr Kant, with or without the sheep on his head.

Gaia did her best not to laugh and set out to reassure her friend.

'My dear Miss Prim. None of us wants to be experimented on and none of your friends, myself and Councillor Nash included, would ever allow that to happen to you.'

'But Mrs Mulligatawny said ...'

'The lady that you call Mrs Mulligatawny is mistaken. Now banish the thought from your mind and look to the future. You have nothing to worry about. Indeed, the only people who should be worrying are the likes of Hezekiah Porter and Shirley Haytit for being such terrible shopkeepers. There will be much to talk about on Saturday.'

'Saturday?' queried Miss Prim.

Gaia leant forward.

'The tea party at Councillor Nash's house, remember. Here on Gay Street. Next door. You will be among friends. We will all share what we have learned in our quest to save the soufflé. And we will have a decent cup of tea while we're at it.'

NOTES

- Queen Elizabeth I adored dogs and was painted with her Maltese lapdog named Mrs Perico. By contrast, she considered

102

cats to be demons and had one burnt alive at her coronation. Interestingly, this hatred of cats was a leftover from Catholicism. A succession of popes undertook a 500-year feline holocaust typified by Pope Innocent VIII who, in 1484, ordered the Inquisition to burn all cats and cat lovers. Over the centuries, this extended pogrom led to a steep rise in the number of rats that in turn accelerated the spread of bubonic plague.

CHAPTER XI

Scones, finger sandwiches and allusions

SATURDAY HAD COME. As Belle Nash prepared for the arrival of his tea party guests, he considered how much had changed since his birthday dinner. A man of enlightened education, he knew of ancient Indian texts that describe the universe as having a recurring cycle of creation, destruction and rebirth every four million years. It seemed that the cycle of time, at least in Bath, was rather quicker. There was a good chance of the world being turned upside down in the space of a couple of weeks.

It was a topic of conversation that he would gladly have shared with Gerhardt Kant, but his companion was otherwise engaged with Lucius Lush. As Belle arranged the plates of scones, finger sandwiches and petite madeleines on the rosewood table in the drawing room, he could hear the two younger men giggling in the kitchen below. It had seemed a good idea at the time but now he wondered whether he had erred by introducing them. There was no evidence of a jigsaw being undertaken or any other healthy intellectual pursuit.

He went into the corridor and shouted down the stairs.

'Master Lush, when you have finished amusing yourself with Herr Kant, kindly grace me with your presence. The ladies are due any moment and rarely come late. And bring up the teapot while you're at it. Even though the ladies have not yet arrived, if my palate is not bathed by the waters of China in the next five minutes, I shall die.'

Belle returned to the drawing room and made adjustments to

some flowers in a vase. It was a modest display compared to those Gaia Champion provided in Somerset Place but he liked to show that he was as much master of his house as she was of hers. A few moments later there were footsteps and Lush entered – with Belle's second-best teapot, a moulded Minton design in white and pale blue, with colourful flower patterns, gold trim and a handle like a dragon's wing.

'I must apologise for not bringing the tea up earlier, Sir,' Lush said hurriedly as he prepared to pour a cup, 'but Herr Kant never stops talking. He tells me I'm beautiful but that I'm not as beautiful as he. I imagine that, in Prussia, that would be regarded as a compliment and I should take it as such.'

'Is that so?' said Belle, waiting for Lush to pour.

'Yes, indeed. Herr Kant believes we English are inhibited by our upbringing and that if we could only return to our childhoods, we might rid ourselves of our English inhibitions. He says I should cast off mine.'

'You should, Master Lush,' said Belle dryly. 'And the first inhibition to cast off would be the pouring of my tea, for which I am still waiting. Concentrate on the task at hand, Sir. That's the English tradition and we haven't fared too badly from it.'

Lush tipped the pot and handed over a cup of freshly brewed Lapsang to Belle. Behind them, Gerhardt entered the room, having first stopped briefly to inspect himself in the hallway mirror.

'*Ach*, Lucius. I am turning my back, my wig to rearrange, *und* you disappear,' he declared. '*Das ist* naughty, so naughty. I must tickle you in punishment.'

At which point Gerhardt took off towards Lush with his arms outstretched and fingers wiggling.

His victim jumped to one side, imperilling the safety of the teapot, to escape.

'Oh, Gerhardt, stop. My ribs ache from too much laughing.'

Belle had had enough of the younger men's tomfoolery, and of their easy use of each other's first names. They had evidently become too close, too soon.

'Stop it both of you. You need to be in a sober mood for the ladies. As you are well aware, Miss Prim has been unwell and we do not want to overexcite her.' At that moment the front doorbell rang; it seemed that their guests had arrived. 'Master Lush, go answer the door and welcome the ladies. Gerhardt, a word with you, if you'd spare me a second.'

His clerk departed and Belle was left alone with his companion.

He hissed, 'You must calm down, Gerhardt. Remember this afternoon isn't about you and your entertainment. Nor is it about philosophy. It is about far weightier matters: what caused the soufflé to sink. There can never be peace in Bath until the reason is known.'

Having laid down the law, Belle set his mind to receive his guests. Like Grandfather Beau, he understood that a party requires organisation and structure, whether it be a tea party on a Saturday afternoon or a grand ball on a Saturday night.

His checklist included:

Scones, clotted cream and strawberry jam	☑
Selection – minimum, three varieties – of finger sandwiches	☑
Les petites madeleines to be plated *par le douzen*	☑
Cake	☑
The best tea from India or China	☑
Disruptive guests being told in advance to behave	☑

By tradition, his four friends arrived together in Lady Passmore's splendid chaise and four. Accompanied by Mrs Pomeroy, Lady Passmore would collect Gaia Champion first and then Phyllis Prim from Gay Street (for even though she lived next door to Belle, she deserved the same courtesy).

For the ladies, therefore, the fun had begun before they

arrived, so that by the time they stood waiting at the front door, they were in full voice, gaggling like excited geese. The first to appear in the drawing room was Gaia, who walked in backwards, the better to continue face to face the conversation she had been conducting in the carriage with Lady Passmore.

'Mrs Champion, Madam: how lovely to see you!' declared Belle. 'Or at the least, your posterior.'

Gaia spun round with a look of delight on her face. She, too, adored Belle's tea parties.

'Belle, I am as impolite as Menoetius and as uncultivated as Feronia!' she said, appealing to Belle's love of ancient history. 'Can you ever forgive me? My governess tried to teach me never to reverse into a drawing room but evidently failed, in that as in much else.'

They joined hands and Belle greeted the other ladies.

'Lady Passmore of Tewkesbury Manor, a delight. I am beholden to you, Ma'am, for making your carriage available to these other ... goddesses.'

Lady Passmore offered her hand while appearing less than convinced by Belle's greeting.

'I have no idea what you are talking about Councillor Nash.'

'Goddesses such as Mrs Pomeroy,' said Belle, a touch unnerved by Her Ladyship, but deciding to hold the line. 'Ah, Mrs Pomeroy. What a charming bonnet you are wearing – braided as I see by Juno and her maidens. Quite the loveliest bonnet anyone has worn this season.'

Mrs Pomeroy, who had a straw bonnet trimmed with red ribbon over her lace cap, was thrilled. It was most agreeable to be complimented on one's choice of bonnet, and how clever it was of Belle to know the names of the ladies who made it.

'You are too kind. As for the ribbon, I chose and tied it myself,' she replied joyously.

'We can see that,' said Lady Passmore.

Belle wisely chose to ignore the intervention.

'And last but not least, dear Miss Prim. How wonderful that you are here, nursed back to health by Asclepius after an ordeal of which no mortal may speak,' he said, unwisely offering up another Greek allusion. 'Welcome, one and all. Please, take your seats and the younger men among us will pour tea and offer treats.'

The ladies settled themselves and Belle introduced Lush, whom none had so far met.

'You've brought a clerk,' said Lady Passmore dismissively, 'to our tea party?'

'Indeed,' replied Belle. 'Gerhardt had need of an assistant. Pouring tea while balancing a German periwig on his head might be too much even for him! And none of us likes wig powder in our drink.'

Three of the ladies laughed; Miss Prim, by contrast, eyed Gerhardt with suspicion.

'Maybe your clerk could take notes,' suggested Mrs Pomeroy. 'Lady Passmore of Tewkesbury Manor and I have much to report from our secret surveillance. We must honour the purpose of our meeting today, although those scones do look delicious.'

Belle responded to the idea with enthusiasm.

'An excellent suggestion, Ma'am. I have news from Guildhall to pass on and Gerhardt shall detail his visit to the demon store. We may also hear from Miss Prim, if she has the strength following her awful ordeal at the hands of the beldame Haytit. But only if you have the strength, dear Miss Prim.'

'I will do my best.'

Once tea and dainties had been distributed – with Mrs Pomeroy taking for herself a double helping of scones – the group began describing to one another what they had learned from their individual endeavours. Lush, quill and paper to hand, took notes.

Lady Passmore and Mrs Pomeroy read out the names of those they had seen enter Porter's to collective gasps, titters and 'well I nevers'. Then Belle explained, to applause, how by chance he had been elected to the committee to choose the next magistrate, before revealing that Hezekiah Porter had been seen visiting the office of Magistrate Obadiah Wood the Thursday just past.

'I have my spies at Guildhall,' Belle revealed, to which Lush kept his mouth shut. It was he who had witnessed Mr Porter entering the magistrate's office, but he had not been able to hear their conversation through the door. The substance of the shopkeeper's visit to the magistrate, therefore, remained unknown.

'And Gerhardt,' Belle continued, 'what learned you from your visit to Porter's? But before you speak, on behalf of us all, may I acknowledge your bravery in venturing beyond the Styx and down to the ninth circle of Hell. Never was faithful Orpheo so fiercely determined.'

Belle's conversation attracted a mixed reception: were she very honest, Mrs Pomeroy would admit to having little idea who Orpheo was; Miss Prim might be equally candid about not having met the medic Asclepius; and Lady Passmore was prepared to make a formal complaint on the grounds of unspecified vulgarity. Gaia wished she had not got Belle started by mentioning Menoetius and Feronia. It was only Gerhardt who remained enamoured.

'Such bravery is to the German peoples – *die deutschen Völker* – only natural,' he began, 'for we embody the ancient spirit of the Greeks. Are *die Deutschen* not a new Athens from the swamps of Berlin building? *Und* is there not now a new *geistige* Socratic pursuit in favour of *Innerlichkeit*, the inwardness, the internalism ...'

Belle became aware that Lady Passmore was turning purple having had her fill of all things Greek and, now, German. As a consequence, fearing for his companion's life, he intervened.

'Gerhardt, my love, let us stick to the matter at hand. Namely, your visit to Porter's.'

His companion came back down from Mount Olympus with a proverbial thump.

'*Ja*, when you will, Belle. I visited the Porter's shop, *und* found that his carrots, they are from Viltshire.'

'Viltshire?' Mrs Pomeroy enquired.

'Wiltshire,' translated Belle. 'But why Wiltshire, Gerhardt, dear?'

'Because they vilt. Herr Porter explained me to it. This variety is limp, so different to the upstanding *und* proud *deutsche Karotten*.'

Mrs Pomeroy emitted an inappropriate giggle, to Lady Passmore's displeasure.

'Maybe they were farmed in the village of Limpley Stoke,' suggested Gaia, who knew her local geography. 'But what else did you find, Herr Kant?'

'On his bags of *Zucker* the correct weight declares he not; *und* the correct change to the customer tenders he not. This Herr Porter is *ein Dieb*, *er ist ein Lügner*, *und* he would not be allowed a shop in Königsberg to keep.'

'Thank you, Gerhardt,' said Belle, who had taken it upon himself to chair the meeting. 'An admirable report. And duly noted by Master Lush. Now I know Gaia has the results of tests conducted on the flour, but may I first call on Miss Prim? If Gerhardt has been as brave as Perseus ... Damnation, I am affected by the Athenian disease. In plain speech, Miss Prim, would you confide in us your report.'

Miss Prim fidgeted uncomfortably in her chair. In her opinion, the world would be a better place if people stuck to British history. Talk of Perseus, Andromache, Orpheo, Asclepius, Menoetius, Feronia and Juno, not to mention the group of unidentified maidens, was too much to bear on a Somerset Saturday afternoon.

Seeing her friend in distress, Gaia intervened.

'Perhaps the time is not yet right for dear Miss Prim,' she said simply.

Her opinion found support in Mrs Pomeroy.

'I agree. There is no need for Miss Prim to speak if to do so is painful. After all, there remain more scones waiting to find a home. And there is cake yet to enjoy.'

Bath's foremost knitter, however, wanted to have her say. She just needed time to clear her head so she could choose her words carefully.

'I thank you, Mrs Pomeroy,' she said, steeling herself to her task, 'but I am fully recovered from the terrible incident. The problem is quite other than you imagine. In the two days I spent watching Porter's from that most dreadful of tearooms, I ... I ... I saw nothing untoward, and thus have nothing to report.'

Lady Passmore was compelled to intervene with her customary lack of empathy.

'Nothing? Nothing will come of nothing, Miss Prim, as the Bard long ago warned us. Mrs Pomeroy and I made copious observations. You cannot have seen nothing.'

'I assure you. I saw nothing.'

'Then what were you doing in there, Miss Prim? Really, you need to knit yourself a pair of lunettes.'

Miss Prim had an answer to hand.

'It was not that I did not see customers enter and leave, Lady Passmore of Tewkesbury Manor. It's that the identity of the customers shone no light on the issue that occupies us. Nothing at all.'

Lady Passmore was about to respond when Gaia raised her hand.

'May I intervene? I believe that what Miss Prim says is true and is likely to be the key to this case. I can confirm that the poor quality of the flour – if it can be termed flour – was to blame for the soufflé's failure to rise. The esteemed Mrs Mulligatawny and Mme Galette have proved this beyond a doubt. For my own part, I visited Mrs Crust, baker of Bath's most excellent pies. She had confronted the wretched Haytit woman about her foul behaviour, and it struck

111

me that in Mrs Crust we have a lady who has been keeping watch over her neighbours not for hours or days but for years. And she disclosed to me ...'

Gaia paused for dramatic effect.

'What?' asked Mrs Pomeroy.

'You must tell us,' demanded Lady Passmore.

'O righteous Gaia! Spill the fabaceaen legumes,' said Belle.

Gaia adopted an earnest expression.

'Mrs Crust says that the oddest thing about Porter's shop is the hours he receives deliveries. Mrs Crust starts baking well before dawn. By that time Hezekiah Porter is already at his store, taking in supplies.'

'From whom?' queried Lady Passmore.

'The supplier of the Viltshire carrots, perhaps,' said Gerhardt. '*Heiaha!*'

'She is unsure,' replied Gaia. 'The deliveries are always done under cover of darkness, which would explain why Miss Prim, quite correctly, has nothing to report. Mrs Crust suggests that, if we want answers, we need to change the timing of our watch.'

There was a moment's silence as everyone absorbed the suggestion.

'Early birds and worms, then,' said Belle. 'In this case a worm called Hezekiah Porter. Ladies – and Gerhardt, of course: who here is up to the challenge?'

I N ALL THE excitement, the participants of the tea party had failed to discuss why Mr Porter had held a private meeting with Magistrate Wood on the Thursday, and the possibility that their efforts at espionage might have been rumbled. Such was their eagerness to save the soufflé that it passed them by that the opposing camp also had interests to protect: interests of an illicit nature.

It should come as no surprise to onlookers, therefore, that the gathering in Gay Street was not the only one taking place that

Saturday afternoon. At the same time that the tea party was concluding, Magistrate Wood was meeting his erstwhile henchman Special Constable Decimus Dimm in the Dog & Duck tavern in an alleyway beside the abbey.

Wood spoke through lips as full and fat as Jersey cream.

'Mrs Haytit told Mr Porter that the store is being spied on. We cannot sit by while our affairs are pried on by this mixed party of meddling women and interfering bachelors. Eh? Nor should we view these busybodies as foolish. We must take it that the nosey parkers will redouble their efforts. That means they will likely extend the timing of their deployment.'

Dimm was a man of limited intelligence whose main feature was a set of sideburns the size of allotments. He also had a loud voice.

'Yes, Sir!' he shouted, frightening the other drinkers in the tavern. 'They will extend the timing of their deployment!'

Wood winced and continued with instructions.

'In which case they will be vulnerable to a trap that I have conceived. Listen closely, Dimm. You know of course of Molly Jenkins?'

'I know some of her slatterns, Sir. As do quite a few of Bath's worthies.'

'It is one of the most frequented clap houses in the city,' the magistrate continued. 'Ought to be closed down but there are so many advantages in keeping it open. Makes its customers wondrous pliant when arrested! So useful in the administration of the law, I always find. Now, as you know, Molly Jenkins's establishment lies in the alleyway to the side of Porter's ...'

NOTES

- At the opening of the chapter, I believe my uncle was referring to *The Vedas*, which are the earliest texts of Indian philosophy from the second millennium BC. The texts state that the uni-

113

verse lasts a thousandth of a single day of Brahma's life, which equates to 4.32 million Earth years. We are comparatively close to the end of a cycle, with 426,877 years remaining (as of 2021) before the universe implodes.

CHAPTER XII

Interfering ladies

WHEN GAIA CHAMPION had suggested a change to the timing of the watch on Hezekiah Porter's store, there were only two people up to the job, at least in Lady Passmore's mind. Belle Nash had suggested that Gerhardt Kant and Lucius Lush might don cloaks and hats and hide in the shadows of Abbey Green. Her Ladyship was having none of it.

'A foreigner and a clerk!' she had remarked. 'Trusting in amateurs will doom the mission from its inception. No, Mrs Pomeroy and I will undertake the challenge. Not only have we the equipment, we have the experience to succeed.'

'Are you sure, Lady Passmore of Tewkesbury Manor?' Gaia had asked. 'Master Lush has the benefit of being a newcomer to Bath. If seen, he will not be recognised.'

Lady Passmore had dismissed the proposal out of hand. Years of studying guests arriving at parties through a pair of lorgnette had given them, in her opinion, unparalleled expertise. They were, in effect, accomplished spies.

'You're suggesting that we will be seen, Ma'am. But I assure you, we will not. Isn't that the case, Mrs Pomeroy? We are mistresses of disguise!'

So it was that at midnight the following Monday, Lady Passmore's magnificent carriage could be found parked on the side of Abbey Green, looking as inconspicuous as Noah's Ark on the top of Mount Ararat after the Flood.

The curtains of the carriage were all but closed except for the tiniest gap through which to push the lorgnette, a detail that assured Lady Passmore that they could not in consequence be seen. In addition, it was a dark and cloudy night, so that the only light on Abbey Green was from the two gas streetlamps.

'This is perfect,' said Her Ladyship. 'We're completely hidden.'

Mrs Pomeroy was a little less than convinced.

'If you say so, Lady Passmore of Tewkesbury Manor. I'm aware that we can't see much of what is happening outside. But what steps have we taken to disguise the carriage?'

Lady Passmore was nothing if not a meticulous planner.

'I have ordered the coachman to stand down from his position. So far as the onlooker is concerned, ours is just another carriage parked by the roadside while a young fool visits the gaming tables, or a young blade his paramour. No one will guess that it's us.'

By such means do the wealthy among us meld into the world.

Having learned that the coachman had been dispensed with, Mrs Pomeroy manoeuvred her stool into place and took up her usual position by the window. The other side of the green was a mere thirty feet away, giving her a direct view onto the side door of Porter's where deliveries would be made. To its left was an alley-way fronted by a stone arch that admitted wayfarers but not light.

'Is there anything going on?' asked Lady Passmore, who once again adopted the role of note-taker from the comfort of an upholstered seat.

'It's terribly dark out there. I might be able to see a little more if I adjust the curtain,' said Mrs Pomeroy.

'And expose us to the world? Never! We have to balance risk and reward, Subaltern Pomeroy. For the moment, leave the curtain as it is, if you please.'

Anyone who has undertaken an all-night watch will know that the hardest part is staying alert during the long hours of inactivity. On this particular night, there was little of interest for Mrs Pomeroy to report, other than a train of furtive visitors to Molly

116

Jenkins's parlour and the sound of raucous and ribald merriment from inside.

At close to one o'clock, she saw a slim-figured man walk across the green in the direction of the river.

'Could he be a narrowboat worker heading back to the canal?' suggested Lady Passmore.

'No, too well dressed for that. If only the lamplight were better, I am sure I would have recognised him.'

An hour later, the same man returned, passing within two feet of the carriage. This time Mrs Pomeroy saw his face.

'Oh, my goodness,' she squealed. 'The person I saw earlier was Councillor Pollard. He has just walked by again in the opposite direction. And – how odd! – he appears to have mud on his knees and stinging nettles on the back of his coat. How peculiar.'

Lady Passmore agreed and made a note to say as much.

'Odd indeed. But scarcely anything to do with Porter's.'

As the night wore on, the silence continued to be broken by sounds from the alleyway, the opening and closing of a door onto the street and the sound of drunken shrieks.

'I do apologise, Lady Passmore of Tewkesbury Manor, but I fear that our sensitive hearing is being assaulted by the sound of men and women – together,' reported Mrs Pomeroy.

'How vulgar,' commented Lady Passmore, making another note. 'And so early in the morning. Do people never sleep?'

More than once the sounds of laughter and passion were followed by the shadow of men crossing to the far side of the green, but none stopped by Porter's and none was identified by the watch.

'They have their collars up and hats pulled down,' said Mrs Pomeroy. 'It's almost as if they had something to hide. If only we knew why they were being so secretive.'

Then at four o'clock, just before the birds started their chorus, something did happen. It seemed that the long hours of effort were about to pay off. In the rooms above the store where Hezekiah

Porter lived, a candle was lit. Mrs Pomeroy immediately raised a hand, a signal that events were stirring. This was not seen by Lady Passmore, however, for she had nodded off.

'There's a candle in a first-floor window,' hissed Mrs Pomeroy. Then a second, brighter light in the same room, almost certainly that of an oil lamp. 'Mr Porter is awake and on the move.'

'Mmm? What did you say?' said Lady Passmore, momentarily disorientated. 'Oh, my goodness, I'm in my carriage. And you're with me, Mrs Pomeroy. Do I know why?'

Her companion turned towards her, her face full of excitement.

'Lady Passmore of Tewkesbury Manor, have your notebook at the ready. Mr Porter is awake. More than that, a cart has just pulled up to the side door. He's taking a delivery.'

The news brought Lady Passmore to her senses. She edged to the window and pulled the curtains a little more open.

Mrs Pomeroy said, 'I thought we weren't supposed to do that with the curtains.'

'Never question the line of authority, Madam. It's a case of risk versus reward. Who is doing the delivery? Do you recognise him?'

Mrs Pomeroy shook her head. Although the distance was short, the light from the streetlamps was too dim for her to make an identification.

The owner of the cart stepped down and knocked on the side door. Within a few seconds, it was opened by Mr Porter and the addition of his lamplight helped to illuminate events.

'I recognise him!' hissed Mrs Pomeroy. 'I saw his face. It's Mr Cudworth, the one who collects kitchen scraps for chickens. Perhaps he collects from Porter's too.'

'He's not collecting, he's unloading,' said Lady Passmore. 'Now what would a man like Mr Cudworth be delivering to a rogue like Mr Porter?'

The two fell silent as they pondered the question, and then arrived at the answer together.

'It's whatever goes into that terrible flour!' said Mrs Pomeroy.

'My thoughts exactly,' confirmed Lady Passmore. 'This is our breakthrough.'

'But we still don't know what it is that he's delivering.'

'Which is what you're about to find out.'

Mrs Pomeroy had spent her life having Lady Passmore pull rank on her. Although on occasion she had protested, it would be true to say that in their battle of wills, Mrs Pomeroy consistently lost. It was one of the reasons for her having developed a liking for cake, for no cake, whatever its pretensions, had ever told her what to do.

'Must I?' asked Mrs Pomeroy after Lady Passmore had outlined her plan.

'If the opportunity arises, yes. The moment Mr Cudworth and Mr Porter both go indoors, you are to run over to the cart and see what's in it. Then we'll have Mr Porter where we want him. Now get ready by the door and await my signal.'

Mrs Pomeroy reluctantly crouched as she prepared to spring, or perhaps roll, into action. Above her, Lady Passmore watched for a suitable opportunity. It came soon enough. Mr Cudworth hauled a bag over his shoulder and followed Mr Porter into the storeroom.

'Go, go, go – forsooth,' cried Lady Passmore urgently, as she opened the carriage door and pushed Mrs Pomeroy out.

There was in principle nothing wrong with the plan, except that Mrs Pomeroy's unathleticism told against her. The descent from the carriage was steep and the hours of sitting stationary on the stool had left her legs stiff. She hobbled as well as she could across the cobbles, snatched a glance in the cart but was interrupted by the sound of voices returning to the side door. Unable to reach the safe haven of the carriage in time, she dodged under the adjacent arch and into the darkness of the alley.

Pressed against a wall, her heart pounding, she strained to hear the two men talking.

'One hundredweight of feed, then,' said Mr Cudworth. 'Will that do you for the week?'

'Expect so,' said Mr Porter. 'Although you never know what's around the corner in this business.'

Which was as true a statement as the man had ever made. Mrs Pomeroy breathed in sharply and hugged the shadows.

'No one knows I'm here,' she said to herself, which seemed a reasonable assumption until she felt an unexpected tap on the shoulder from behind.

'Aaargh!' she yelped involuntarily, her cry revealing her presence to all.

The sound of a female cry in the night might normally be taken as a call for help but that of a woman at night in a dark alleyway next to Porter's left more scope for interpretation. Mr Cudworth started to make a move but Mr Porter restrained him. As a result, Mrs Pomeroy found herself alone with a mystery assailant.

'What you doin' 'ere? I'll strangle you, I will.'

To her surprise it was the rasping voice of another woman. Mrs Pomeroy turned and was confronted with a face that, even in the dark, was of a shocking ugliness. The eyes were masked by a filthy cotton cap beneath which fell strands of lank grey hair, but the mouth was only too evident. It was ulcerated and nothing much was left of the teeth or the gums that had once held them. There were suppurating blisters on the cheeks.

'I'm Molly Jenkins, and them's my girls what works this alley. It's what we like to call a proper molly house and I ain't having no newcomers invading my patch.'

Despite her refinement, the name of Molly Jenkins was known to Mrs Pomeroy.

'I am so terribly sorry, Mrs Jenkins,' she blustered. 'I had not the slightest idea.'

Molly Jenkins pressed herself to Mrs Pomeroy and breathed foul vapours in her face.

'Don't you come all innocent with me. Anyone in this alley at this time in the mornin' is a tart, and that means you're stealing my immoral earnings.'

Mrs Pomeroy, overwhelmed as much by her attacker's smell as by her aggression, nonetheless pulled herself together. 'I'm nothing of the sort. I'll have you know that I'm a personal friend of Lady Passmore of Tewkesbury Manor.'

'That's what you call your madam, is it?' hissed Bath's most celebrated brothel-keeper. 'Well, I don't tolerate competition, no matter what it calls itself and I'm going to teach you a lesson, here and now.'

At which point, a strange thing happened. As Molly Jenkins launched herself at Mrs Pomeroy, a posse of men emerged from the shadows of the abbey: Special Constable Decimus Dimm and two sidekicks.

'That's enough of that!' shouted Dimm as he led the charge across the cobbles.

'Oh, Special Constable, thank you!' Mrs Pomeroy cried. 'I'm Mrs Pomeroy of Lansdown Hill. This vile creature has attacked me.'

Dimm pulled the two women apart.

'Did she now? That's not what I saw. I'm arresting you, Mrs Pomeroy, for importuning, as we upholders of the law like to say. And to think what airs you give yourself in daylight.'

Mrs Pomeroy could not believe her ears.

'I'm not importuning. She is!'

'Molly Jenkins? Importuning? That's cruel, very cruel,' the special constable replied. 'I'll tell you what she's doing: she's witnessing your crime. You run along now, Molly, and take care of yourself. And give your girls a good smack on their behinds from me.'

Having followed to the letter the instructions given to her several hours earlier, Molly Jenkins waved goodbye.

'I will, Mr Dimm. And compliments of the night to Magistrate Wood. Ta-raah!'

'But she attacked me! These fine men saw it all,' cried Mrs Pomeroy, indicating Messrs Porter and Cudworth.

The two men turned to each other and grinned.

'You can keep all that for the court,' Dimm replied. 'Magistrate Wood will see you in the morning, and you'd better have a better story than that.'

The seriousness of the situation only now began to dawn on Mrs Pomeroy. She played her final card.

'But I'm with Lady Passmore of Tewkesbury Manor. She's in the carriage over there. If you don't believe me, Her Ladyship will vouch for my good character.'

'Lady Passmore's in the carriage, d'you say?' said Dimm, with a raised eyebrow. 'So, Molly Jenkins was right: it's Her Ladyship what's runnin' the Tewkesbury trollops.' He turned to his sidekicks and barked an order. 'You two, go to the carriage and arrest Lady Passmore. It's time us men cleaned up the streets of Bath once and for all.'

Dimm smiled to himself. When Magistrate Wood insisted that no quarter be given, there was no reason not to up the stakes.

NOTES

- A molly house in the eighteenth and nineteenth centuries was the common name for clubs for gay men (despite homosexuality being wholly illegal). Molly Jenkins clearly wants to claim back the title for her den of heterosexual vice.

CHAPTER XIII

A defence counsel is required

THE ENGLISH JUDICIAL process has no respect for privacy when it comes to the accused. Title and wealth count for nothing in a trial and humiliation awaits all who consider themselves above the law. To its credit, this egalitarian approach to justice subjects the system to public scrutiny.

Not that the public made a habit of attending Obadiah Wood's court, let alone scrutinising its workings, for they were too fearful that they might become incriminated too. Wood was famous for his swift injustice and his court was a place best avoided.

The magistrate's starting assumption was that anyone accused of a crime must be guilty of something. He also believed that there were better things to do, such as having a long lunch, than to listen to the gobbledygook of the typical defence.

'In and out, in and out, that's how I handle it,' he liked telling Decimus Dimm.

'Just like Molly Jenkins, Sir!' the special constable joked.

For his first few years in office, Wood had employed a small boy to count the seconds and thereby determine how quickly he could prosecute a case. First the five-minute barrier fell, then the four-minute. His finest achievement was in finding a farmhand guilty of theft before the man had even made it to the dock.

'You're guilty,' he had declared, then stopped to check with the boy. 'Three seconds? Excellent!'

'Is that my sentence, Sir?' the confused and entirely innocent farmhand had asked.

'That's my timing, you wretch,' Wood had replied, to Dimm's chuckles. 'Your sentence will be five years — with hard labour. Take the thief away!'

Given this blatant abuse of power, it was no surprise that the magistrate preferred to preside over an empty court, free from watchful eyes, and that the public was happy to defer to his wish. It was to his consternation, therefore, that when he arrived at Guildhall on Tuesday morning, he was told that the court was unusually well attended. Indeed, it was heaving to the gunnels and not with the type of people he wished to see.

'There are how many people on the public benches?' he asked Dimm.

'Sixty and rising, Sir. Mostly women and nancies, if you know what I mean!'

'How in the Devil's name did word get out so quickly? You brought Lady Passmore and Mrs Pomeroy to the gaol under cover of dark. Someone's let the cat out the bag.'

His suspicions were poorly founded. The truth was that on witnessing Mrs Pomeroy being assaulted by Molly Jenkins, then arrested by Dimm, Lady Passmore had acted soundly, not by single-handedly descending from the carriage — that was out of the question for a woman of her rank — but by writing a clear and unambiguous note for her coachman to find on his return:

Mrs Pomeroy has been falsely arrested by Special Constable Dimm. I, too, am in immediate danger of seizure. All is lost. If you find this note, alert Mrs Gaia Champion and Councillor Belle Nash immediately. Time is of the essence.
By order of,
Lady Passmore of ...

She had been prevented from stating her full title, so rapidly and ignominiously had events proceeded. When the coachman

124

returned at dawn, he had found the carriage empty and the note lying on the floor. He had acted promptly, riding like the wind to alert Gaia and, with her blessing, to Gay Street to wake and return with Belle.

By the time Belle had arrived in Somerset Place, a plan of action was unfolding. Having read Lady Passmore's note and assessed the situation, Gaia knew that determined action was required – and that none in Bath was better suited for the task than herself. Ensconced at her desk, Gaia had set about writing a flurry of messages, which she had passed to her footmen for immediate delivery, and to additional footmen drafted in from her neighbours.

Somerset Place had become a hive of frenetic activity.

'Do we know on what grounds they have been arrested?' Belle had asked, still shocked by the news that his friends lay behind bars.

'That will be revealed in court,' Gaia had replied, her quill flying across a sheet of paper.

'Damnably awkward, though. How do we mount a defence?'

Gaia had looked up from her writing.

'Our immediate tactic is to put pressure on Magistrate Wood. What he is doing is not acceptable. It must not be allowed.'

'And your plan?'

'To flood the court, not with water but with people. We must cram the court with supporters of justice and, to that end, I am sending out these missives.'

'To whom?'

'To sympathetic friends. To as many people as we can muster. You must do the same. Grab a quill and paper and plead. We have but two hours before the courtroom opens.'

Two hours for Gaia and Belle had proved more than sufficient and so it was that the public benches of the court were overflowing. Gaia and Belle now sat in the front row along with Phyllis Prim, Arthur Quigley and Lucius Lush. Mrs Crust, whom Gaia had identified as a key ally, was behind them, having posted a note on her shop door that anyone wanting a pie had better come to the court. As a result, friends of the accused had been joined by a bevy of concerned pie lovers. Looking over his shoulder, Belle was pleased to see the arrival in court of a large bobbling wig. Prussia had joined the call to arms.

And just in time, for at that moment Decimus Dimm entered and shouted, 'Be upstanding in court for Magistrate Wood!'

Behind him came the elephantine form of the city magistrate, who proceeded to his raised chair with a sneer on his face. The heavy oak of the dais onto which he stepped whimpered as it took the weight of his gargantuan bulk. He seated himself and eyed the throng, looking at Gaia and Belle with disdain before shouting the first order of the day.

'Bring out the accused and place them in the dock!'

With their heads held high, Lady Passmore and Mrs Pomeroy emerged from the rear of the court, prompting a loud cheer from the public. The ladies were shown to the dock by Dimm, who stood guard beside them.

'They're innocent!' declared Mrs Crust. 'And good women too.'

'Your English law is *eine Schande*,' shouted Gerhardt from the back.

'Long live Lady Passmore of Tewkesbury Manor,' cried a young woman. 'And her friend, whatever her name is!'

Further demonstrations of support were curtailed by the magistrate slamming down his gavel.

Looking daggers at the crowd he bellowed, 'If I hear one more word, I will clear the court and have the accused sent down for twenty years.' Silence descended. 'Special Constable Dimm, what is the charge facing the accused?'

Dimm took a step forward.

'These two women were found improperly importuning themselves this past night in Abbey Green, My Lord, a place well known for such activity. So I am told.'

There was a collective gasp from the public that such an accusation could be made. Wood picked up his quill and wrote the charge in the court record.

Then as if to conclude the matter, he said, 'I presume that the accused have no worthless protests to make before I sentence them?'

For ten years and more, this fast-track approach to justice had rarely been challenged, but on this occasion, the magistrate failed to have his way. Against a background of mutterings from the public benches, Lady Passmore rose to her feet.

'Ah,' growled Wood, 'I see that one of the accused has a worthless protest to make. Right then. Proceed if you must. But every minute you keep me from my lunch will cost you another year in chains.'

'I have something to say,' announced Lady Passmore, unmoved, 'as would Admiral Lord Passmore, were he here today. I demand that Mrs Pomeroy and I be properly represented by legal counsel, so we can clear our good names of this false and grotesque accusation.'

Wood pursed his lips.

'Do you, indeed? Well, it's a pointless exercise but if you insist on legal counsel, you'll have to choose a person from among this rabble in court, and good luck to you.'

The magistrate, however, was mistaken in thinking he had called Lady Passmore's bluff. She turned towards the public benches and pointed a finger in a forthright manner. She knew exactly who she wanted to defend her and Mrs Pomeroy.

'I appoint Mrs Gaia Champion as our legal counsel. She has the experience of having worked for many years alongside her esteemed late husband, Mr Hercules Champion.'

Her decision was greeted with approval from the public and

another swipe of the gavel from Wood. As the noise subsided, all eyes turned to Gaia who, after a moment's consideration, rose.

'I would be honoured to undertake the role,' she announced. 'All innocent souls deserve to be defended. *Tuti innocentes*.'

There were further cheers, prompting Wood, his face as sour and large as a pumpkin-sized lemon, to shout for order.

'Silence in court. This is your final warning!'

The noise receded only when Gaia raised a hand and spoke in a clear, firm voice.

'I call as my first witness Special Constable Dimm, on whose order these women were wrongfully arrested and held in gaol.'

It was a line of attack that neither Wood nor Dimm had anticipated but it could not be denied.

'Do you not intend to call the accused?' asked the magistrate.

'I may. But I will question the arresting officer first. Mr Dimm, please take the stand.'

Reluctantly, Dimm moved to the front of the court. He was not accustomed to being cross-examined.

Gaia continued, 'Please tell the court on what grounds you concluded that these two ladies, both highly respected and without a blemish on their characters, were importuning themselves?'

Dimm swallowed hard.

'That one on the left, Mrs Pomeroy, was recognised as being a person of an importuning nature by Molly Jenkins, who has knowledge of such things. I was close by Abbey Green and heard her identify Mrs Pomeroy as such.'

Gaia nodded. While she had no direct experience as a defence counsel, it immediately felt natural to her.

'So, on the dubious word of Madame Jenkins, owner of Bath's most notorious brothel, you arrested Mrs Pomeroy. Constable Dimm, what is your view of the accusation made by Mrs Jenkins?'

The public fell silent in anticipation, and Dimm, sensing that he was being hemmed in, fell back on a statement that has served

128

many an officer of the law across the centuries. It was, he believed, one that would carry weight.

'Credible. And true.'

Silence gave ways to cries of incredulity in court, but before Wood could intervene, Gaia again raised her hand for silence.

'With due respect,' she said in the hush that followed, 'your decision to arrest these two irreproachable ladies on the basis of an overheard accusation of a brothel-keeper seems fantastical. Molly Jenkins's accusation is neither credible nor true. It is *in*credible and *false*!'

Dimm coughed awkwardly.

'You are entitled to your opinion, Ma'am.'

'As you might be to yours, had you attempted to corroborate the claim made by Molly Jenkins. To that end, did you ask the ladies you arrested why they were in Abbey Green?'

Dimm hesitated.

'No, Ma'am, there was no point, given the credible and true nature of the accusation.'

'And was there any legal objection to their being in Abbey Green? Were they trespassing? Have public rights of access to the green suddenly been withdrawn?'

'No, Ma'am.'

'They had every right to be there, if they wished, did they not?'

Gaia looked the special constable in the eye. With every passing word she felt more distinctly the righteousness of her cause, and with it, a great sense of oneness with Mary Wollstonecraft, Jane Gomeldon and other heroines of human rights. Her bosom swelled.

'Let me suggest an answer to you, Mr Dimm. On Abbey Green stands a shop in the possession of a pie-maker. Is that not true?'

'It is,' agreed Dimm, sounding punctured.

There was a rustling of interest on the public benches.

'Would you please name that pie-maker?'

'Mrs Crust, Ma'am.

A chorus of 'hurrahs' was sounded, and a rolling pin was waved by Mrs Crust herself.

'I suggest to you that Lady Passmore of Tewkesbury Manor and her friend Mrs Pomeroy had come to Abbey Green with the intention of purchasing one of Mrs Crust's excellent pies. I suggest they were planning a celebratory meal ahead of the forthcoming visit of Her Royal Highness Princess Victoria and wished for a pie that was freshly baked. Perhaps these two women of impeccable character wanted to be the first customers of the day, to be sure of the widest choice of pies. That, of course, was their prerogative, was it not, Special Constable?'

Dimm mumbled an incoherent reply. He did not know the meaning of prerogative.

Gaia responded sharply, 'I could not hear you, Special Constable. Speak louder, if you will, so the full court can hear your reply. Was it or was it not their prerogative to buy fresh pies first thing in the morning?'

'Yes, Ma'am, I expect it was.'

'And is there any English law or custom or practice that precludes a woman of virtuous character from buying a fresh pie first thing in the morning?'

'No, Ma'am.'

Gaia turned to address the public.

'Clearly not. Your lack of understanding of the female mind and of the rights of womankind led you falsely to arrest two innocents on the most specious of charges. You, Sir, should be ashamed of your actions and should apologise forthwith!'

The ranks of the public rose as one in support of Gaia.

'Shame on you, Dimm!' a lady in the second row shouted.

'You're a buffoon!' yelled a pie lover at the back.

'I'd queue up all night for one of Mrs Crust's specials!' called another.

'You need to get them early so Magistrate Wood don't nab 'em all for himself,' joked a fourth.

This was too much for Wood. It was time, he deemed, to call an end to the proceedings. That did not mean he wished to concede defeat. Instead, consumed with rage, he took advantage of the revolutionary mêlée and ordered the court to be cleared.

'Enough,' he barked. 'I won't listen to another word. Empty the court. Except for the accused. They remain in custody, bail denied. I shall deliver my verdict tomorrow.'

After which he rose from his chair and, with his fat feet thumping from the dais, stormed from the courtroom.

ALTHOUGH IT WAS disappointing to see Lady Passmore and Mrs Pomeroy escorted back to a cell, there was a sense of jubilation that left the two accused ladies with smiles on their faces.

'Great goddess, Gaia, you were a marvel,' said Belle, shaking her hand. 'Hark, hear you not Hesiod rewriting his Theogony? Be Gaia no more, he cries; henceforth be thou Dike.'

'Dike?' said Gaia, confused. 'Who's Dike?'

Belle was surprised by his friend's apparent ignorance.

'Daughter of Themis, author of justice, holder of the scales.'

'Then, truly, I am flattered,' she replied, her face pale from the effort she had made.

'You made Decimus Dimm and Wood look like fools.'

'But will it free Lady Passmore and Mrs Pomeroy?'

Belle nodded confidently.

'There is no basis for the charge. And your defence: brilliant! You provided a reason for our dear friends' being in Abbey Green without ever revealing the truth of why they were there. You countered a fictional charge with a fictional alibi.'

Gaia was not so convinced.

'We cannot celebrate victory until they're safely released,

Belle. I don't trust that magistrate. He's bought himself time and he'll make use of it. He's not a man to throw the game so easily.'

And Gaia was right. Behind them, Dimm had already returned to the courtroom and approached them.

'Don't think your clever words are going to get your friends freed,' he snapped. 'It's not how justice operates in this city! I'll tell you how it works. You meet Magistrate Wood at four o'clock this afternoon at Mrs Haytit's tearoom. His invitation, but you'll be paying. Now get out. And think twice before you cross me again.'

Belle and Gaia bowed courteously and went outside to join the jubilant crowd.

'What do you think Wood wants?' asked Gaia.

'To negotiate,' replied Belle. 'He calls himself a magistrate but he's a corrupt politician at heart. We should prepare for the meeting – which I suggest we do over a good lunch. It may be too early to celebrate victory, but the last thing we want is Mrs Haytit's tea.'

NOTES

- Jane Gomeldon (1720–1779) was an English writer and poet from Newcastle upon Tyne. Married young and independently wealthy, she fled domestic violence to France and adopted the guise of a man. Her many French adventures included her courting – and attempting to elope with – a young nun. Unusually, her husband advertised for her return in a Newcastle paper, in response to which she took out an advert of her own, detailing that she had left him on account of his cruelty and his efforts to obtain the fortune left to her by her mother. Among the causes she supported in her lifetime were lying-in hospitals for pregnant women.

CHAPTER XIV

Rock cake and crumpets

A TEAROOM MIGHT seem an unusual location for a duel. Loaded éclairs at twenty paces are not the most common of weapons. We are rarely, however, in control of our destiny, or the manner of our death.

By way of example, Sophocles died unexpectedly of exhaustion after reciting an excessively long sentence from *Antigone*; and paranoid Pope John XX, fearing twenty to be an unlucky number and declaring himself thereby to be John XXI, within a year was crushed to death by the collapse of his bedchamber ceiling – a punishment for lying, perhaps, and for claiming infallibility.

After their lunch, and without a clear sense of what might be coming their way, Gaia Champion and Belle Nash walked to Abbey Green and peered through the window of Shirley Haytit's tearoom. Both tried to suppress a sense of foreboding.

'I agree, Gaia,' Belle said. 'We must be as watchful as an owl and have the acumen of Minerva. Magistrate Wood wishes us ill. He's in league with Hezekiah Porter and he, in turn, must be in league with Mrs Haytit. Why else would he insist on our meeting in this vomitorium?'

They entered and immediately gagged on the smell of rancid butter.

'Two days poor Miss Prim sat in vigil here, keeping watch on Porter's. I wonder how she did it?' said Gaia.

Ahead of them, Mrs Haytit stopped picking at her head lice and peeled herself off a stool.

'A table for three,' requested Belle. 'We meet Magistrate Wood here at four.'

'So they told me,' said Mrs Haytit. 'I've prepared a little table in the corner. You won't be disturbed.'

Belle looked around. Mrs Haytit was spot on in her assessment. They wouldn't be disturbed. Given her tearoom's dire reputation, it was, as ever, devoid of patrons.

'Most kind,' Belle noted. 'Let us order some tea in advance of the weighty magistrate's arrival. A pot of your finest Darjeeling, please, and three cups.'

Mrs Haytit was not used to her customers being quite so specific in their demands.

'I'll see what I can find,' she replied. 'You can have a plate of our famous rock cakes. They was fresh out of the oven last week.'

Belle and Gaia took their seats. The place was a misery. Where there should be joy and laughter, there was soullessness and solitude, as if in rebellion against the tradition of what a good English tearoom should be.

Within a couple of minutes, the proprietor returned. She carried a tray with cups, a pot of tea, a small jug of milk and six stale rock cakes on a platter. She laid the tray on their table and returned to her stool.

Gaia leaned over and poured tea from the pot.

'I'd offer you the milk but as you'll have noticed, it's off,' she grimaced. 'As for the rock cakes ...'

Belle reached for one, not with any intention of eating it but as a potential weapon.

'If Wood turns nasty, don't you reckon a fusillade of these would knock him out? We shall be as the *psiloi*, in want only of slings for these outrageous missiles.'

'We can be twin Davids to his Goliath,' commented Gaia, thinking of a biblical equivalent to match. 'He's picked the wrong fight this time.'

Belle laughed, before inspecting the rock cake closely.

'He'd stand not a chance, the lubber fiend. The raisins in this thing are hard as gunshot.'

Belle would have continued to dissect the object verbally – this being the only treatment of it possible – had a movement in Gaia's eyes not alerted him. Mrs Haytit had returned to the table.

'Everything to your satisfaction or don't you like rock cakes? I've got scones that'll go down a treat, if you'd rather.'

'And bring me down with them,' Belle was tempted to say, but managed to respond instead with his usual courtesy.

'Thank you kindly, charming lady, but do you perchance have something a little softer on the palate? I suffer the most terrible toothache and fear that both rock cake and scone might be the end of me.'

'And you, Ma'am?' Mrs Haytit asked Gaia suspiciously.

'Similarly afflicted,' Gaia responded, rubbing her jaw. 'Tragic coincidence.'

'I'll get you buttered crumpets, then. If you can't eat them, you ain't got no business being here.'

As she stomped off to shout at a cook, the teashop door swung open and Magistrate Wood entered, larger than a prize bull. There was something about his sheer mass that inspired awe. It was as if his body, an oblate spheroid in shape, demonstrated Sir Isaac Newton's laws by asserting its own gravitational pull.

'Here we go,' said Gaia. 'Remember, we must stand fast. We won the argument in court and we can do it again.'

As Wood marched over to them, they stood to greet him.

'Sit down,' he barked sharply.

Belle and Gaia both remained standing.

'We'll sit when you do, Wood,' said Belle to the magistrate. 'Unless you find this small table too constraining.'

'You mind your tongue, boy. You're in my court now. Or your women are.'

'I appreciate the reminder but I'm confident you'll be acquitting 'em soon. As was clear from this morning's hearing, Lady Passmore and Mrs Pomeroy have no case to answer. The sooner you let them go, the more time you'll have to prepare for your own downfall.'

Wood's face lit up.

'My downfall?! At whose hands? I run the law in this city. I'd gaol Mother Mary if she washed up in front of my bench. Appeal to a higher court, if you wish. Your women's reputations are already in tatters, and they'll remain so.'

Mrs Haytit emerged from the kitchen and replaced the untouched rock cakes with hot-toasted crumpets soaked, like sponges, in rancid butter.

'That will be sixpence, Sir,' she said. 'And for Your Honour? A slice of caraway cake, perhaps? – on the house, of course.'

'On the house, Ma'am?' Wood guffawed. 'No magistrate can be seen to accept favours. Have the goodness to add the cake to the councillor's account.'

As Mrs Haytit departed, Gaia decided to seize the opportunity that Wood had opened up and played the only card that fate had dealt her.

'No magistrate can be seen to accept favours, indeed, Magistrate Wood. But there are plenty that have been accepted unseen. Councillor Nash knows this, and I know it too. You are very close to being exposed. We've got you, Sir, and we mean to bring you down.'

'Is that a fact?' Wood sneered. 'With your friends as my hostages? I think not.' And, so saying, he picked up a crumpet, salting it thoroughly. 'There's always a choice in life. Back off from matters that do not concern you, or consign your friends to the tender mercies of my gaolers for the rest of their lives.'

Gaia and Belle looked at each other. Wood had a point. He had called Gaia's play and she had no card to follow. Without solid evidence, there was nothing specific to throw at Wood. If she and Belle prevaricated, there was no knowing how long their friends might languish in Bath's worst hell. But if they backed down, their fight to end corruption was lost – and with it, their mission to save the soufflé. They were snared by their own snare.

Wood now stuffed the salted crumpet in his mouth, ignoring the way the cooling, slightly green butter was congealing.

'So, what do you say?'

As his jaw closed, a mixture of festering, oleaginous butter squirted down the back of his throat. Not being used to turning down food, he grabbed at his milky tea to wash it down. The sour liquid, like a bowl of greasy slops, only worsened his plight.

'You wretch,' said Belle.

And retch is exactly what Wood did.

'Damnation,' he cried, spluttering and choking. 'Hell ... I say hell ... I say help me!'

With his eyes spinning, he gagged, revealing a ball of half-chewed rancid crumpet mixed with sour tea stuck in his mouth like a wedge. He flung his arms out as his upper body fell forward, his head lurching into the remaining crumpets on the plate. Liquid green butter spurted into his face, cementing his nostrils closed and burning away his eyeballs.

'What a disgusting sight,' said Belle, stepping away from the table to allow Wood more room.

'A revolting performance,' agreed Gaia. 'Is he always like this at mealtimes, do you think?'

Mrs Haytit, who had answered the call for help, did not think so.

'Oh, Magistrate Wood!' she cried. 'With Your Honour's permission, Sir ...' and she banged the magistrate on his back, but such was the bulk of the magistrate that she made no impression on him. He remained immobile, his jowls glued to the table by the remaining crumpets as they set hard.

137

Sizing up the situation, Gaia took a napkin and wiped his face so she could check for signs of life. Of which, it became quickly apparent, there were none.

'He would appear to be dead,' she declared.

'Undeniably,' agreed Belle. 'What food giveth, food hath taken away.'

'What?!' wept Mrs Haytit. 'My best customer! He can't be dead.'

Belle, however, determined otherwise.

'In fact, he can, Ma'am. Your teatime fayre has finished him off. There is nothing more to be done. He has stopped breathing. Moments ago, he was the colour of one of your delightful plum puddings, he is now the colour of one of your no less delicious curd tarts. I suggest you call for Decimus Dimm and have the gentleman taken to a morgue to be examined. If you can find any strong enough to carry him.'

Mrs Haytit staggered backwards at the thought of how her tearoom's reputation might now suffer.

'I suggest you also shut the shop for the rest of the day, Ma'am,' said Belle. 'Or longer. At the very minimum, I advise you put a tablecloth over the deceased or you might frighten any other customers foolish enough to venture inside. Oh, I see you have none. How fortunes do change. As for us, we'll be on our way. Come, Gaia. Let us find the special constable and deliver the news that his master's coil has been shuffled off.'

'Is that it?' asked Mrs Haytit plaintively. 'You're leaving me with a corpse?'

Belle reached into a waistcoat pocket.

'I do apologise, Mrs Haytit, Ma'am. You're quite right. Here's a shilling for your troubles. That should more than cover the bill. Indeed, keep the change. I suspect you'll be needing it.'

NOTES

- The éclair (and by reputation, too, the soufflé) was created by the first celebrity chef, Monsieur Marie-Antoine Carême (1783–1833). Named after the Queen of France – for boys and girls were often given names designed for the opposite gender – he was born into an impoverished family and was one of twenty-five siblings. Abandoned by his parents, he worked as a kitchen-boy before honing his art as a chef. During his career, he was employed by the French gourmand, diplomat Talleyrand, George IV of England, Czar Alexander I of Russia and the banker James Mayer Rothschild. He wrote the encyclo-paedic *L'Art de la Cuisine Française*.

- My uncle has a habit of making reference to the great Bachelors of History. The physicist Sir Isaac Newton (1642–1726) enjoyed a close friendship with the Swiss mathematician Nicolas Fatio de Duillier, although it is not known if their mutual interest in gravitational pull extended to other types of pull.

PART BUBBLE

CHAPTER XV

Death concentrates the mind

THE FROTH COLLAPSES, like foam upon the sea, riding the waves of human nonsense. Pop-pop-poppity-pop, it goes, until only a single bubble remains. Its surface shining, reflecting the good and ill of the world, buffeted by the wind, anxious to avoid the sun, at risk of a single drop of rain shed by the sky.

Look into the bubble's mirrored, convex surface while you can, and observe your own distended face: a bulbous nose, giant almond eyes, disconsolate mouth. It is a face you may not recognise as your own but touch it, feel it with your hand and pinch your skin. True enough, it is yours: a living reflection of your being. And you would do well to watch it while you can, for we all know what happens to a bubble.

It bursts, like a dying species. Its existence expires.

AFTER THE SHOCKING events at Dame Shirley Haytit's tearoom, Gaia Champion and Belle Nash had tracked down Decimus Dimm at the Dog & Duck and revealed that Obadiah Wood had consumed his last. While the special constable took in the news, Gaia recommended that he release Lady Passmore and Mrs Pomeroy forthwith or risk a riot of women and the razing of Pulteney Gaol by Bath's fairer sex.

'They'd hazard their pretty frocks and petticoats?' Dimm had shouted. 'I think not.'

'You think not, indeed,' Belle had interposed. 'We will

143

therefore think for you. You, you Cerberus, will accompany Mrs Champion to the gaol and instruct kind Charon to ferry our dear friends back up into light-filled Pheneus, paying Charon yourself for their passage. After that you can collect the corpse of the unlovely Dolos and feed on it, for all I care. I shall meanwhile alert Chairman Camshaft of his untimely demise.'

The torrent of Greek allusions had left Dimm unsure and disorientated.

'We can't leave the body unattended,' he had declared.

'It is safe with Mrs Haytit's rock cakes,' Belle had replied. 'Neither of them is going anywhere. The crumpet, however, will need rescuing for Dr Sturridge's observation at the post-mortem.'

A minute later and back to the present, the three of them were on the move, Gaia with Dimm to the gaol and Belle to Guildhall. His gait was always light, but the events of the day had vitalised him further, and he leapt through the main entrance like Pan in spring.

'Good evening, Councillor Nash,' said Bullard, the doorman.

'Beautiful indeed, Bullard. Is our beloved chairman at hand?'

'He left but then came back for something he'd forgotten, like every evening.'

'And my clerk, young whippersnapper Lush?'

'Left earlier hand in hand with Herr Kant,' Bullard reported.

'Those boys,' laughed Belle. 'Just think what they'd do if I wasn't around.'

Belle made straight for the chairman's office, where he found an oil lamp burning but no one present. On the other side of the corridor, however, and entirely in the dark, was the small figure of Camshaft, with his head buried in a bureau in the clerks' ante-chamber.

Belle knocked to alert the old man to his presence.

'Who's there?' said the chairman, removing his head from a drawer.

'Belle Nash. One of your councillors, you'll recall.'

Camshaft turned towards the sound of Belle's voice.

'Councillor Nash? Ah, yes. You're the bachelor who's looking after my great-grandson. I remember your father. Bright as a button. Now, where are you, Sir? Come to think of it, where am I?'

'You're in the clerks' room, Sir,' said Belle. 'And the candles have all been snuffed.'

'That explains it,' said Camshaft. 'Thought I'd lost my eyesight. And why am I here?'

'I'd venture that you left something behind and you're now looking for it.'

''Pon my soul, Sir, you're right. Now, if I had my spectacles, I might be able to see what it was.'

Belle sighed.

'Might it be your spectacles you're looking for?' he suggested. 'Maybe you left them in your office. Here, Chairman, let me lead you into the light.'

As Belle took Camshaft by the hand, Camshaft rested his weight on Belle's arm and shuffled into his own room, where a small pair of spectacles lay in the middle of his empty desk.

'Are these the ones?' Belle asked.

'Maybe. What are they?'

'Your spectacles, Chairman. Now you can put them on to see what you came back to look for. Unless it was ...'

'My spectacles! By Jove, you're right. You're bright as a button, Nash,' Camshaft declared again. 'Just like your father.'

Belle smiled and handed over the spectacles. 'You honour me, Sir. And now, to return the favour, may I detain you a moment longer? I have important news to impart.'

The chairman sensed trouble and his hands began to shake as he eased himself into his chair.

'News, eh? Don't tell me my wife's died. Tough as old boots but when the moment comes ... .'

145

'It's not your wife, Sir.'

'General McCarthy, then?'

'No, Sir, Governor McCarthy died a few years ago in the Gold Coast, killed by Ashanti warriors.'

Camshaft was unimpressed.

'Not the actual General McCarthy. Don't take me for a fool, young man. I'm talking about my golden retriever General McCarthy, a dog with a brain the size of a pea.'

Belle sighed again. Conversations with the chairman rarely proved straightforward – but Belle could wander too.

'Not your dog either, Sir. But you're right that a death has occurred. Indeed, as we speak, Minos, Rhadamanthus and Aecus are preparing to deliver their funerary verdict on our esteemed, now former-esteemed magistrate, Obadiah Wood.'

'What? You're losing me, Nash.'

'I have to report that Wood met a similar fate to that of King Adolf Frederick of Sweden and barked his last an hour ago in Shirley Haytit's tearoom.'

'The King of Sweden died in Haytit's tearoom?'

'No. Magistrate Wood, Sir, of crumpets.'

Camshaft nodded as he absorbed the news.

'I wish you didn't speak in riddles, Nash, but I get your drift. Magistrate Wood died of crumpet poisoning. We must shut the establishment down. Good of you to tell me. I'll get on to it in the morning.'

'Not just that, Chairman,' Belle went on, giving Camshaft his victory. 'Wood's sad demise leaves us with a crisis on our hands. Princess Victoria is due here in a few days' time and we can't afford distractions. The Magistrate Selection Committee has to appoint a replacement. Can its meeting be postponed until after the visit?'

For the first time, Camshaft appeared to have his wits about him.

'You're right, Nash. Nothing must get in the way of royalty, least of all death. Choosing a new magistrate can wait a few days and will give us time to identify the best candidate. *De mortuis nil nisi bonum*, etc. etc., but I suggest we elect someone more attuned to the law than Wood. Any thoughts on the matter?'

I T WAS THE first time that Gaia had been inside a gaol and it reminded her of the workhouses that she and Hercules had visited and deplored. Situated in Grove Street on the east side of Pulteney Bridge, the building could have been the gracious twin of Bath's Theatre Royal, had it had a portico stuck on the front. Instead, it was dank and miserable, with a pervasive smell of the subterranean. Although built above the water line, water from the River Avon seemed to seep through every wall. Gaia gasped for air as if drowning.

'My friends are being held in this?' she exclaimed.

'Well, we haven't put them up in the Sydney Hotel,' said Dimm.

Gaia was sharp in her reply.

'You'd do well to rein in your tongue, Special Constable, or you may find yourself ending up here in their place.'

'You'd do well to rein in yours, Mrs Champion,' Dimm snapped back, 'because I'm the one with the keys.'

The two stood facing each other in silence. Seconds ticked but it was Dimm who backed down. With his very next sentence, he ordered the release of the women and Gaia watched as Lady Passmore and Mrs Pomeroy were escorted to the front entrance and to freedom. They emerged from the gloom, blinking but defiant and proud, into Gaia's embrace.

'Oh, Lady Passmore of Tewkesbury Manor and Mrs Pomeroy, your ordeal is over. You poor creatures. What torments have you endured.'

Lady Passmore fanned the air in front of her face with her hand.

'No words, Mrs Champion, no words.'

147

'As for the latrines!' declared Mrs Pomeroy, but Lady Passmore interrupted.

'No words, I said. Please.'

'"What torments have you endured" was a rhetorical statement, my dears, not a question,' Gaia explained. 'Now is not the time for detail. Now is the time for flight. Come. Lady Passmore of Tewkesbury's carriage is waiting for us in Grove Street.'

At the sight of the carriage, even Lady Passmore's eyes teared up, for its presence provided a physical reminder of their former standing in Bath society.

'I presume that we have been declared innocent,' said Lady Passmore as she took her seat and relaxed into the luxuriant velvet.

'Not exactly,' replied Gaia, 'but there is other news. Death visited Magistrate Wood this afternoon in the strangest of circumstances. As a result, there will be no prosecution. The case is withdrawn.'

Lady Passmore and Mrs Pomeroy sat up straight.

'The magistrate is dead?' said Her Ladyship, as if dying was an offence against polite society.

'You mean, he died?' asked Mrs Pomeroy, by way of clarification.

'He choked on a buttered crumpet. And a cup of sour tea.'

The two friends stared at Gaia. They did not know whether to be more amazed at the speed of their release or the manner of Wood's death.

'On a crumpet?' declared Lady Passmore. 'But how common. To choke on a madeleine, perhaps, although never with tea. But a crumpet!'

'And buttered, you say,' enquired Mrs Pomeroy. 'Was it salted or unsalted butter? My own taste tends more to the salted.'

Gaia was pleased to have her friends back, and on their usual form, despite their travails.

'The butter was both green and rancid, making one suppose

that it was unsalted, a speculation confirmed when the magistrate added copious quantities of salt to it. Whether it was the crumpet, the butter or the salt that dealt the blow, I could not say. But he choked and is now dead.'

'... and unable, therefore, to halt us in our triumph,' declared Lady Passmore proudly. 'We have news of our own to impart, do we not, Mrs Pomeroy? Our night-time vigil in Abbey Green bore fruit. Through stealth and deception, we have unearthed the truth behind Porter's flour. It's all coming nicely to a head, Mrs Champion. Magistrate Wood is dead. And Hezekiah Porter's days are numbered.'

NOTES
- Brigadier-General Sir Charles McCarthy (1764–1824) was governor of the Gold Coast, modern-day Ghana. The powerful Ashanti tribe rebelled and McCarthy, described by one historian as a 'decent, proud, but stupid man', confronted a 10,000-strong Ashanti force with just 500 men. His tactic of playing *God Save the King* to scare the enemy failed. Battle ensued and the British force was overcome when it was discovered that the cases of reserve gunpowder contained macaroni. Only twenty of the British force survived. McCarthy was killed, his heart plucked out and his head kept as a trophy by the victors.
- Gluttonous King Adolf Frederick of Sweden (1710–1771) died enjoying a cream bun at the end of a meal of lobster, caviar, sauerkraut, kippers and Champagne. Being Shrove Tuesday and the final meal before Lent, the king was not satisfied with one cream bun, or even two. He died whilst consuming his fourteenth.

CHAPTER XVI

Rhyming couplets

A S IS COMMON in most Georgian houses in Bath, the Nash residence at Gay Street had both a drawing room and a withdrawing room, for what else is one to do, having completed a heavy day's reading or water colouring, if not retire to an adjoining salon?

With Belle yet to return home, Gerhardt Kant had commandeered the withdrawing room for the evening, pushing the furniture against the walls and leaving one solitary, straight-backed chair in its centre. On the chair sat Lucius Lush, his feet planted side by side, his ankles touching, his hands on his knees, his eyes looking straight ahead like the very best boy in class, precisely as instructed by his Prussian tutor.

'So, Master Lush, your *Professor* asks you: what have you today in your lesson learned?' asked Gerhardt, who stood six feet in front of him, with a mortar board balanced precariously on his wig.

Lush did his best not to smirk, but it was hard. He wore his woollen work suit, with his white cotton shirt untucked from his trousers in the manner of a schoolboy's smock. He was also wearing a small top hat that had been part of Belle's uniform at Bath's Abbey School for Boys. He felt very silly and was rather glad that Belle was not at home to witness the scene.

'Oh, great and good Professor Kant,' he replied, 'You have taught me algebra and physics. In return, for recitation, I have memorised a poem by England's greatest poet, Henry James Pye.'

Gerhardt threw his hands into the air.

'Pye? Pei? Pigh? Never *von* such a name have I hearing been.'

'Oh Professor, Pye was a lyric god. No poet in the history of verse knew better how to rhyme. Shakespeare and Milton were but dunces compared with him. He matches *food* with *mood*, *delight* with *appetite*, *inhales* with *gales* and *unbends* with *offends*. There's not a word in the English language that Pye has not coupled with another:

> Incessant down the stream of Time
> And days, and years, and ages, roll,
> Speeding through Error's iron clime
> To dark Oblivion's goal.'

'This is poetry?' protested Gerhardt. 'This is *Mumpitz*! I will teach you poetry. Attend – *passt auf*:

> *Da ihr noch die schöne Welt regieret,*
> *An der Freude leichtem Gängelband*
> *Selige Geschlechter noch geführet,*
> *Schöne Wesen aus dem Fabelland!*

'That, Master Lucius, is from Friedrich von Schiller's *The Grecian Gods*. It is *Fantastisch*! *So schön*. A quality that is good to contemplate, *nicht wahr*?'

Lush giggled. German hegemony was to be contested.

'Tum-tee-tum-tee-tum-tee gengelband. Tum-tee-tum-tee-tum-tee fatherland! Your Schiller sounds like nonsense verse. Silly Schiller!'

'*Du Schlingel*!' roared Gerhardt, flapping his arms angrily. '*Du Teufel*! Pye is *peinlich*! Now listen *und* learn:

> *Er stand auf seines Daches Zinnen,*
> *Er schaute mit vergnügten Sinnen ...*'

'Not bad, Sir,' Lush interrupted. 'In fact, it sounds not unlike the worthy Pye:

151

On earth's green bosom lavish fling,
When genial Zephyr breathes the spring ...'

At this, Gerhardt stepped in. 'Pye – like Schiller?! *Ach*: the boy is deaf!

'Dies alles ist mir untertänig,'
Begann er zu Ägyptens König ...'

Only for Lush to have his repost:

From all that copious Fancy sings
Of fabled demi-gods and kings ...

Lush would have continued had he not begun to laugh uncontrollably.

'*Abuse – obtuse. Breast – dressed. Dispense – eloquence,*' he giggled. 'Mr Pye was truly a marriage-broker of verbality, capable of teaching Mr Schiller a trick or two. Can we not declare this contest a draw, Sir?'

Gerhardt stamped his feet.

'A draw? You should be beaten! I declare *einen Krieg*. Take up arms!'

In response, Lush lifted his arms in the air.

'Not like that!'

Lush dropped his arms and hid them behind his back.

'*Nein!*' said Gerhardt, now also laughing. A moment later, the tutor had collapsed to the floor and was clutching his chest in merriment.

'*Hör auf*, Master Lucius. Stop! You have killed the art of poetry *und* now you kill the poet.'

He beat his head with his fist, and Lush followed suit. Toppling off the chair, he fell in a mock faint and joined Gerhardt on the floor, tears streaming down his face at the idiocy of their play-acting. They both lay on their backs, chests heaving.

'That's the funniest thing ever!' said Lush, gasping. 'Whoever thought poetry could be so hilarious. Shilly Schiller!'

'*Peinlicher* Pye! *Ach*, the *Dummkopf* English,' replied Gerhardt breathlessly, before turning onto his side to face the younger man. As was his character, he needed affirmation. 'But now you must tell me: have you enjoyed *die Efahrung* – the experience – that I constructed? Have you achieved an *Innerlichkeit* of the mind? Do you, by chance, feel less miserable?'

Lush stared at the rosette on the high ceiling. So much had changed in such a short time. One week he was in his great-grandfather's dusty library, drained of all life; the next he was immersed in the world of Councillor Nash and his exotic second cousin once removed.

'I am loving your *Efahrung*. I am thrilled by your *Innerlichkeit*. I'm amazed by what life suddenly has to offer. You make the serious such fun!'

Gerhardt was delighted.

'*Ja*, that is how it should be. *Ernsthafter Spaß*. Life is beautiful. Like myself, *ja*?'

Lush smiled. He had anticipated the question but found that, lying next to Gerhardt, it now carried more meaning. A willing participant, Lush could no longer deny that Gerhardt's close proximity excited him.

'I think life should be more like you,' he said, almost answering the question.

But Gerhardt wanted an unequivocal response. He fondled his wig with one hand, while running the other down a thigh.

'So, you think I am beautiful, *ja*? That I have a beautiful body?'

It was not the first occasion on which Gerhardt had asked, but this time Lush recognised it as an invitation to push their friendship further.

153

An awkward thrill ran through him. He wanted to respond. To engage.

'Of course, Gerhardt. The human body is a beautiful thing. Although with mine ...'

'Then let yourself go, Lucius,' pled Gerhardt. 'Let yourself enter the *Traum*.'

Lush closed his eyes to dream, and imagined a life in which he could be free of inhibition. Comfortable with his body. Was that not the path to happiness? To pleasure? He felt himself relax, to accept that there was no shame in being with another. More than that, that he could take pride in being different.

'Hmmm,' he whispered. 'You're right. That feels good.'

'As a cup of tea would, once you've finished burbling,' said a familiar voice. Lush opened his eyes in fright. There was no sign of Gerhardt. Instead, Belle Nash was looming over him. 'In the name of slothful Aergia, what are you doing down there, Master Lush?'

The young clerk went red with embarrassment.

'Sorry, Sir. I was taking a rest.'

'On the floor of my withdrawing room.'

'I wasn't aware you'd come home.'

'There are chairs to rest on,' Belle pointed out. 'Far be it for me to tell the youth of today how to act, but it seems most peculiar to lie down on the floor. What's my school hat doing over there? And where's Gerhardt?'

Lush looked about, perplexed. It seemed that, having heard Belle arrive, Gerhardt had scampered from the room.

'I'm not sure, Sir. He's definitely about.'

Belle huffed. The young were forever taking liberties.

'I'll go and look for him. In the meantime, I suggest you get up, put the furniture back where it belongs and pop the kettle on. It's been a long and arduous day. Tomorrow I have to rise early to finalise the plans for the princess's visit – which I will be able to do only if no more of my friends get arrested.'

154

A T THAT MOMENT, Gaia Champion was arriving back at Somerset Place, having seen Mrs Pomeroy and Lady Passmore to their own front doors. Each woman had been welcomed warmly by their respective staff. After descending from the carriage, Mrs Pomeroy had been hugged by her maid and cook. Lady Passmore's staff had not dared cross the Rubicon of physical contact in the same way, but Gaia had noted that tears were shed. The women had been received as goddesses.

Gaia's intention on her return home had been to take a glass of fine whisky before heading quickly to bed. The events of the day had left her tired beyond measure. Her heart momentarily sank, therefore, on being told by Pritchard that Phyllis Prim was waiting in the drawing room and had been there the past three hours.

'She appeared most agitated, Ma'am,' explained the butler. 'I took it upon myself to offer her refuge until your return. I understand that you were successful in your endeavours, although at some cost to the city magistrate.'

Bath's rumour mill had evidently been as efficient as ever.

'Our friends are indeed free,' said Gaia. 'And it is true that we have seen the last of Magistrate Wood. As for Miss Prim, you acted correctly. I will impart to her briefly what has transpired and then she may return home. Make sure to hold the carriage. But, first and most importantly ...'

Pritchard guessed correctly.

'A glass of Scotland's best, Ma'am. I will accompany you to the drawing room and deliver the amber nectar forthwith.'

They climbed the stairs, Pritchard attentively, Gaia with a purposeful step. The experience of visiting the gaol had focussed her mind on what mattered most in life now that Hercules was gone. The ill treatment of her women friends had, in particular, shocked her. There was something wrong with a city that did not respect its own female citizens, nor recognise the contribution they made to its wellbeing.

She entered the drawing room and stopped. There, beside the fireplace, was one such citizen fast asleep on a chaise, her small head gently hanging to one side, a half-finished shawl spread across a lap on which were cradled two balls of wool and a pair of knitting needles.

After a moment's thought, Gaia decided to wake the slumbering spinster. Though blissful in the arms of Morpheus, Miss Prim would wish to know that Lady Passmore and Mrs Pomeroy were safe. And Gaia needed to sleep.

She sat down beside her friend and touched her on the shoulder.

'Miss Prim, wake up. I have news.'

The bundle of knitting emitted a slight whimper.

'Mrs Champion, is that you?'

'Yes, dear. Don't panic. Take time to gather your senses and I will be your *Evening Clarion*.'

Miss Prim rubbed her eyes.

'I fear the worst. I was knitting a shawl for a suffering soul in Trim Street. Will it now be needed for Lady Passmore and her companion?'

Gaia laughed.

'Lady Passmore and Mrs Pomeroy were freed from gaol this afternoon and are returned home.'

Miss Prim felt faint with relief.

'Wonderful, wonderful. I feared they might catch a chill. Prison cell windows are unglazed, you see, and the drafts are fierce. But tell me about Magistrate Wood. Everyone in society is saying that he choked to death on a buttered crumpet.'

'And a cup of tea – to be precise,' said Gaia.

Reminded of her own ordeal, Miss Prim gasped for breath.

'And did Mrs Haytit douse him with water?'

'With rancid butter, in fact. It was not a pleasant sight. But there is more.'

156

'More?' said Miss Prim suspiciously. Miss Prim rarely liked the sound of more.

'Before their arrest, our intrepid spies uncovered the secret of Porter's flour. They witnessed a delivery of cattle-feed into the store in the early hours. It is their belief that Mr Porter mixes stale flour and cattle-feed and sells it into many of the best kitchens in Bath. That, Miss Prim, would explain Mme Galette's stodgy soufflé.'

For a second time, Miss Prim's eyes widened.

'He's been mixing cattle-feed with flour! What a crime! But can we bring him to book?'

'His real crime, I suggest, is to have taken advantage of the women of Bath. Men do not buy flour, Miss Prim. It is the wives and cooks and housekeepers and kitchen staff who make up Porter's clientèle. There is a lot more than the soufflé now at stake. Porter's is an assault against our entire sex and I for one am not prepared to tolerate such a state of affairs. It is time for women to rise up against injustice, to occupy the roles of authority that have for so long been betrayed by men.'

Miss Prim began to shake.

'Must *all* women rise up, Mrs Champion?' she asked nervously. 'My own passion, as you know, is for the knit and purl, though I believe the rib stitch and the cable deserve greater recognition. Could you do the rising up for me?'

Gaia smiled. In this instance, she was happy to compromise.

'Yes, Miss Prim,' she said. 'It would be my privilege. Although right now, my dear, what I need to do is to collapse into bed. So, if you don't mind ...'

Gaia knocked back the rest of her whisky in one gulp. Then she stood, held out her arm and escorted Miss Prim to the front door and the waiting carriage.

157

NOTES

- The kindest view of Henry James Pye (1744–1813) is that he had an obsession with rhyming couplets better suited to modern rap music than traditional verse. Some have said he was born in the wrong century. A crueller assessment is that of the historian Lord Blake, who described Pye as 'the worst poet laureate in English history'. Pye was a Member of Parliament and his appointment as laureate was an ill-judged reward for his political fealty to William Pitt the Younger. Ridiculed even in his own lifetime, the unfortunate Pye is commonly classified as a 'poetaster', a derogatory term applied to bad poets.

CHAPTER XVII

The rotten old king is dead ...

BELLE NASH FOUND Gerhardt Kant innocently filing his fingernails in the bedchamber. Heedless of distracting him from such a vital task, Belle manoeuvred him back to the withdrawing room, where Lucius Lush had restored some order, and prepared to enlarge on the day's events. But what should have been a tale of derring-do – of ladies freed and magistrates dispatched – fell unaccountably flat. The fizz of their earlier encounters had disappeared.

Clearly uncomfortable, Lush welcomed the suggestion that he return to his lodgings. Now alone with Gerhardt, Belle enquired about domestic matters: why the furniture in the room had been moved; and what Lush had been doing on the floor.

'I will not the truth conceal, Belle. I am with the young man's mind a great experiment making. I am opening him up to *Efahrung und Innerlichkeit, und* he is great promise showing. A remarkable boy. He unlocked for me his insights into the greatest poet, Friedrich von Schiller. Misguided but innovative he is. A *Philosoph* in the making, I am thinking.'

Belle experienced a sinking feeling. The Prussian had evidently switched his attention from the matron of the knitting needles to Camshaft's young pup, and not in a helpful way. In bringing the two of them together, Belle realised, he had scored a dramatic own goal.

'I'll need a little more detail,' he said curtly. 'I fear for the sanity of Gay Street.'

There followed a ten-minute psychological treatise by Gerhardt on his ambition to return a human mind to its childhood state. It ended when Belle could take no more.

'Enough, please! Even Perseus, assisted by Ariadne's endless ball of thread, would lose his way in the labyrinth of your mind. As for how my school hat might help the boy's cerebral development is beyond me. I'd have thought it would restrict its growth. And who but a child would want to return to their childhood? I hated mine. Couldn't wait to grow up and escape the backwaters of Frome.'

But Gerhardt was adamant that he was on the verge of a great discovery.

'*Das Englisch* are miserable – you, Lucius, *alle* – but Lucius at least a willing pupil is. To be saved, he must be transported to the earliest stage of his *Kindheit*. *Ja*, infancy, *Kindesalter*, is the necessary first step. But how does one take the mind back to the beginning of life?'

Belle huffed dismissively. He was tired and was not in an indulging mood.

'I give up, Gerhardt. And, at the moment, with so much on my plate with the royal visit, I'm beyond caring. Just don't try your ludicrous theory out on me, and please take note: if you choose to experiment again in the future, do so without disarranging the furniture. I'm going to bed now. Goodnight.'

THE NEXT MORNING Belle sat in his Guildhall office in a state of despair. It was not that Lush had failed to bring him tea; indeed, his clerk had been particularly solicitous of his needs. Nor had the paradigm of his world undergone a notable change. His socks had been in their usual drawer, the abbey bells chimed every quarter and Mrs Crust's slice of breakfast pie had been, as ever, excellent.

But he could not deny that the previous evening's hollowness of spirit continued to afflict him. Looking out towards Sham Castle, he wondered anew what went on in the Prussian mind and how his own scepticism of Gerhardt's theories reflected on their relationship. He wanted to do the right thing, but it was hard to know what that was.

'Damn it, Gerhardt, I don't know whether I am coming or going with your *Innerlichkeits* and your *Outerlichkeits*,' he mused out loud. 'And I really have more important matters to deal with.'

At that moment, Lush returned to the office from a meaningless errand. It would be nice to report that the clerk was his normal, bubbly self but he was not. He was a man out of sorts, the inevitable consequence of his first toying with improper desire. Guilt, like a drop of iodine in water, coloured his soul. Though loyal to Belle, he had come within a whisker of betraying his trust.

'Is something wrong, Sir?' he asked, on hearing Belle talking to himself.

'Not at all, young fellow. I was lost in thought, but none of any matter.'

'A fresh cup of tea, perhaps?'

At risk to his bladder, it seemed the only way to get the boy out of his office was to agree.

'There's always room for one more, I suppose.'

Lush bowed and was all set to fetch the kettle when he stopped. He was a well-meaning youth and one who preferred to face the facts than sidestep them. His body shook with emotion as he spoke.

'About last night, Sir. I have something to say.'

The clerk, however, had misjudged the moment. Belle's mind was set on Bath's royal visitor and the papers on his desk.

'Not now. I need to concentrate on the princess's schedule.'

'But, Sir, I should explain myself.'

In response, Belle fixed him with the sternest of expressions.

'No, Master Lush. I have not the time. I spoke to Gerhardt last

161

night and he regaled me at unnecessary length with tales of your forays into experience and inwardness. It sounds fascinating but I have a lot more to worry about than reversion to childhood. If it pleases you, I'm delighted. But please don't involve me.'

This clear and apparently unambiguous statement came as a great relief to Lush. He was thankful beyond telling that his feared transgression had the councillor's seal of approval.

'That's generous, Sir. But should you ever say otherwise ...'

Belle waved his hand.

'For goodness' sake, get your priorities right. Tea first, then everything else. Off you go.'

As the clerk left, Belle turned back to the royal itinerary. Princess Victoria was to arrive in two days' time and would stay in Royal Crescent. The next morning, civic dignitaries would gather in the Assembly Rooms and then walk or travel by carriage the short distance to the new park.

He checked and double-checked the plan.

Of the several thousand people expected to attend, only a select few would meet the princess, among whom would be Gaia Champion and himself: he had made sure of that. Of the key dignitaries, he had received news that his godfather the Revd. George Monstrance, Bishop of Bath & Wells, was unable to travel because of the ill health of his cat, and the late Obadiah Wood would not now be attending. Belle decided to take advantage of their absence and invite in their place Lady Passmore and Mrs Pomeroy.

His one concern remained the reliability of the ancient music master who had yet to divulge details of his programme for the Abbey School for Boys' Choir. Given that Arthur Quigley's repertoire included such bawdy numbers as *Hunt the Squirrel* and *The Old Fumbler* Belle felt pangs of concern but had no choice beyond that of trusting his old teacher.

At this point, Belle became aware of a visitor standing by his

162

office door. The good news was that it was someone who could drink the tea when Lush returned with it. The bad news was that it was Belle's least favourite councillor.

'Jacob Pollard! Let joy be unconfined! To what do I owe the honour, Sir? I pray you're not petitioning me for an introduction to the princess. My list is full, I regret. You'll have to gather with the narrowboat boys and watch the event from afar, but I'm sure you won't find their company disagreeable.'

Pollard took note of the insult but chose not to respond.

'I shall be attending with my lady wife, thank you, Councillor Nash. But I am not here about the royal visit. It is about another matter that I wish to bend your ear.'

The two looked at the other with suspicion.

'Enlighten me.'

Pollard stepped into the office.

'I am informed that our respected magistrate, Obadiah Wood, died yesterday in the most unfortunate of circumstances. The Magistrate Selection Committee, of which we are both members, will be required to choose his replacement.'

'But not until the royal visit is over, Sir. I have spoken with Chairman Camshaft and he has agreed to delay the appointment by a few days.'

'So I understand,' said Pollard. 'At which point, I presume that we will follow tradition.'

Belle looked up cautiously. He did not trust Pollard.

'And what tradition would that be? I'm not necessarily a follower of tradition.'

A smirk fell across Pollard's face.

'The new magistrate will be elected from within the committee, of course,' he replied. 'There will be others who apply – there always are – but the committee by tradition chooses one of its own, as it did in the case of Obadiah Wood. And, of the current committee, it isn't going to be Chairman Camshaft, and you are so

163

lately arrived as barely to qualify, which makes me the sole candidate, as I'm sure you'll agree.'

Belle did not – far from it, and the thought that Pollard might become magistrate was unconscionable. But now was not the moment to voice his opposition.

'I will give it some thought,' he replied. 'I certainly agree that it should not be me.'

Pollard left with his spirits buoyed but distrustful of Belle, and rightly so. For his part, Belle had his own idea who the next magistrate should be and was delighted that Pollard had shown his hand. The information Pollard had imparted had also provided the opportunity to spring a trap.

I T WAS AT three in the afternoon, or at seven cups of tea and five biscuits into the day, when Belle received his second visitor, and it was someone a good deal more welcome than his first.

'Dare I to hope that I'm not interrupting, dear Belle?' said Gaia, standing in the doorway with a large smile across her hand-some face. Dressed in a riding habit of brown wool and a feathered hat, she cut a powerful figure. She had, without a doubt, broken free of mourning.

Belle greeted her with genuine joy.

'I see an apparition of Diana, fresh from coursing in the glades! Enter, nymph! You could not have come at a better time. I have been desirous of intercourse with you all day.'

Gaia beamed. She had woken with a freshness of spirit and had carried it with her.

'What a coincidence, Belle. I have been wanting the same. But we will need privacy, if our tongues are to speak trippingly. Would Master Lush oblige?'

Somewhat bemused, Lush stepped out from behind his clerk's bureau.

'Of course, Mrs Champion. Please excuse me, Ma'am.'

But Belle had a better idea.

'No, wait. Gaia, if you would accompany me, I believe the magistrate's court is unoccupied for the day. We can talk there and allow Master Lush to continue his important work.'

They left Belle's office and traversed the corridors of Guildhall. Belle opened the double doors of the courtroom and, making a dramatic flourish with one arm, stepped aside for Gaia to enter.

'The King is dead,' he said dramatically. 'Long live the ...'

He halted as Gaia turned to face him. Such was their bond of friendship that they had reached the same conclusion independently.

'Long live the Queen? Oh, Belle, could it be? Even the thought seems treasonous.'

Belle was having none of it.

'You'd make a splendid magistrate, Ma'am. None could do it better — no man, certainly. Bath would be eternally in your debt. You were your husband's equal and he was a great lawyer. You and the role are made for each other.'

'But will it be allowed?'

He gave a shrug of his shoulders.

'It's without precedent. But that's the thing about precedents. As King James the First learned to his cost, precedents can be created. And if the divine right of monarchs can be overruled, then the monopoly of men can be as well.'

Together they moved down the aisle between the public benches, their minds working in tandem.

'You're right,' said Gaia. 'Something has to change if society is to progress.'

They stopped at the magistrate's chair.

'Try it for size,' Belle suggested.

Gaia did not hesitate. She climbed the dais, looked out over the dock and the witness stand, then lowered herself into the magistrate's seat.

'It's surprisingly comfortable.'

'A perfect fit. Like Cinderella's shoe.'

'But we delude ourselves, dear Councillor Nash. In our beloved nation's history, never has a lady magistrate been appointed. The other members of your committee will oppose my selection.'

Belle knew she was right, and that was without the added complications of Pollard's covetousness. Hers seemed a pointless ambition. But Belle stood firm.

'The battle cannot be won until the argument is made. Remember the brave Parthians who, though heavily outnumbered, defeated the mighty Crassus at Carrhae. Put yourself forward, Mrs Champion, and challenge the Fates.'

Suddenly, however, Gaia sounded timid.

'People will laugh.'

It was undeniably true.

'Some will, but more will cheer. And do not doubt this: you are the best candidate.'

This time, she nodded. Gaia was not a woman who doubted her ability.

'True, but I need more time to think. That I crave the role, I do not deny, but neither do I wish to look a fool. The dice are loaded against me; my defeat, an inevitability. And if, by chance, I succeeded to the post, opposition to me would not end there.'

Belle joined her on the dais.

'The choice is yours, Madam, but make it soon. The committee meets immediately Princess Victoria's visit has concluded. You have three days to make up your mind.'

NOTES

- *Hunt the Squirrel* is an olde English folk tune with indecipherable lyrics:

Hunt the squirrel through the wood,
I lost him, I found him;
I have a little dog at home,
He won't bite you, He won't bite you.

The Old Fumbler is another classic of the same genre:

Smug rich and fantastic Old Fumbler was known,
That wedded a brisk juicy girl of the town,
Her face like an angel, fair plump and a maid,
Her lute when in tune, too, could he have but played,
But lost is his skill, let him do what he can,
She finds him in bed a weak silly old man.

CHAPTER XVIII

The secret to British greatness ...

I T WAS A delightfully sunny spring morning and great crowds of
people had come out to celebrate the opening of Bath's new
park by Princess Alexandrina Victoria of Kent, better known
as plain Princess Victoria, for plain she was. Among them were a
certain Prussian of our acquaintance and his new friend, one
Lucius Lush. They filled the time before the princess's arrival by
playing a game of who could say the longest title of a monarch or
statesman without drawing breath.

'George *Vierte*, by the grace of God, of the United Kingdom of
Great Britain *und* Ireland, King, Defender of the Faith, King of
Hanover, Duke of Brunswick,' managed Gerhardt, his face
momentarily turning purple.

'By all the heavens, Gerti, I can't beat that,' replied Lush.

'Then I am *der Gewinner*! Huzzah!'

They had chosen a spot close to the arboretum. This gave them
a vantage point across an area of open grass and to the bandstand,
where the main action was to occur. Lush checked to see if the
royal party had arrived, but it was not yet in evidence.

'Yes, you win,' he conceded. 'But how do you know so long a
title?'

The answer was that Gerhardt had an obsession with royalty,
and in particular the House of Hanover that had now gifted the
British their monarch. It was that fascination that had emboldened
him to follow Belle Nash to Bath and experience first-hand how an
alien realm was faring under a Lower-Saxon monarch.

England had not impressed him. Bewildered by its citizens' misguided self-belief, Gerhardt had once asked Belle what made the country the way it was.

'Sausages, gin and beer, of course,' Belle had replied promptly. 'World-beaters in every category.'

Gerhardt, however, profoundly disagreed. In his opinion the *Knipp wurst*, made with pig's head, belly, rind and liver mixed with oats was second to none. *Schnapps* was superior to gin – a drink for women with neither rank nor prospects – and the idea that the stinking brown liquids that the British called beer were of higher rank than the classic *Weizenbier*, whose purity was controlled by *Reinheitsgebot* decree, was risible.

He had been close to concluding that there was nothing great about Great Britain when he had an epiphany. What made the country great – or on course to be great – was that its monarchy was resolutely German.

Having won the game of saying the longest title of a monarch or statesman without drawing breath, he started to explain his theory of British greatness to Lush.

'Is our royal family really so completely Germanic?' asked the young man.

'*Ja, ja. Absolut.* Take the Princess Victoria. Her grandmother Queen Charlotte was German *und* the family, they all marry Germans. Her Uncle William is married to Adelaide of Saxe-Meiningen. Her Uncle Frederick is married to Frederica Charlotte of Prussia, who must not be confused with Frederica of Mecklenburg-Strelitz who is the wife of Uncle Ernest. Her Aunt Charlotte's husband is Frederick of Wurttemberg, *und* her Aunt Elizabeth is married to Frederick of Hesse-Homburg.'

Lush was amazed.

'I could never remember all that. Too many Charlottes and Fredericks for a start. I'm amazed they know how to keep out of each other's beds. Do they sometimes make mistakes?'

Gerhardt touched Lush gently on the arm. He was determined to find a way of protecting Belle's clerk from the melancholia that clung to the Sceptred Isle like clouds and rain.

'They do not make mistakes. You have much to learn from the royal family *und* their night-time wanderings: much. In my country the use of the *Schlafgemach* – the bedchamber – is an art. Nor are they miserable like *das Englisch*. So, for now, *süßer Mann*, let us enjoy the day. We will continue struggling to free your mind later.'

A SHORT DISTANCE FROM the two beaux was Councillor Jacob Pollard, through whose veins English misery ran like blood. On this day, thanks to Belle Nash's unwillingness to intercede on his behalf, he was having to mix with the uninvited masses and was not happy. As a city councillor, he had expected to be on the other side of the rope with the royal party. Since he was not, he would rather have stayed at home, but his wife Clarissa had insisted they come, so their poodle Panto could experience the sight of royalty.

For Mrs Pollard, the day was a celebration of royalty and civic pride. There was bunting galore, which is guaranteed to stir any crowd to fever pitch all over England, and she could see the Abbey School for Boys' Choir being assembled on the nearby bandstand by an oddly dressed teacher.

'What on Earth is that man wearing?' she asked her husband. 'It looks like a red military frock coat and a pair of knee-breeches. But what does he have on his head?'

Pollard's mood was not improved on seeing Arthur Quigley.

'It is a tea cosy, Ma'am, a tea cosy. The man is mad and an embarrassment to the city. In my opinion, he shouldn't be allowed near Princess Victoria, or the boys in the choir. But what else do you expect when you make that fool Nash responsible for the day?'

Mrs Pollard would not let her spirits be dampened by her husband.

'I think it is all hoofloads of fun! After all, the princess is still only twelve. I am confident, Mr Pollard, that she will be charmed by all she sees. And look how many boys and girls have been brought here by their parents and governesses. This is their day to enjoy, Sir, truly it is.'

Her husband did not answer. His attention had been caught by a group of three young men standing to one side. Their linen shirts, waistcoats and flat caps set them apart as narrowboat workers. Belle had anticipated their presence and they were giving Pollard the eye. He knew them well, lads who loaded the boats at the Malt House on the Kennet & Avon Canal, and who at dusk would seek an extra shilling.

'Let's get closer to the bandstand,' suggested his wife. 'It would be nice for Panto to hear the children sing.'

She took her husband's arm, following a path that led directly past the lads. One of them winked at the councillor and started to walk alongside him.

'I want you, Sir,' the lad whispered in his ear.

Pollard's heart quickened. There was too much risk in the situation, but at that moment Panto caught sight of a pair of Pekinese and pulled Mrs Pollard away. This gave him the chance to respond.

'Later, Liam,' he hissed. 'Not here.'

'When? I won't leave you, Sir, until you tell me.'

In the near distance, Pollard could hear his wife's voice.

'Get down from those Pekinese, Panto. Stop that at once.'

Pollard felt his mouth go dry and his throat tighten.

'Very well. The canal pump house by Sydney Gardens at eight o'clock tonight.'

L OOK OVER THERE! I can see Councillor Nash and Mrs Champion!' proclaimed Lush in excitement, peering over the gathering crowd. 'Princess Victoria must be here. Can you see her?'

Gerhardt's wig wobbled at the thought of espying royalty. Lush was right. Thirty dignitaries including Belle and Gaia were walking across the open grass towards the bandstand. With them were Lady Passmore and Mrs Pomeroy.

'*Nein*, I can't see her. Where are you, my little German princess?'

'There ... I think,' said Lush, uncertainly. 'For an instant I saw a girl, but terribly small. Maybe it wasn't her. Does the royal court employ dwarfs?'

Gerhardt's excitement rose.

'A dwarf, you say? *Ja, das ist* Victoria! The family of the House of Hanover are all *winzig*. Tiny. Queen Charlotte of Mecklenburg-Strelitz was less than four foot tall.'

Lush gave Gerhardt a quizzical look.

'She was? I'd never heard that before.'

'It is a secret. Her womb required the miracle of German engineering — *deutsche Technik* — to deliver her *fünfzehn* children.'

The worthies had collected in front of the bandstand to listen to the choir. At their front was the girl whom Lush had spotted, small in stature but with an unusual confidence for one so young. As they waited for the singing to start, the crowd fell silent.

'Councillor Nash has been very worried,' Lush whispered to Gerhardt. 'Mr Quigley, the music teacher, refused to divulge the programme of songs. Councillor Nash suggested Bach or Handel.'

'*Ja*, both good German composers. *Und* excellent wearers of the wig.'

'But Mr Quigley declined. He said he had something far more interesting in mind.'

'We shall see. Belle *und* I had tea *und* buns with Herr Quigley, *und* he is quite mad, yes? *Übergeschnappt*!'

In the near distance, the choir was arranged with three lines of angelic boys in pristine uniforms. Lush shifted his gaze to Belle

172

and saw that he had removed a glove and was biting his nails. Gaia was at his side, whispering reassurances.

Mr Quigley stood before the boys. He beat an introductory bar and the children began to sing.

'Oh,' said Lush. 'That is neither Bach nor Mozart.'

It was not. Nor, fortunately, was it *Hunt the Squirrel*. Instead, a simple teasing melody drifted through the air.

> *Ring around the rosy,*
> *A pocket full of posies,*
> *A-tishoo, a-tishoo,*
> *We all fall down!*

Lush and Gerhardt listened intently.

'I'm not sure that's what Councillor Nash was hoping for,' said the clerk.

Gerhardt did not speak. For once, he was too taken by the spectacle to comment. The verse was repeated and after each verse one or more child from the choir fell to the ground as if in a faint. The crowd, which had at first been silent, began to laugh and clap as the children sang and fell. Most importantly, by the fourth repeat of the verse, they were joined in their clapping by Princess Victoria.

Gerhardt was equally enamoured. He was clapping, smiling and singing the nursery rhyme in German.

> *Ringel, Ringel, Rosen,*
> *Schöne Aprikosen,*
> *Veilchen blau, Vergissmeinnicht,*
> *Alle Kinder setzen sich!*

The general merriment spread to Lush, who saw that Belle, aware that the performance had met with royal approval, had also begun to clap. People across the park were dancing and falling over in merriment. Mr Quigley had come up trumps.

'This is marvellous!' Lush declared. 'How clever of mad Mr Quigley. He has won the princess round. And me too.'

He turned to Gerhardt and, to his surprise, found himself being embraced. Gerhardt was in a state of intellectual ecstasy not seen since Newton watched an apple fall from a tree. Tears of joy were streaming from his eyes.

'The man with the tea cosy on his head is a *Genius*. Lucius, listen to me. We must this evening invite Mr Quigley to Gay Street. With his help, we can perfect the technique of what I have termed *Regression*. This will go down in history as the day misery was banished from the world! *Alle Kinder setzen sich!*'

T O BELLE'S RELIEF, the day was passing without a hitch. Initially, he had feared the worst, worried that the tiny princess might topple under the weight of the large shears that had been provided to cut the ribbon at the entrance to the park. Her Royal Lowness, however, had experience of such events. She had grabbed the shears with both hands and closed the blades on the ribbon with a firm snap.

The greatest worry — the performance by the Abbey School for Boys' Choir — had been a triumph. *Ring Around the Rosy* had been followed by *Humpty Dumpty* and *Sing a Song of Sixpence*. Having cursed Mr Quigley for keeping the programme from him, Belle had been thrilled with the outcome.

There remained the final item of the day's itinerary: the introducing of the princess to the city's grandees. Normally the honour would have gone to the chairman of the Corporation, but he had passed it down to Belle. With admirable candour, Ernest Camshaft had admitted that his memory and eyesight were too poor to carry it out.

When the time came, Belle steered the princess down the row

of notables, taking care not to knee her in the side of the head as they went. The dignitaries had all practised their bowing and curtseying, and now put on an excellent display of public obeisance. In return, Princess Victoria proved herself an expert in the very English art of formal conversation.

'Are we not lucky with the weather today?' she asked the owner of the Radstock colliery.

To Bath's principal banker, she remarked, 'Such a pleasure to be opening a park. As you know, my grandmother was a keen botanist.'

And for Chairman Camshaft she reserved her greatest compliment.

'In recognition of your city's gracious hospitality, Chairman Camshaft, I hereby declare this a royal park. From this day forth, it shall be called Royal Victoria Park.'

'Such kindness, Your Royal Highness,' said Camshaft. 'The citizens of Bath will be forever grateful.'

Belle and the princess soon reached the middle of the line. There stood Lady Passmore and Mrs Pomeroy who, on being introduced, curtseyed together.

'And what do you do in this city?' asked the royal visitor.

It was not a question that either lady had previously considered.

'I am Lady Passmore of Tewkesbury Manor, Your Royal Highness,' said Lady Passmore, who could think of no other answer.

'And I have the honour to be her companion, Your Royal Highness,' said Mrs Pomeroy. 'We keep each other company.'

'These ladies are inspectors of the city's prisons, Your Royal Highness,' Belle intervened, to fend off embarrassment. 'They visited Pulteney Gaol only last week.'

The answer seemed to satisfy the princess.

'Maybe you could come to London and inspect the Tower,' she said, with unexpectedly mature poise and wit. 'One never knows when one might end up there.'

175

After a dozen more introductions, they reached the end of the line, where Belle had placed Gaia as the final dignitary.

'Mrs Gaia Champion,' he announced.

'Your Royal Highness,' Gaia dutifully proclaimed with a neat curtsey.

The princess looked up at Gaia.

'And what is your role in the city?'

Like her friends, Gaia hesitated but this time Belle did not intervene. Gaia chose to speak from the heart.

'I supported my late husband in his law practice. Since his death from cholera, I have been in need of a new occupation.'

Princess Victoria listened and nodded.

'I wish you well in your search, Mrs Champion. For myself, I shall be Queen. There is no reason for women not to occupy the highest offices in this nation.'

With that, the princess moved on. Belle followed, but not before glancing back at Gaia. He knew by the way she stood that any doubts she might have held had gone. As if by royal command, Gaia would apply for the post of magistrate. It was now up to him to make it happen.

NOTES

- Queen Victoria was small, reportedly no more than five foot, which is a polite way of saying less than five foot. As for Queen Charlotte, I have found no evidence for my uncle's suggestion that she was a dwarf.

CHAPTER XIX

We must be true to ourselves

WHILE GAIA CHAMPION did not wish to overreach herself, she also understood the need for advance planning. Becoming the city magistrate involved two challenges: getting into the saddle and then staying there. The latter required popular approval and that was best achieved by winning a high-profile prosecution. Without it she could be unseated at any time.

Gaia knew, however, that the right case would not just fall into her lap. Finding a suitable prosecution would need a little help and there was no time like the present to put the wheels in motion. For Gaia had a target in mind: Hezekiah Porter.

Princess Victoria's opening of the park was over by early afternoon and Gaia had agreed to meet Belle Nash at Somerset Place at sunset. Before heading home, she walked into the city centre, returning for the first time since the magistrate's death to Abbey Green.

If Obadiah Wood had been the first victim of his own demise, Shirley Haytit's tearoom had been the second. The sight of the magistrate's bloated body had drawn a crowd to the premises, but none had subsequently been tempted to enter. That a heavyweight pugilist such as Wood had been felled by the Haytit one-two of crumpet and tea had sealed the tearoom's reputation as the worst in Somerset. Without customers to serve, Mrs Haytit had closed her establishment and disappeared.

Mrs Crust, by contrast, was doing a roaring trade with people as eager for the latest gossip as for extra slices of her excellent pies. It was to her shop that Gaia now went, for she was keen to enlist its proprietor in her efforts against Mr Porter. This would, however, require her first to listen to the shopkeeper's views on life before outlining her own plans.

As she opened the door to the emporium, Gaia was met with the delectable aroma of freshly baked pastry, game and fruit with tots of brandy and slugs of cider thrown in. Standing behind the counter, Mrs Crust appeared at the top of her profession.

'Mrs Champion, Ma'am, we are honoured to see you,' declared Mrs Crust. 'And on such a royal day.'

'Thank you, Mrs Crust. It has, indeed, been a royal day. And judging by your counter, the visit seems to have been good for trade too.'

Mrs Crust smiled. She had made extra pies in the morning and would have to make an equal number tomorrow to restock the shelves.

'I won't deny it's been beneficial, Ma'am. My shelves are nearly clear.'

'But I see there is less competition on Abbey Green than hitherto! Is Mrs Haytit no longer open?'

Mrs Crust licked her lips.

'She's gone, all right, and good riddance. The damage that woman and Hezekiah Porter have done to the reputation of this area, it's a wonder I'm still in business.'

Gaia was pleased to hear Mr Porter criticised. Mrs Crust would be a natural ally.

'There's only one person who knows how to bake a pie, Mrs Crust, and that's you.'

Mrs Crust's face shone with pride.

'I can do no more than my best. There's those that appreciate quality and those that don't. I'll mention no names, but I've been shocked to see who frequents Porter's store. That man has no shame, though he'll have to watch out for himself, now he's got no Magistrate Wood to protect him.'

'He certainly will,' agreed Gaia, who was happy to let Mrs Crust's diatribe run its natural course.

'We've had a few magistrates come and go, but Wood was the worst. There's a hundred crooks in Bath who need to have been put away and not one of them did he reel in, which is no surprise seeing as Decimus Dimm was his special constable. Look what happened to Lady Passmore and Mrs Pomeroy, two decent women. As you said yourself in court, they wanted nothing more than a freshly baked pie, and for that Dimm put them in gaol. It's not right.'

Gaia was enjoying letting Mrs Crust lead the conversation.

'And the event today. I'm not against the city hosting royalty, don't get me wrong. But the corruption, Mrs Champion: that should be our priority! It's time we took a stand.'

Which gave Gaia exactly the entry she needed. She raised both her arms in agreement, as if the thought had only just occurred to her.

'I believe you're right, Mrs Crust. We should take that stand. Imagine what the massed forces of womankind could achieve with their arms interlinked. Would you join forces with me to root out crime in Bath? Be so good as to assent to this wish and I will surely persuade Lady Passmore and Mrs Pomeroy to support us too.'

Mrs Crust was taken aback. Though she had spent her adult life complaining about corruption, this was the first occasion that anyone had agreed to do anything about it.

'As women, can we do this?'

'If we stand together, truly we can. I suggest we start with your neighbour Hezekiah Porter. It's high time a man who sells cattle-feed for flour at fourteen ounces to a pound got his comeuppance. I have a proposal to make, Mrs Crust. Would you join me to discuss it over a slice of delicious pie?'

That had been the easy part of the plan. The harder part came later when, in the library of her Somerset Place home, Gaia sat down, with quill and ink to hand, to pen the oratorical masterpiece of a lifetime. The one that would win her the role of magistrate.

Her shelves were packed with the law books and Acts of Parliament that had been necessary for her and Hercules's work, leather-bound volumes that should now have inspired her. But after an hour she had written nothing down on paper. The ink on the tip of the quill was dry.

Belle arrived and they resorted to the whisky decanter for inspiration.

'Deciding to stand was the easy part,' she said. 'It was all very well Princess Victoria saying that women can occupy the highest offices, but her place is hereditary and mine is not. It has to be won. I have to persuade Chairman Camshaft and Councillor Pollard of my merits. It's like asking approval for a revolution.'

'Then, Madam, do not portray it as a revolution. Make it look like the restoration of a time-honoured custom.'

Gaia raised an eyebrow.

'But Mr Bentham and others portray it as a revolution: when they say that women should have the right to participate fully in society, they make it sound like a call to arms.'

'And that is why they struggle to find support from those of us of the masculine sex – even from those on the distaff side,' said Belle. To encourage her, he clenched a fist. 'But you can outwit them all, Madam. Outwit Bentham; outwit the chairman and the awful Pollard; outwit the stinking populace.'

Gaia scanned the shelves for books that might support her cause.

'Argue that enabling female rights has higher legal precedent than excluding them ...' she said. 'Regrettably, Belle, I see nothing in the great armoury of English law and jurisprudence that will help. Although – odds bodkins! – there was a case closer to home.'

Gaia ran to an old chest and, from its lowest drawer, pulled out a folder of notes.

'Hercules and I worked on this case together. A Mrs Louisa Anderson desired to become a doctor, a profession restricted to men by the Society of Apothecaries' charter. It was never concluded for lack of funds, but our research was constructive, I recall. First, we looked at history ... .'

Gaia pulled out one of the papers and flourished it at Belle.

'Yes, here it is in Hercules's hand,' she declared. '"In Tudor times, women were excluded from public office, that situation continuing largely to this day ... etc., etc. ..." but I know there was more ... .'

Her finger ran down the page searching for a passage.

'I have it! "Tudor lawyers held that, in theory, a woman could occupy public office, even though there are no known examples from this period." Hercules wrote that "the exclusion of women from public office, in the Tudor period at least, was a matter of convention, not legal dogma – *res ipsa loquitur*, *inter alles*, women being *sui juris*, whether *de facto* or *de jure*, allowing for *de minimis non curat Lex, et cetera*." Thank you! It could not be clearer.'

'My own thoughts exactly,' Belle nodded. 'Not least the Latin.'

Gaia passed the folder over to him.

'See how Hercules or I underscored seven words: that excluding women from public office is *a matter of convention, not legal dogma*. After this case dried up, we wrote to the esteemed peer Lord Brougham, lately appointed Lord Chancellor, who outlined the principle. If you would please return to me the folder ... .'

She shuffled through more papers.

'Yes, here is Brougham's letter. He writes that "unless women were specifically excluded in a statute or charter, any reference to

181

the masculine could be taken as a reference also to the feminine". Brougham was clear that for legal purposes, men and women are interchangeable! To put it simply, men cannot have it all their own way.'

Belle slapped his thigh. Now he understood, and had ammunition of his own to offer.

'The troops are marching to your side, Madam. For is not Lord Brougham's comrade-in-arms the formidable William Wilberforce MP, both with their muskets loaded to abolish slavery? In the context of which, would you esteem me the courtesy of mentioning my dear Aunt Sarah? There is a connection if you bear with me.'

The mention of another woman indeed interested Gaia.

'What of your aunt, then?'

'I received by yesterday's mail a letter she had written to me. In it, she reports the death of a distant cousin and the reading of his Last Will & Testament, in consequence of which, she is now the inheritor of a sugar plantation on the island of Grenada, in the West Indies.'

Gaia nodded solemnly.

'An uncomfortable position to be in. Does your aunt mention the accounts of the freed slaves Cugoano and Equiano?'

'Exactly where I was headed, Madam: you're on the trail of my fox, by gad! She has read them and is aghast at this unwanted bounty. She wishes to turn misfortune to fortune, however, and has determined that the slaves who work the plantation must be freed – and in the full meaning of the word, not simply turned into indentured apprentices. What she especially stressed was, "These men and women must have title to the land!" *Men and women*, you see, Ma'am. We are equals. As a woman, you have as much right to the magistracy as any man!'

Gaia clenched her fist. Her resolve had returned.

'Like your aunt, I abhor slavery, which in turn means that I oppose serfdom. And women are treated by our nation as serfs.

The time for change has come. Leave me, Belle. I will write the speech, put myself forward for the role and trust that good fortune will prevail.'

He stood up and kissed Gaia on her outstretched hand, assured that she would arrive at Guildhall the next day fully confident of how to frame her case.

As he turned, his face hidden for a moment from view, he allowed himself a private smile — one that he did not wish his friend to see. Unlike Gaia, Belle had no intention in relying solely on good fortune and a well-written speech for her success. At this moment, only he was aware of Pollard's intention to stand as magistrate and the danger that this posed to her chances. He had, therefore, put in play a secret operation regarding the despised councillor, knowing that Gaia would strongly disapprove, were she to learn of it.

NOTES

- My uncle is accurate in his account of the history of women in public office. Women may have held public office before Tudor times (although evidence is scant), when the misogyny of Church and State took hold. The Catholic Church, with entrenched views on the primacy of the male, led a Europe-wide campaign of terror against so-called witches in which an estimated 40,000 women were brutally executed. In Great Britain, King Henry VIII, supported by his chief minister Thomas Cromwell, turned to uxoricide in his efforts to secure a male heir, establishing a culture of misogyny. An assumption took root that women were barred from public office, but this was solely a matter of convention supported by the fact that, when written, statutes and charters typically referred only to the male gender. Parliamentary clarification that a legal reference to 'men' also included 'women' was made in The Interpretation Act of 1850 (known as Lord Brougham's Act).

- Citing Lord Brougham's Act, a key case was won in 1865 by Elizabeth Anderson (1836–1917), who became the first woman to qualify in Britain as a physician and surgeon having challenged the Society of Apothecaries' 'male-only' charter. She co-founded the first hospital staffed by women, was the first dean of a British medical school and was the first female mayor (of the town of Aldridge) in Britain. My uncle suggests that her mother, too, desired to be a doctor.

- Jeremy Bentham (1748–1832) was the founder of modern utilitarianism and is another Bachelor of History. He advocated separation of Church and State, freedom of expression, equal rights for women and the decriminalisation of same-sex acts. He called for the abolition of slavery, the death penalty and corporal punishment. He had a certain vanity, ordering that his corpse be mummified and kept on display by University College London.

- Ottobah Cugoano (c.1757–c.1791) and Olaudah Equiano (c.1745–1797) were two West Africans who suffered enslavement but secured their freedom (in Grenada and Virginia, respectively). When in England, they published their experiences: Cugoano's *Thoughts and Sentiments on the Evil and Wicked Traffic of Slavery and Commerce of the Human Species* (1797); and *The Interesting Narrative of the Life of Olaudah Equiano* (1789).

- When the Slavery Abolition Act was passed in 1833, it required nothing more than the transformation of slaves into indentured apprentices (who were nonetheless required to work for nothing to 'earn' their freedom). The nations of the British West Indies recognise 1838, the year that indentured apprenticeship was abolished, as marking emancipation.

CHAPTER XX

Twinkle, twinkle, little star

FEELING THE NEED for a walk to clear his mind, like the refuse cart a fortnight earlier, Belle Nash went home by skirting the residence of William Beckford on Lansdown Crescent. He was soon lengthening his stride and a few minutes later had turned into another of the royal city's great crescents, Camden Crescent. There, he took a seat on a bench that looked across the valley.

It was one of his favourite spots, with a view that stretched over the River Avon to Sydney Gardens and beyond. In the fading light, on Bathwick Hill he could see the outline of Sydney Buildings that bordered the Kennet & Avon Canal.

Belle breathed in the cool, evening air and looked east of the river to where Great Pulteney Street lay. From this wide boulevard, a new district of Bath had been intended but the grand plan had failed, brought low by financial woes, a cholera epidemic and the great flood of 1809. Incomplete, Johnstone Street and Sunderland Street jutted into green fields, stumps instead of fingers on an otherwise fine hand.

Looking out from Camden Crescent, Belle considered the glory and the failure of human ambition. Ambition is both the wonder and the curse of humanity; when mixed with vanity, it can foment human tragedy.

'Are we heroes or fools to dream of a better world?' he thought.

He looked at his fob watch and noted the time. It was half past six. In a day's time, he would either be toasting Gaia as Bath's new magistrate or drowning his sorrows with her. And in an hour, an event would be taking place that would dramatically influence her chances of success.

'Forgive me for not telling you,' he whispered. 'But some things are best kept to oneself.'

For good reason. When Belle first conceived the plan, he had nearly baulked at it himself, so outlandish was its nature. For Gaia to succeed, Councillor Pollard must fail to attend the meeting to appoint Magistrate Wood's successor. An absent Pollard could not promote his own nomination; and in his absence, only Chairman Camshaft need be persuaded of Gaia's suitability.

But how might this be achieved?

'No one likes you, Pollard,' Belle had thought. 'Not even the wretched narrowboat boys after whom you lust. I pity those lost souls. They would do anything for a shilling, even with a twisted hypocrite like you. Which makes me wonder what they might do for five pounds ... .'

The answer, Belle had ascertained on meeting the lads, was that for five pounds they could hold Pollard hostage for a day. That much had been their pledge, with two pounds paid up front. The meeting with Liam and his mates that morning in the park had not been the chance event that Pollard had imagined.

'Will it work, though?' Belle asked as he looked across the half-mile to the canal pump house. It was there that the entrapment would soon occur. 'To think that the emergence of a new social order might depend on the narrowboat lads. There's no sense in the world.'

Sitting on the bench, Belle hugged himself. The evening was turning cold, and it had been a long day. What he needed was a nice cup of tea and a chair next to a log fire. Maybe he could get Gerhardt Kant to rub his toes.

'And speaking of nonsense,' he said to himself as he rose to his feet, 'I'd better get back to Gay Street before Gerhardt rearranges the furniture. I wonder what he's been up to all day. And what he's doing to poor Master Lush.'

IGNORANCE IS BLISS, and it might have been better for Belle to have stayed on the bench, for while he sat there, Gerhardt's exploration of Lucius Lush's mind was continuing apace in Gay Street.

It is an irony of psychoanalysis that a traditional cure for melancholia is to return the patient to a state of ignorance. Experience of life has often been regarded by medics as a curse to be drawn from a patient like pus from a boil. By excising the past, they have thought, the inflammation of the mind may be soothed.

In Europe, Greeks were the pioneers. Aristotle conceived of the *tabula rasa* nature of the mind, a state the physician Themison of Laodicea thought could be attained by chaining and starving mentally ill people in conditions of total darkness. By the seventh century, Paul of Aegina had refined the practice by tying patients inside wicker baskets suspended from the ceiling to be watered occasionally, like hanging flowers.

It was hardly surprising, therefore, that the innocent citizenry of Europe preferred to self-medicate than trust physicians. After all, if the solution to stress was to annihilate memory, recourse to liquor provided a readier remedy. Thus, the Greeks turned to *ouzo*, the Germans to *schnapps*, the Scandinavians to *brännvin*, and the southern Italians to *limoncello*. The choice of the British tribes was gin and whisky.

Now enter Gerhardt Kant into the history of the mind. He was as determined as any of his forebears to put right the injured mind but, unlike them, did not consider sobriety essential to the cure. On this merry evening, he was joined by the ingenue Lush and old Arthur Quigley — who had met the two younger men after his triumphant concert in the park. Together, they were finishing off their fourth bottle of claret.

187

The three men sat in the drawing room enjoying each other's company and telling stories, which was exactly what Gerhardt intended. Relaxation, he had concluded, was a prerequisite for successful *Regression*.

'A tremendous wine, Herr Kant: tremendous,' said Mr Quigley, still dressed in his frock coat and tea cosy. 'I am reminded of the time I spent in Paris before the revolution. Say what you will of the French aristocrat, but he had the measure of fun, Sir. As did the boys of the Left Bank. Drank wine by the flagon, but none so good as this.'

Lush found it difficult to conceive of anyone being so old as to remember the time before the French Revolution.

'Were you born in Paris, Mr Quigley?' he asked, refilling the older man's glass before replenishing his own.

'Born, Sir? My *joie de vivre* was born there, yes! I was returning from Italy with my Landolfi and was invited to fill in as third violin with the *Olympique* orchestra. Wonderful musicians, all of 'em, and conducted by an extraordinary French West Indian by the name of Chevalier de Saint-Georges. Ever heard of him? Beautiful-looking man. Couldn't take my eyes off him. You would have been similarly smitten, if I judge you aright!'

'So interesting, these French,' Gerhardt butted in. 'A nation that achieved *Befreiung* – liberation – through the guillotine. But there are other ways to freedom. Lucius, please to open more wine *und* then let us tonight's experiment begin.'

Mr Quigley's face lit up.

'Experiment, Sir? Splendid! What experiment would that be?'

Lush laughed as he pulled the cork from a fifth bottle of claret.

'Gerhardt is convinced that all English people are miserable. He believes he can make us happy again by returning us to our childhoods. He calls it *Regression*. It's hilarious. Last week he took me back to when I was ten years old by having me pretend I was a schoolboy.'

188

Mr Quigley clapped his hands together in delight.

'Brilliant, Sir, brilliant! I have been pretending to be a school-boy since I was a schoolboy! Another glass, if you please.'

Gerhardt stood up and inspected the room.

'To undertake this experiment, we will keep the daybed facing the fireplace, but everything else we will push back, *ja*? *Und* let us more logs on the fire put, *und* the fire into a fierce blaze stoke. *Perfekt*! So, now we must prepare Lucius.'

'Oh, goody!' said Lush. 'What would you like me to dress as this time?'

Gerhardt crossed his arms.

'*Nichts.*'

Lush was disappointed. He had enjoyed dressing up and was eager to do so again.

'Nothing? You want me to stay as I am?'

'*Nein*. I want you to wear nothing. This evening must you as naked as the moment you were born once more become. *Nackt wie ein Baby*. Without the clothes, *danke schon*,' Gerhardt ordered.

Lush suddenly felt very shy.

'I'm not sure I would feel comfortable taking my clothes off, Gerhardt. Certainly not in front of Mr Quigley.'

'Don't worry about me,' commented Mr Quigley, who thought Gerhardt's suggestion an excellent idea. 'I've seen it all before.'

'I am not sure you have, Sir. And ...'

Gerhardt was determined to dictate the conditions of the experiment.

'It is *wesentlich*. You cannot have *Regression* to *Baby* when you are dressed as a man. So much is obvious – *selbstverständlich*. Remember, what we are doing is to advance humanity. It is a noble cause.'

Lush defended himself.

'I understand the concept, but it is not what I was expecting. What were you planning to do once I had undressed?'

189

Gerhardt stepped into the centre of the room by the daybed.

'This will be your cot. You will in the cot lie, as you when you a Baby did, *und* then we will sing to you the *Kinderreime* and *Schlaflieder*. That way, your mind will return to the state of the infant.'

'A wondrous proposal, Sir,' commented Mr Quigley in eager anticipation. 'And another glass of wine first, perhaps?'

'It's fine apart from my getting naked,' said Lush.

Gerhardt pushed his case one more time, this time forcefully.

'*Die Zurückhaltung* – the reticence – of the English is part of your miserable nature. Take off *die* clothes! Experience *die Freude* of the naked body, as the Germans *und* the Prussians do!'

Lush remained unconvinced.

'I do enjoy being naked, but normally when I'm taking a bath. Can I not at least wear a sheet? Even babies have swaddling clothes.'

There was silence. Neither Gerhardt nor Mr Quigley supported the idea but Lush had made a fair point and Gerhardt eventually relented.

'It will the experiment more difficult make but – *ach*, we will try. There is a cupboard on the landing that has the sheets. Please, if you would go to the *Schlafgemach* – the bedchamber. Undress there *und* return to us. Meanwhile Mr Quigley *und* I will agree on the nursery rhymes *und* lullabies we will sing.'

Upstairs, Lush found the cupboard and took out a sheet. He also found a maid's cotton mob cap that he felt would add realism to the scene. The last thing he wanted was to be remembered for having scuppered a scientific discovery. Rather uncertainly, he went into Belle's bedchamber, stripped off and wrapped the sheet between his legs and around his midriff, hiding all he deemed necessary to hide. Then, catching sight of his reflection in the mirror, he laughed at himself. Good-naturedly, he went downstairs to make history and push back the frontiers of knowledge.

And it was fun, too, or so Lush thought. That, however, was not the reaction of Belle when he returned home fifteen minutes later. Surprised by the sound of two-and-a-half grown men giggling helplessly in the drawing room as he entered the house, he slipped his head round the door and saw, to his astonishment, the sight of his clerk, all but naked, lying on the daybed pretending to be a baby.

For its participants, the experiment was progressing well, with improvisation and claret proving the key to progress in *Regression*. Lush had rejected Gerhardt's suggestion that baby should be spanked; Mr Quigley's proposal for feeding baby had been similarly dispatched. Instead, he had agreed to emit baby-like sounds if Gerhardt and Mr Quigley consented to be his devoted parents.

'Ga-ga,' said Lush. 'Goo-goo.'

By his side knelt his adopted procreators, Gerhardt and Mr Quigley, holding hands and stroking him. As they stroked, Mr Quigley removed his tea cosy and, holding it to his heart, sang:

> *Twinkle, twinkle, little star,*
> *How I wonder what you are!*
> *Up above the world so high,*
> *Like a diamond in the sky.*

Tears gathered in his eyes as he leant forward and kissed baby on the forehead.

'Sleep well, young man. Your mother loves you *so* much. You're such a beautiful boy.'

'*Ja*, so beautiful,' added Gerhardt. 'Almost as beautiful as *dein* father.'

'Ga-goo-ga,' Lush responded dreamily.

It was Gerhardt's turn to sing. Head held high and wig reaching for the sky, he sang the second verse.

191

Wenn die lodernde Sonne fort ist
Wenn nichts da ist, auf das er scheint
Dann zeigst du dein kleines Lict,
Funkel, funkel durch die Nacht.'

There might have been a third verse, sung by both parents in harmony, but we shall never know for Belle, unable to remain silent any longer, now made his presence known.

'*Funkel, funkel durch die Nacht*?' he cried, stepping forthrightly into the room. 'What in damnation is going on here?! How many gallons of wine have you drunk? And who's moved my blasted furniture again?'

Gerhardt sprang to his feet and Mr Quigley followed him. Lush sat up on the daybed, for a second the sheet falling away before, once more, he covered his naked torso.

'It's an experiment in German science, Sir,' said Lush, nervously. 'Gerhardt says it's very important.'

'We make discoveries of value to *alle* mankind,' declared Gerhardt.

'Whoops! You've caught us at it,' bleated Mr Quigley. 'Just when the fun was starting too.'

Belle declined to listen to their pleading.

'Get dressed Mistress Lush, and then get out,' he said. 'And make sure you come to work on time tomorrow or I'll cuff your ears!'

'Yes, Sir,' said Lush. 'I'm so terribly sorry, Sir.'

As the young man hurried out, clutching the sheet in one hand and the mob cap in the other, Belle turned on the other two men.

'Gerhardt, I cannot leave you for five minutes without you imposing your lunatic fancies on your physical lusts. As for you Mr Quigley, Sir, is this an honourable way to celebrate your musical triumph this morning? What do you think the princess might say if she could see you now?'

192

The music master looked remorseful and replaced the tea cosy on his head.

'Music hath charms to soothe a savage breast, young Nash,' Mr Quigley replied meekly. 'And you have misunderstood the scene. Herr Kant had admired the choral performance in the park, and he saw a further application for it with Master Lush ... whose best interests, of course, we all hold dear.'

'Exactly,' said the Prussian. 'We were the limits of *Regression* exploring *und* great progress making.'

But Belle was having none of it. More importantly, he sensed an opportunity that he could exploit to his advantage.

'Silence, both of you. I'm deeply disappointed. Our reputations are at stake. Imagine if word of this got out. You have risked exposing to public ridicule not just yourselves and not just me, but the entire bachelor community.'

From the corridor, they heard the front door open and close as Lush let himself out into Gay Street.

He continued, 'And now you are going to atone for your sins by assisting me. Even now, an extremely tawdry event is occurring on the canal. I need to assure myself that certain boys have behaved more reliably than you three have done. Listen closely as I explain what is happening, and then get yourselves ready for a walk.'

BELLE WAS RIGHT to have had his doubts about the narrow-boat lads. For once, knowing that his friends were there to pounce, Liam had enjoyed dropping his trousers for Jacob Pollard in the pump house. For his part, Pollard had got more pump house than he had paid for, and not in a good way. The other lads had sniggered as they watched Liam get to work, then jumped Pollard and trussed him up like a turkey, stuffing his mouth with a gag. But they had done a poor job of the knots and had then left their victim unattended without even barring the pump-room door. Worse, the gag they had put in his mouth had come loose.

'Help! Help!' he cried as Gerhardt and Mr Quigley – as directed by Belle – approached along the towpath, wearing scarves and hats to disguise their identities. 'Help, help! Let me out.'

Pushing open the door, they could see Pollard lying on the dirt floor, his breeches still round his ankles.

'Praise the Lord!' he said. 'I'm Councillor Pollard and I've been attacked by a band of rascals. Untie me quickly, so I can call the constable.'

Mr Quigley bent down to take a look.

'Oh, in the name of heaven,' he said. 'The boys have used a cleat hitch when they should have used a poacher's hitch. No matter: the harp string knot used for the violin will serve as well.'

'What?! Who are you?!' cried Pollard, as Gerhardt held the councillor down. 'Don't tie me up again, you idiots!'

In the near dark, Mr Quigley's eyes looked at the councillor contemptuously.

'While I'm about it, let me fix that gag for you, Sir. There, that's how the Marquis de Sade told me it should be done. I think that should do the trick.'

NOTES

- The great Joseph Bologne, Chevalier de Saint-Georges (1745–1799), was born in Guadeloupe, the son of a French plantation owner and an African slave. The couple returned to France, where the multi-talented Joseph – one of the finest fencers, violinists, composers and conductors of the era – became a darling of the French court. Come the revolution, however, he turned against the monarchy and founded the Légion Saint-Georges, a pro-revolutionary all-Black regiment. He was at the forefront of the movement to abolish the slave trade.

CHAPTER XXI

Progress by subterfuge

L UCIUS LUSH HAD spent a sleepless night worrying about his behaviour after being sent home from Gay Street a second time with his tail between his legs. He had truly not intended to upset anyone, nor to create a rift among friends.

But Belle Nash, it seemed, had forgotten that he had provided unambiguous permission for his clerk to enjoy the company of Gerhardt Kant, and this now left Lush terribly confused. He enjoyed the company of bachelors – spending time with Gerhardt, Belle and old Arthur Quigley was liberating – and he was fearful of being ostracised from a group to which he naturally belonged.

He arrived at work on time the next day and waited nervously for his irascible employer to appear. It was going to be a big day, with the Magistrate Selection Committee scheduled to meet later that morning, so he tidied Belle's desk and placed primroses that he had cut from a hedgerow in a small vase beside the inkpot. He opened the office window to freshen the air and readied himself to make tea. But all the time he worried about whether he had lost his job.

And this was unfair on him because Belle was far less upset than he had pretended to be. Catching Gerhardt, Mr Quigley and Lush *in flagrante* had played into his hands, giving him the excuse to deploy Gerhardt and Mr Quigley in the pump-house entrapment of Joseph Pollard.

Belle had every intention of putting Lush to similar use and conveyed his stern intention even as he strode down the corridor to his office in Guildhall the next morning. His anxious clerk heard the sense of purpose in his footsteps and jumped to attention with more alacrity than a private on parade.

'Good morning, Sir, and I most humbly apologise for my reckless dereliction of duty last night and may I offer you a cup of tea or anything else that might placate your understandable malaise or in other ways ... .'

'Enough of your fol-di-rol, Mr Twinkle-Funkel, enough. This morning there is a matter that takes precedence over tea, and it will take more than a bunch of primroses to calm my temper.'

Lush dropped his head meekly.

'Yes, Sir. I understand what a disappointment I have been to you and willingly accept whatever penalty you feel it most fit to chastise me with.'

Belle arched an eyebrow as he handed over his coat and gloves.

'I learned much of your predilections – more than either of us might wish to have known – last night. Playing Cardinal Alberoni to my Duc de Vendôme now does not help. Rather, let us talk of reparations. I shall offer you the opportunity to make good on your night's excesses, assuming you have the strength of character for the task.'

Lush's face brightened a shade.

'Anything, Sir.'

'Good, for I believe at heart you remain a fine young man. Gerhardt attempted to explain matters after you had left. He said you have a passion for men of an older generation – what he termed the *Papa-Syndrom* – engendered by the kindness of your great-grandfather, Chairman Camshaft, and your devotion to him.'

This was news to Lush and would have been news to Gerhardt, who had said no such thing. In fact, that morning Belle and Gerhardt had had – and not for the first time – a furious argument about Belle's failure to take seriously his Prussian cousin's philosophical practices. Belle, however, was a practised deceiver when he needed to be and knew how to exhibit sincerity when telling a falsehood. Lush was taken in and aback by the revelation.

'Do I have such a passion?'

'Like the Apostle Peter, you may deny it – three times if you must – but it was clear that when Mr Quigley stroked and kissed your forehead, his feelings were reciprocated, for you did not seem to object or tell him to desist.'

'But we were conducting an experiment in German science, Sir,' said Lush nervously. 'German science is different from English science, Gerhardt says. Clothes have to be removed.'

'Indeed, Master Lush. And as a man of liberal outlook, I am open to each avenue that science invites us to explore. Even German science. In matters of natural philosophy and other pursuits, let Gerhardt and, indeed, Mr Quigley be your guides. You are young and have much to discover. You will not find me standing in your way.'

'How strange are the workings of the world,' thought Lush. Once more, Belle seemed to have granted him clear permission to consort with Gerhardt in whatever way they desired. Or had he misunderstood?

'Are you sure?' he asked, nervous and more than a little confused. 'If you are sympathetic to my nature, then I have caused no offence. In which case, Sir, on what grounds are reparations, as you termed them, required?'

It was time for Belle to press home his advantage and to do so without mercy. There remained a vital element in his plan to elevate Gaia Champion to the position of magistrate, and it required the special participation of his clerk.

Belle reverted to a stern voice.

'I was not a happy man when I greeted the dawn this morning. My list of grievances included a soiled sheet; five bottles of my finest claret; and ...'

Lush's face turned white, and his eyes dropped to the floor.

'The sheet, Sir, was not soiled, I assure you.'

Belle would not be halted. He drove the sword onward into his clerk's exposed breast.

'... and the most heinous crime of all – more frightful than ever Medea meted out to her offspring – the movement of furniture, for a second time, without my permission. Moved, indeed, against my express instructions. For that, young Funkel-Twink, there is a grievous price to pay!'

Lush gulped.

'Which is?'

E RNEST CAMSHAFT HAD agreed that the magistrate's courtroom would be the most appropriate place to meet the candidates. When Belle entered with the chairman, he did so with a degree of confidence. Not only was Pollard tied up in the pump house but hidden inside Belle's jacket pocket were the chairman's spectacles.

Lush had been sent to his great-grandfather's office with the specific instruction to steal them and had excelled in his errand.

'I'm obliged to you, loyal clerk,' Belle had said, taking the spectacles into his safekeeping. 'All is now forgiven. And fret not: the eyeglasses will be restored in due course.'

'I hope so, Sir. I feel a dreadful cad stealing from my great-grandpapa.'

Belle had laughed.

'An emotion you seem not to have had when partaking of your employer's wine.'

Lush was relieved that he and Belle were back on good terms but was intrigued to know the spectacles' importance.

'May I enquire as to your purpose, Sir? Great-grandpapa cannot see a thing without lenses.'

'That is why I asked you for them, young fellow. Now, don't rush away. I need your help in another matter.'

Belle held in his hand the list of candidates who had applied for the role of magistrate. In addition to Pollard, three other councillors were throwing their hats in the ring, all of them hidebound conventionalists. With Pollard tucked safely away, it was Belle's intention that these other three should be interviewed first. Gaia would be seen last.

'Only after Councillor Bunce has left the courtroom should you allow Mrs Champion to enter,' he instructed Lush. 'Until that point, keep her from public view in my office. I don't want her arousing anyone's suspicions.'

After that, he had gone to collect the chairman and was pleased to find him already flustered and ripe for further flustering.

'Is that you, young Nash? It's a confounded bore but I've misplaced my spectacles again.'

Belle put on his most innocent expression.

'Fortunately, Chairman, we shan't be judging the candidates on their appearance. I thought you and I should sit on the dais and put the candidates in the dock. Give them the sense of what a courtroom is like, eh!'

Camshaft agreed.

'I like your thinking, Nash. Bright as a button, eh?!'

Belle took the old man by the elbow and led him down the corridors to the courtroom, where he guided him up the steps.

'As chairman, the magistrate's chair is for you. I had arranged for another couple of chairs for myself and Councillor Pollard, but I regret to report that my fellow councillor is nowhere to be found.'

Camshaft huffed in disapproval.

'What's the man up to? Isn't he supposed to be one of the candidates?'

Belle shrugged.

'You and I make up a quorum, Sir, so I suggest we conduct the interviews ourselves. Bath needs a magistrate and Councillor Pollard's dallying should not be honoured by dallying of our own.'

Rather than rush through the interviews, Belle made sure that they were long and tedious. Camshaft was duly sedated. Deprived of his spectacles, he drifted through the interviews like a rudderless boat. Occasionally, he nodded off. Meanwhile, Belle enjoyed testing the candidates with his knowledge of obscure laws.

'You say you wish to become Bath's magistrate, Councillor Wrigglesworth. Expand for me then what bounties must be paid, in addition to the export of herring, under the British Fisheries Act of 1820.'

Later, he admonished Councillor Buckley.

'You cannot recall the fee charged for noncompliance with the Buried in Woollen Act 1666–80 or how to notate compliance? For shame, Sir.'

As for Councillor Bunce, Belle was unsparing in his criticism.

'Indeed, you should know whether sheep and bulls are covered by the Cruel Treatment of Cattle Act 1822! If you are uninformed about the protection of our bovine friends in court, how will you deal fairly with your fellow man?'

All the while, Belle kept half an eye on the chairman. On hearing the sound of sustained snoring, he drew to an end the interview with Bunce and congratulated himself on a couple of hours well spent.

'Thank you, Councillor Bunce. You may step down from the dock. We will let you know our decision shortly.'

Bunce, who correctly surmised that he had failed the interview, strode indignantly from the courtroom and Belle nudged the chairman awake.

'Time to rouse yourself, Chairman Camshaft. It's over. Open your eyes.'

'What?! Thank the elements. By heavens, I'd forgotten how tedious interviews are. I'm glad you know what you're on about, Nash. Deplorably dull bunch. Still, there's no getting around the fact that one of 'em has to be appointed.'

Belle strummed his fingers on the table. The moment of truth had arrived.

'I beg to disagree with you, Sir. One had the strength of Gaius Gracchus in his prime. Could we but resurrect Rome's finest magistrate in our own fair Bath, how blessed our city would be.'

Camshaft rubbed his eyes.

'One of them impressed you, Sir? I must have missed it.'

Belle remained polite.

'It was the second of the four. Head and shoulders above the rest.'

'Four, y'say. Did we see that many?'

Belle lied.

'Indeed, we did. I suggest we call the candidate back to confirm our decision.'

Camshaft nodded.

'I agree. The quicker this business is over, the sooner I can go and walk the dog. Will you get him?'

Belle descended the dais and hurried back to his office in order to escort Gaia to the courtroom. She was attired in a dress of dark blue, elegant but conservative, with a matching wide-brimmed hat. She had been awake since the early hours of the morning, readying herself.

'Whatever you do,' he whispered as they walked, 'say nothing.'

'Nothing?' she hissed back. 'I've prepared a speech. I spent all night writing it.'

They entered the courtroom.

'Madam, trust me. Speak not a word except at my command. And stand close to the bench. He's long-sighted, to the extent he has any sight at all. I'll do the rest.'

'"At your command"? Are you now my lord?'

'No, Ma'am: I am your friend.'

With reluctance, Gaia stepped forward. Belle returned to the dais and found Camshaft staring at the candidate with a befuddled expression. Though unable to see anything in detail, he knew that something was not quite right about the person in front of him. Guildhall was home to councillors of all shapes and sizes, but none with so large a head.

Belle made the introduction.

'You'll recall Guy er ... Champion. Excellent legal pedigree! Twenty years' experience. And, as you'll recall, the *primus inter pares* at the interviews.'

'Was he?'

'Most definitely. Bath is fortunate that this candidate competed for the post.'

Camshaft continued to squint, closing one eye, then another, in an attempt to see clearly.

'You don't have a lorgnette on you, do you, Nash?'

Belle shook his head.

'Sadly, my vision is perfect, Sir. But even if I had cataracts in both eyes, I'd have no need for lenses when it is clear that the best candidate stands before us.'

Camshaft gave up his efforts and blew his nose instead.

'Damned annoying. Most peculiar fellow I've seen in a long time,' he muttered. 'Reminds me of someone but I'm dashed if I know who.' Then a thought occurred to him. 'You're not a relative of that lawyer who died a year or so ago? What was his name now? Ah – I have it! Hercules Champion: that was the man.'

Gaia stood stock-still. Belle lifted a warning finger to his lips.

'You knew him, Sir?' replied Belle. 'He was a close relative of the candidate.'

He prayed that the chairman would not require Gaia to speak, and that Gaia would remain quiet.

'A fine fellow, from what I've heard,' Camshaft continued. 'My wife Audrey has widow friends who still speak very warmly of his intelligence and kindness. Hercules Champion had a good brain, by all accounts. And a remarkable wife too, I believe.'

202

A tear gathered in Gaia's eye.

'Thank you,' she whispered.

Belle rose from his chair.

'So, that's agreed. By unanimous verdict of the committee. I feel congratulations are in order.'

'Indeed, they are,' said Camshaft, picking up a gavel and slamming it down. 'I hereby declare you the new magistrate of the Royal City of Bath, young chap. Congratulations.'

TEN MINUTES LATER, Belle had in his hand the signed minutes of the meeting and the announcement of Gaia's appointment, authorised by Chairman Camshaft. It had been a triumph of duplicity. Waiting outside in the corridor were Gaia and Lush.

Belle spoke to his clerk first, handing over the spectacles.

'There you go, Miss Lucy. I suggest you pop them back in your great-grandfather's office.'

Lush took the spectacles gratefully and hurried off.

'Miss Lucy?' remarked Gaia. 'What sort of a name is that for a young man? It sounds most inappropriate.'

Belle huffed.

'There's more to that young man than meets the eye. But it's a long story — much of it private, and the bits that can be told are best kept for a glass of whisky. More important, are you happy with your new appointment?'

'With the appointment, yes; but not with the manner of its making. I wanted to win it fair and square, and on my own terms. Not by subterfuge. I feel ashamed.'

Belle looked Gaia directly in the eye.

'Then you do not fully know the workings of the world, Ma'am. It was the only way. But you will make a name for yourself in this court and that will be all your own doing.'

To his relief, Gaia accepted his statement.

'In truth, I had guessed you were up to something – you usually are – and it worked out well, so I will let you off with a caution this time. But be aware: I won't stand for nonsense like this in the future. D'you hear, Sir?'

Belle laughed nervously and then blushed at the thought of what had been done to Councillor Pollard. He had been on the point of revealing all to Gaia but now considered it best that the pump-house entrapment remain a secret.

Instead, he guided Gaia along the corridor.

'Let's post the notice of your appointment and await the up-roar. You'll need to start work quickly to counter any opposition.'

'I already have plans in place,' she replied. 'In private, I have been preparing for the first serious prosecution.'

Belle smiled at her in amazement.

'Oh, great Dike, I say again. Remove the divine blindfold and reveal what hangeth in the scales!'

She laughed at the allusion.

'You're not the only one, Belle, who can play at games. Speak not a word but – '

His grin widened. Gaia would be the greatest of magistrates.

' – by midday tomorrow I hope to have Hezekiah Porter in my dock with enough evidence to close his tawdry store forever. Action is happening in Abbey Green as we speak. A cup of tea?'

NOTES

- The Duc de Vendôme (1654–1712), commander of the French forces in Italy, had the habit of granting audience to an envoy while sitting on a commode, famously wiping his arse in front of a bishop. On repeating this unseemly act to Cardinal Giulio Alberoni, envoy to the Duke of Parma, in an act of supreme diplomatic sycophancy Alberoni ran forward to kiss the Duc's buttocks, crying out, 'Oh, the arse of an angel!'

CHAPTER XXII

Beware the angry bee

GAIA CHAMPION HAD indeed been busy in her effort to bring Hezekiah Porter to the court, as had Mrs Crust, Lady Passmore, Mrs Pomeroy and Phyllis Prim. Blue moons recur more often than the appointment of a woman magistrate and Gaia had all her lady friends' support.

The masterplan – now retitled the *mistress-plan* – was to record overwhelming evidence of Hezekiah Porter's malpractice. Gaia already had Gerhardt Kant's receipt and his statement about being overcharged for sugar, but a lot more besides was needed to build a case.

She had shared her thoughts with Mrs Crust, who had agreed to persuade her customers to make purchases at Porter's and report back. A flurry of messages primed close friends to undertake further evidence-gathering.

'I've spent twenty years telling customers not to go near that place but for one day I'm happy to do as you ask,' Mrs Crust had told Gaia. 'I'll even offer a slice of fruit pie as a reward for everyone who does!'

As a result, Mr Porter had had his best day ever, and marvelled at his good fortune. The closure of Mrs Haytit's teashop and her departure from Bath had deprived him of one of his best buyers and landed him with an unpaid debt. True to form, he had compensated for his loss by adjusting his scales a tad, so his customers got even less for their money.

'Every little helps,' he said to himself.

He had also increased the ratio of cattle-feed to flour. By such means, he reckoned he would recoup his loss within a fortnight, and maybe in just a few days, given the unexpected upturn in trade driven by Mrs Crust.

What baffled him was what had caused it.

'The customers seem to like the new cattle-feed mix,' he had concluded. 'I think I may congratulate myself on my good judgement and order a fresh hundredweight from Cudworth.'

The non-stop tinkling of the bell on his shop door seemed to prove his surmise.

'Good morning, Mrs Gladwell, Ma'am,' he said to his latest customer. 'Not seen you in my premises for ten years or more. Glad to see you back. More of the same?'

'I think not,' Mrs Gladwell replied. 'Last time I returned home with a bag of slugs for potatoes, but I hear you have a special offer on flour, and I could not resist.'

'Come this way, Mrs Gladwell. I have some lovely strong white just for you. No chaff in Porter's finest, that's our promise. How much would you like?'

Mrs Crust had given precise instructions to her customers.

'Two bags, each of a pound in weight,' she requested. 'And a receipt, if you will. My husband demands to see such things.'

Mr Porter raised an eyebrow. There seemed to be a lot of demanding husbands this morning. When had husbands ever occupied themselves with domestic expenses? Especially below stairs.

'Naturally, Ma'am. And can I help you with anything else?'

Mrs Gladwell looked around at the baskets of unwholesome fruit and sprouting vegetables. Having agreed to return to Porter's for one expedition only, she was now eager to get away.

'Just the flour and receipt, Mr Porter.'

Mr Porter completed the transaction and, having short-changed Mrs Gladwell, waved her farewell.

'Slugs for potatoes, indeed,' he muttered, once she had gone outside. 'Well, I took an extra penny for the insult, you miserable madam.'

A more generous-hearted shopkeeper might have escorted his customers to the door. Had he done so, he might then have observed, as they turned the corner, that they made straight for the door of a splendid carriage belonging to none other than Lady Passmore. He might then have looked inside and seen the set of true scales onto which Mrs Pomeroy placed the goods. He would also have seen Lady Passmore, who noted each item's sold weight and correct weight in her little black book. And, finally, he would have seen them troop across the Green to collect their slice of Mrs Crust's promised fruit pie. Sadly for him, his meanness of spirit veiled from him the truth.

Meanwhile, the operation to ensnare him was conducted with the efficiency of the Royal Army Ordnance Corps.

Every entry was countersigned by the purchaser, with an added comment on whether they had been overcharged or short-changed. Finally, the items and receipts were set to one side by Mrs Pomeroy to be used as evidence in court.

There was an atmosphere of joy among all the participants that comes with the righting of a long-held wrong. And as a memento of thanks, in addition to the slice of pie, everyone involved received a pair of newly knitted bed socks, courtesy of Miss Prim and Mrs Mulligatawny, who proved as speedy with the knitting needles as her mistress.

'That's the thirty-fifth bag of underweight flour and sugar I've recorded,' said Mrs Pomeroy.

'Almost as many bed socks as we've knitted,' remarked Miss Prim, perspiration dripping from her forehead to the floor of the carriage.

Mrs Mulligatawny, too, cast a weary expression from her seat on the other side of the carriage.

'Only the English wear socks in bed.'

Even with such a sizable chariot, the space inside was becoming congested. In order to appear plausible, the ladies had bought not only flour and sugar but turnips, potatoes, leeks and swedes.

'Must we keep these vegetables, Lady Passmore of Tewkesbury Manor?' Mrs Pomeroy asked, eyeing them with distaste. 'Waste is a heinous sin against the Lord but many of these vegetables seem to have been sinning on their own behalf for several months.'

Lady Passmore looked up from her notebook.

'I could not say, Mrs Pomeroy. What does anyone do with a tired vegetable?'

The three English ladies turned to Miss Prim's Tamil cook for advice.

'Don't ask,' Mrs Mulligatawny answered, not even raising her eyes from her knitting, 'or I'll carrot the lot of you.'

A LTHOUGH GUILDHALL WAS alive with the sound of males – the great and the not-so-great – affronted by the thought of a female taking on the mantle of authority, Gaia felt immediately at home in its environs. Not all, however, was as she would wish.

Soon after entering her new office with Belle Nash, she summoned the clerk to the court. He was a gentleman half her age by the name of Wallop – one of the Wallops of Nether Wallop – and made little attempt to disguise his shock at her appointment.

'I believe I need to check my calendar, Ma'am,' was his opening remark, foolishly looking to Belle Nash for support. 'The first of April seems to have crept up on us earlier than hitherto.'

It was an inauspicious start.

'I want a list of pending cases on my desk in ten minutes, young man,' replied Gaia brusquely, 'and please don't consider me a fool or make such comments again. I will not be footled with.'

Other than by his mother and his nursemaid, Wallop had never been spoken to in such a manner before by a woman and his face turned red – not with embarrassment but fury.

'Yes, Ma'am,' he responded, without apology.

Gaia continued in a typically forthright manner.

'And kindly send a message to Special Constable Dimm to be here in one hour's time. Then fetch tea and biscuits for Councillor Nash and myself. After that, you can leave us for the day. I will hold my first session tomorrow morning.'

For thirty minutes Gaia kept the office door wide open while she shared a pot of tea with Belle. He had been right that the appointment would cause a stir. Cries of protest and derision could be heard, and a stream of men peered through the open door to witness for themselves the incredible occurrence of a woman being appointed to a public post.

'D'you think there's a danger that Chairman Camshaft will renege on his decision?' asked Gaia quietly.

'It's a danger but I think not,' said Belle, weighing up her question. 'The climbdown would be more damaging than the criticism. And the chairman is a good man at heart, and wise – a *senex sapiens*, if ever Bath knew one. For all we know, his eyesight may not be as bad as he lets on.'

'It would certainly be good to have his support,' Gaia said. 'And now I think I shall close the door. Maledom has had its chance to gawp. I feel like an exhibit in a fairground of grotesques.'

For the next ten minutes, Gaia rifled through the drawers of the desk and the cabinets while Belle drank more tea.

'Much to see?' he asked.

Gaia picked out a wizened object from a file.

'It resembles the Acgean stables *before* they were cleaned. Look, a stale pie, though whether one of Mrs Crust's or Mrs Haytit's I cannot tell, so elderly is it. Belle, I hate to think what miscarriages may have occurred under the late Obadiah Wood.'

Belle finished off his third biscuit.

'Then look to the future, Ma'am. If past injustices are raised, then investigate them with the application of a proconsul, but you will find more than enough on your plate without rehearsing Wood's misdeeds, I imagine.'

Gaia closed the cabinet.

'With reluctance, I agree with you. The first demand is to run my own office and those who serve it. I don't see Mr Wallop lasting long in that regard. Nor Special Constable Dimm, for that matter.'

'A clean sweep is in order, Ma'am,' agreed Belle. 'You don't want the past to tie your hands.'

It was a chance remark that made him swallow his tea the wrong way, reminding him, as it did, that the narrowboat lads were still owed three pounds and that the order had yet to be given to free the unlovely Jacob Pollard.

'On the subject of tied hands, I will take my leave. Decimus Dimm will be here any moment and you will require privacy. Send word if you need me. I am, as ever, your devoted servant.'

Gaia crossed the room to hug him.

'Of course, Belle, and forgive my lack of grace earlier. It was haughty of me. Had I but won the position on my own, I would have been kinder. But I allow that a little trickery was required, and you are a magician in that regard. As for my speech, there will be others after me who will speak its words.'

Belle smiled.

'So, you are content?'

'I am delighted. And I should like you to dine with me tonight at Somerset Place. Lady Passmore, Mrs Pomeroy and Miss Prim will be attending. It will be an opportunity for us to explain to you how Hezekiah Porter is being ensnared. And do bring Herr Kant.'

Belle waved as he left.

'I hope to. But Gerhardt's in a sullen mood with me, so I cannot promise his attendance. When I left Gay Street this morning, he was plucking hair out of his wig in anger like fur from a rabbit.

210

He will more than likely wish to spend the evening with Mistress Lush, a willing supplicant for *Regression*.'

He closed the door and Gaia set to work. On her desk, she had a list of the constabulary of the county and she marked the names of the officers she believed she might trust. A few minutes later, there was a knock on the door.

'It's me, Ma'am. Special Constable Dimm at your request.'

'Very good. Do come in, Special Constable.'

Dimm entered, conspicuously ill at ease. In the space of a few days his patron had died and been replaced by his polar opposite: a person of impeccable morality, impeccable legal knowledge and impeccable womanhood.

He stood in her office and gawped.

'I don't know how to address you, Mrs Champion, Ma'am.'

Gaia remained seated behind her desk.

'How did you address Magistrate Wood?'

'As Your Honour. Or as Magistrate Wood, that being his title.'

'And why would you think to treat me any differently? Your Honour will be fine, as will Magistrate Champion. Madam Magistrate gives you a third option. You may take potluck.'

Dimm sounded like a dog that had lost its bark.

'I'm not sure, Honour Champion, Magistrate. It just doesn't seem right somehow. Ma'am. Your magistracy. Sir. I mean ...'

It was the wrong answer. Gaia fixed him with an unforgiving glare.

'What's not right, Special Constable, are unfounded prosecutions. What is not right is wrongful convictions. What is not right is the persecution of the innocent. What is not right is giving the lawbreakers of the city free rein to pursue their pernicious activities without fear of legal penalty. Do I make myself abundantly clear?'

Apparently, she did not.

'That's not how it's been done in the past.'

211

Gaia brought her fist down on the desk. She had no time for men like Dimm.

'And that is why I am placing you under review. I shall, over the next twenty-four hours, consider your record as special constable and then decide on your future. For now, you may leave. I will see you in a day.'

As Dimm left, Gaia sat seething behind her desk. She had a mind to call Dimm back and sack him on the spot, but she was not entirely sure whether she had the authority to do so. That was unfortunate, for early decisions on assuming a new role are often the most important. As many have learned to their cost, the perception of weakness in authority, even for an instant, can have the most calamitous effect.

B ELLE STILL RECALLED the day when, as a child, he trapped a bumblebee inside an empty jar and taunted it by shaking its glass prison. He was in the garden of his grandparents' house, close to the Somerset town of Frome. The bee became angry, indeed more than angry: it was consumed by rage. Uncertain what to do, the young Belle panicked and threw the jar as far as he could across the lawn.

At first, he was relieved to see the bee free and in flight. Then he froze in horror as the bee turned and, with merciless intent, flew directly at him. Too scared to run, he watched as the bee, closing fast, reversed its body in flight and directed its sting – and with that its life – at his right eye. Only at the last moment did Belle throw back his head. The sting entered an inch below his eye; his sight was saved but to this day he bore its mark.

Belle had left Gaia's new office to instruct the narrowboat lads to wrap scarves around their faces and go and free Jacob Pollard. He had assumed that, once freed, the chastened councillor would go straight home, make some excuse to his wife and return to work the next day.

But Belle was mistaken, for Pollard was not a chastened man. He was an angry bee.

In the middle of the afternoon, what looked like two young highwaymen with knotted handkerchiefs around their mouths had entered the pump house and untied the councillor. They had then run as fast as their legs could carry them towards Bathwick village.

Pollard did not chase them because he was wise enough to know that they must be mere pawns in a bigger game. He had had nearly twenty hours to consider who might be the master of the chessboard and had reduced his list of suspects to one: Belle Nash, the only man with the knowledge and the gall to defy him.

It was to Guildhall that Pollard now went, not caring that his trousers were covered with dirt from the pump-house floor, that his shirt was torn and that his hair was matted with filth. At the entrance door, he pushed past a startled Bullard and made directly for Belle's office.

Lucius Lush was absent, having been sent on a pointless errand, and Belle was admiring the primroses on his desk when his door was suddenly flung open.

'Councillor Pollard, by all the gods! Breath courses through your lungs, blood through your veins! Need I say what fears attended us when you failed to appear this morning and yet here you are in all your glory! Let pipes be piped, let acrobats tumble, let great bulls be garlanded and sacrificed! I myself shall ply Dionysus with wine. But – Councillor Pollard: you seem vexed.'

Pollard was beyond vexed.

'These were your doings – you and your bestial friends, Nash. Don't deny it!'

Belle remained unruffled and pled ignorance.

'My doings, Sir? What are the doings of which you speak?'

'You incapacitated me, Sir, and I will not let it pass! Once I become magistrate, I will lock you up and I will personally throw away the key.'

213

Belle laughed. It seemed that Pollard had not considered the motive for his seizure.

'Once you become magistrate? Sadly, Sir, there is no vacancy, or did you not hear? In your absence, Chairman Camshaft and I made the necessary appointment. We did note your non-attendance in the minutes, however, "with regret".'

The news that the Magistrate Selection Committee had convened in his absence made Pollard even more distraught.

'You dared make the appointment without me? Who? Not Wrigglesworth? Surely not Bunce?'

Belle was enjoying the moment.

'Please give the chairman credit, Councillor. The chairman appointed Champion as the new magistrate.'

'Champion?' Surprise now trumped Pollard's distress. 'There's no official by the name of Champion.'

'Correct, Sir. We looked outside Guildhall for the candidate. Fresh blood and a new approach. Chairman Camshaft thought that someone beholden to the principles of justice would make a pretty change and so we chose Gaia Champion as magistrate. Mrs Gaia Champion, widow of the late Hercules Champion. Now Magistrate Champion. Or, to give her her full title, Her Honour Magistrate Champion. Trips off the tongue nicely, methinks.'

'You ...!'

'Of course, if you have just cause for complaint, you should make application to the law, as anyone wronged in our fair city should do, and the magistrate will in due course be only too happy to consider your case. You may have my word for it, Sir.'

Belle was used to having the final word and was pleased with his closing remarks. It had been altogether an excellent day, with Gaia installed as magistrate and Pollard humiliated in the process. Angry bees, however, are unforgiving in their nature. Though he left the room in silence, Pollard was already plotting his revenge.

214

CHAPTER XXIII

Beware the act of hubris

GAIA CHAMPION'S COOK, the excellent Mme Galette, had hoped never to see another bag of Porter's flour again in her life and was extremely unhappy when close to fifty bags – with a similar quantity of poor-grade sugar – were unloaded from Lady Passmore's carriage. As for the baskets of vegetables, they went straight into the bin.

'*Nom de Dieu*, it turns *mon ventre* to see *ze* devil's goods *dans la maison*. I am not having them in *ma cuisine* for fear of *ze* contamination.'

In the two weeks since the birthday party, the kitchen had rediscovered its rhythm. A small dinner party on less than a day's notice from her mistress was easily arranged. In quick order, Mme Galette prepared an onion soup, followed by *coq au vin* and *babas au rhum* for pudding.

'*Savez vous combien de* guests there will be for dinner, John?' she asked the butler, who had come down to the kitchen from the drawing room.

'Four guests and Mrs Champion, Mme Galette, making five for dinner. Sadly, Herr Kant will not be with us tonight, although Councillor Nash is here.'

'*Je suis désolé* to hear that. He is *un personage merveilleux*.'

Upstairs in the drawing room, some of the guests were less sorry. Phyllis Prim was relieved that, after a hard day's knitting, she did not have to confront the airborne sheep from Gay Street; and Lady Passmore was delighted that victory could be celebrated without Prussian interference. As for Mrs Pomeroy, she was saddened by Gerhardt's absence.

'I have been wondering all day, whilst watching Miss Prim knit, if a glove is a cow's udder, what a bed sock might be. I was hoping to hear Herr Kant's opinion on the subject.'

'Such unseemly thoughts should be kept to oneself, Mrs Pomeroy,' responded Lady Passmore. 'A sock is a sock, not a ...'

There was an awkward pause.

'A what, Lady Passmore of Tewkesbury Manor?' interposed Belle Nash naughtily.

Her Ladyship pursed her lips.

'Whatever that dreadful poet laureate may have rhymed it with,' she replied, closing off the subject.

Pritchard arrived with a tray of coupes filled with Champagne and proceeded to circulate them.

'Thank you, John,' said Belle. 'We have much to celebrate. It is a little out of order for a man to speak on what has been most definitely a day for women, but if I may ... .'

Gaia was in high spirits.

'We should be delighted. Consider yourself an honorary woman for the evening, Belle, if you will. I am only sad that Herr Kant is not here.'

'As am I, Ma'am, but alas: he is still in a sulk at what he considers to be my unfair criticism of *Regression*. I spent an hour at Gay Street trying to cajole him this afternoon but he would not be cajoled.'

'Regression?' queried Lady Passmore. 'It sounds Prussian and unpleasant. Does it involve cold baths and parade grounds?'

'It is Herr Kant's word for returning the mind to its childhood state,' explained Belle, 'to put right whatever may have gone wrong the first time.'

Mrs Pomeroy was intrigued.

'What is this technique, and does it work, Councillor?'

216

'From observation,' he replied, sipping on his Champagne, 'it mostly involves the act of moving furniture about a room.'

'Oooah,' piped up Miss Prim, who hated change of any sort. As a consequence, she spilled a little Champagne from her coupe. 'Oooah.'

'There, what did I tell you?' confirmed Her Ladyship. 'John: a cloth for Miss Prim, please, so she can wipe herself down.'

Pritchard produced a cotton cloth and, a minute later, with Miss Prim dried, the five friends resumed their discussion, and Belle asked permission to make some introductory remarks.

'If Calliope would but lend me her silver tongue,' he declared, 'I call on us to remember the great woman Agnodice, who in ancient Athens had to practise medicine disguised as a man. She resisted the intrigue of her male colleagues who all plotted against her … .'

Emboldened by Champagne and flushed with pride, there were cries of 'Shame!' from the women in the room.

'… and finally persuaded great Athens to overturn its law prohibiting female physicians.'

Cries of 'Hoorah!'

Belle continued, 'My dear ladies, there will be an end to subterfuge in Bath when Magistrate Champion – yes, Magistrate Champion! – occupies the bench. She will hear and defend the law as a woman, openly; and when she wears the lawyer's chiton, she will wear it to the ankle and not to the knee. Ladies, let us celebrate Gaia's appointment not only as our magistrate but as the first lady magistrate in the entire kingdom. Truly, this is an occasion of great moment!'

It was, indeed, a fabulous cause for celebration. They raised their coupes and drank to Gaia's success.

'There was much good fortune along the way,' Gaia responded. 'It was fortuitous that Councillor Pollard was indisposed and Chairman Camshaft pliable. But the result was the right one. I shall bring to the role commitment and integrity. The corrupt councillors, burghers and traders of this fine city shall all be brought to account.'

'None more so than Hezekiah Porter,' said Mrs Pomeroy. 'Are we to expect an arrest soon?'

Gaia nodded.

'Most likely, tomorrow. I have asked one of the younger constables to sit up and watch in case Mr Cudworth delivers another supply of cattle-feed to Porter's. I cannot trust Dimm to do the task, but the man I have chosen is honest; his brother was a clerk in Hercules's office. But regardless of what happens overnight, by midday Mr Porter will have been arrested and charged.'

'That is excellent news,' said Lady Passmore. 'So, our efforts will bear fruit. There will be no more sunken soufflés.'

'Most definitely not, much to the relief of Mme Galette,' replied Gaia. 'Which is why it is not only my appointment we should be applauding, but the brave endeavours of you all. It is thanks to you and countless ladies of Bath that the evidence against Mr Porter has been collected.'

Once again, they raised their glasses, which Belle politely waited to be lowered before asking for more information.

'I have to admit my partial ignorance, fair ladies. Such has been the pace of events today that I have scant understanding of what occurred in Abbey Green. As an honorary gossib – yes, *Mesdames*, you heard the word right – let me inhabit the spirit of Geoffrey Chaucer and call on you, the fair Wyves & Wymen of Bath, to enlighten me. What exactly have you been up to, O Amazons of retribution, to tip the scales in favour of righteousness and against Mr Porter?'

SELF-CONGRATULATION IS inherently dangerous for, by definition, it is an act of hubris. Horace Walpole, the self-styled man of letters, provided a useful list of things to avoid in life to keep hubris at bay. A vain man and a dandy, he nevertheless warned against monogrammed shirts. Wearing an outsized wig on a windy day to impress others was similarly to court disaster. He did not include, but one may add, drinking Champagne in a fine crescent house in celebration of gender equality.

Hubris disregards right and wrong. Only recall Odysseus, who having blinded and then taunted Polyphemus, unwisely revealed his identity before making his getaway. Polyphemus had been in the wrong – he had eaten six of Odysseus's men – but his prayer to Poseidon that Odysseus be cursed was honoured. Odysseus should have stayed silent.

Belle had not given himself away to Councillor Pollard, but he might just as well have done, for Pollard was left in no doubt who had orchestrated his humiliation. And Gaia would have been wiser to have removed Decimus Dimm at once, rather than threatening to do so in a day's time. There were, therefore, at large two embittered opponents who, at the very moment Champagne was being uncorked high on Sion Hill, were drinking gin and scheming revenge in the Dog & Duck tavern in the city down below.

'Magistrate Wood and me would meet here regular,' Dimm told Pollard, having already drunk the best part of a bottle before the councillor had arrived. 'This is where true power lay, he used to say; not in the court.'

'It's not a tavern that I usually frequent,' replied Pollard.

'Oh yes, there's many a gill we drank here while deciding who to turn the screws on. And it was good money, protecting the likes of Molly Jenkins and her girls. He had a saying for them as he helped, did Magistrate Wood: "Pay up, without dread, and sleep easy in bed."'

'He was a noble man,' stated the councillor.

Dimm looked misty-eyed and not just because of the alcohol. He was in a maudlin frame of mind.

'I shall miss him, I will. And now this Mrs Champion is magistrate! It's beyond belief. I only had her friends in gaol last week. I don't know what I'll do.'

Pollard picked up the bottle and poured the special constable another glass of gin.

'Fight back, man. In fact, let us join forces. I was the rightful successor to Obadiah Wood and that damn woman usurped me. If I were magistrate, you'd have nothing to fear.'

Dimm sniffed and wiped away a tear.

'But fight back how, Councillor Pollard? I am a man of low intelligence. Magistrate Wood told me that and he was right.'

'I don't give a fig for intelligence,' said the councillor. 'You are a man of action and that's more important in the constabulary of today. We must strike hard and fast. And we must do it tonight before Mrs Champion opens the court tomorrow morning and consolidates her hold.'

Dimm had nothing to lose and, emboldened by gin, was up for a fight.

'I'm ready to do whatever it takes.'

Pollard grinned. He was desperate for revenge and Dimm had told him just what he had wanted to hear.

'She has a weakness, this Mrs Champion: her confidante and supporter, Belle Nash.'

Dimm cocked his head to one side. He knew how Magistrate Wood had hated Councillor Nash.

'And ...'

'And, in turn, Nash has a weakness. He's a pederast. We won't catch him in the act, he's too sharp for that, but he has a Prussian mollyboy, and I have a good idea where he can be found after dark. If we're lucky, we can catch the Prussian and put him in the dock. Then we'll watch how that high-and-mighty Magistrate Gaia Champion reacts.'

Dimm reached for the bottle but Pollard intervened. It was time for the special constable to sober up. Dimm pushed his glass away.

'That's alright, Councillor Pollard. I've had enough. You can count on me. There's a couple of men I can call on. You tell us where the Prussian is and we'll do the rest. As of now, I'm still Special Constable and I won't let Mrs Champion forget it.'

Pollard stood and slapped his ally on the back.

'You're not as stupid as Magistrate Wood suggested. So, we have an understanding?'

Dimm looked up at the councillor, his dim mind made dimmer by alcohol.

'We do, Sir. Almost. I'm unclear on one thing. About Councillor Nash being a pedestal ... .'

I T HAD BEEN an excellent dinner, with Mme Galette back to her finest form in the kitchen. Belle had laughed merrily as the ladies described their day by Abbey Green.

'Mrs Crust was an absolute wonder persuading her customers to trick Mr Porter,' said Lady Passmore.

'As were Miss Prim and Mrs Mulligatawny for sewing such a multitude of socks,' added Mrs Pomeroy. 'Yes, Miss Prim, you were a marvel.'

It was an hour before midnight and the three ladies were preparing to depart in Lady Passmore's carriage.

'They say the pen is mightier than the sword. So, it would appear, is the knitting needle!' joked Belle, standing in the entrance hall of Somerset Place with Gaia, as the guests made their farewells.

'A whisky in the library before you go?' asked Gaia, as the front door closed.

'Why not, Ma'am? But only one. You have a long day tomorrow with the reopening of the court, and the public benches will be full of spiteful men, hectoring you and making trouble. You will need all your strength.'

They crossed the hall to the library.

221

He said, 'I wonder what your first case will be, before Mr Porter is hauled in.'

'An affray outside the Assembly Rooms, most likely, or a break-in. They make up the bulk of any magistrate's work.'

Gaia had allowed Pritchard to retire and so poured the whiskies herself. It was the first time in weeks she had felt able to relax, and she took the opportunity to discuss matters of a personal nature.

'Tell me how things are with Herr Kant,' she said as she handed over the whisky. 'Are you happy together?'

Belle smiled but his thoughts were melancholic.

'No, Gaia, we are not, and it is I who is to blame. Events have distracted me these last weeks. Gerhardt is an energetic and demanding soul. He won't stay still and there is, at the moment, a distance between us. But now the park is opened, and you are magistrate and the soufflé is saved, I hope to give him the time he deserves.'

'Poor Belle, you must be exhausted. We expect too much of you. And you are right. If you love Herr Kant, you must dote upon him once again.'

Belle looked into his glass and swirled the amber liquid. In its vortex radiated a single word that Gaia had unintentionally sounded.

'"If",' he whispered. 'A word that defines each human life.'

'Belle?'

He looked up.

'Nothing, Gaia. I do love Gerhardt and his funny ways, but he has been spending more time with Mistress Lucy than with me this past fortnight, and I have been thankful because it has kept him out of harm's way – and been a merry education for my fair clerk.'

Belle sighed.

He continued, 'But in truth, the night is short and the story long. It will keep for another time. For now, I should be on my way and make my peace with the errant Goth before I sleep.'

They both rose.

'My carriage is waiting for you outside,' said Gaia.

He kissed her hand.

'You are a true friend.'

The carriage journey home took no more than ten minutes and Belle barely noticed the passing of time. The streets of Bath were quiet, the gas lanterns softly burning outside the grand houses of Royal Crescent and The Circus. The clattering of horses' hooves was the only evidence of life.

On reaching Gay Street, Belle bade farewell to Gaia's coachman and opened the front door. In the early months of their relationship, he would have found Gerhardt in the drawing room stretched out on the giltwood chaise longue, a low fire in the hearth and a glass of port to hand. Gerhardt had told him he would lie there replaying in his mind the music of his youth. In more recent months, however, Gerhardt had taken his pleasure elsewhere.

The chaise longue was empty and the fire was dead. Belle could have gone upstairs to check the bedchamber but he knew by instinct that Gerhardt would not be there. Instead, he walked to a window and looked outside into the darkness. Somewhere out there ... .

'Oh, dear,' he said, his head bowed. 'So much to do.'

And with those words he went to bed.

CHAPTER XXIV

Waking from a dream into a nightmare

A S MOST SENTIENT beings will acknowledge, thinking and dreaming are strangely intertwined. Nothing is firm. Our perceptions are as fickle as our moods, affected by nothing more solid than a cloud as it passes by the sun.

Some believe that thoughts turn to dreams at night, others that they are one and the same.

Contrast, if you will, the daytime labours of that doughty cleric Martin Luther and the night-time insights of the insomniac bachelor Nicolaus (or Niclas or Mikołaj) Copernicus, the one a dissenting cleric, the other the victim of his own Catholic fealty. After considerable introspection, Luther decided that the Earth must sit stationary at the centre of a universe, where it was ruled by a species – mankind – that he himself would tutor.

Copernicus, on the other hand, looked into the night sky as bats and owls flitted past the stars. He dreamt not that we are at the centre but that we hurtle through the universe in a never-ending journey. Copernicus decided that, for all its arrogance, mankind was carried on God's eternal winds like the seeds of a dandelion.

Who was right? In the fifteenth century, Protestant logic competed with Catholic dreams. In this respect, the dreamer won – not that the Church credited Copernicus with his visions, for not all dreams are blessed, as Belle Nash was discovering. Tucked up in his bed at Gay Street, his sleep was tortured by a fearful, rotten dream.

Belle dreamt it was the night of his birthday party a fortnight earlier and that Gaia Champion's carriage was taking him and Gerhardt Kant back home down Sion Hill. While the journey was all in his mind, Belle could sense the motion of the wheels, the cold air against his face as it seeped into the carriage, the sharp scent of the horses as they ran.

Belle looked out at the gas lamps illuminating the soft yellow stone of the houses. With its Palladian architecture nestling in a West Country valley, Bath was truly a place of dreams, the inspired creation of his ancestor Beau.

In his sleeping mind, Belle looked across the carriage at Gerhardt, who was peering into darkness. Sion Hill is where the boundary of the city lies: on one side elegance and laughter, on the other side the forbidding wilds of nature.

Cities have boundaries. Despite its gaiety, Georgian Bath had a dark side. For all that it embodied the fragrant love of Aphrodite, it spawned a small army of apothecaries ready to supply mercury ointment to the many who suffered from syphilis.

In his sleep, Belle turned uneasily. Gaia's appointment as magistrate had been too easy. All was not as it seemed. All was not right.

One's perception of Bath depends on how one looks at it: directly and honestly as the squire's son does as he entreats the hand of the vicar's daughter; or obliquely and stealthily as the aspiring bridegroom's father does between the thighs of one of Molly Jenkins's girls.

In his dream, Belle watched Gerhardt turn inward from the window of the carriage. His eyes stared out from a white-powdered face. His lips were painted rouge, the colour of blood.

'We are near the park *und* I wish there to go,' insisted Gerhardt. 'I feel in my loins this powerful longing. Come with me, *bitte*. There are men waiting for us.'

Belle sighed. He wanted Gerhardt for himself. To hug him close.

'We have a bed at home. We can lie more comfortably there.'

Gerhardt took Belle's answer for rejection.

'So, you love me not.'

'I do love you. It's the park I detest.'

Belle's reassurance went unacknowledged. Instead, Gerhardt's eyes turned black, his snow-white skin taut with anger.

'*Ihr Englisch* such hypocrites are. In Prussia learn we to accept who we are. To me is clear that with *das Englisch*, something is wrong ... stimms ...'

In the dream, Gerhardt struggled to find the right word.

'"Something is wrong stimms"?'

'... *stimmt. Stimmen. Ach*, you are typical for *das Englisch*, Belle: so verbally unimaginative. *So einfallslos*. Stop the wagon!'

It was an ultimatum not to be denied. The dream was reaching its climax.

'Willingly!' Belle replied, rapping the roof with his knuckles to alert the coachman. He pointed through the window. 'The park is that way. Go, leave me and do what you want.'

Gerhardt needed no second invitation.

He opened the door, pointed his wig into the darkness and descended, his knitted silk breeches catching the light of the moon before he disappeared behind a bush. Alone in the silence, Belle leant back in his carriage and cursed. In his bed, deep in his dream, he grasped hold of his pillow and wept.

T OO MUCH OF what his companion said was true. The English were a mixed-up lot, their attitude to coitus repeatedly interrupted by history. If Wicked Henry had not passed his vile statute, how different England and its dominions might be. And how much more enlightened were those Teutonic states – Bavaria, for example – where men could be men and, if they desired, women too.

Shame on England for its culture of intolerance – and not just

226

to bachelors. Isolate Catholics and confront! Isolate Africans and enslave! Isolate women and disenfranchise! As for the poor ... .

'Damn you, Gerhardt! Damn you for being right. And damn you for not being here, dear Gerhardt – for not supporting me. For leaving me at home. Alone. In our ...'

Belle awoke with a start.

'Gerhardt!' he screamed, reaching out. But the bed, like the fading carriage in his dream, was empty. And cold. 'Gerhardt, where are you?'

Then he heard a rapping on the front door. He sat up and peered towards the window. It was still dark outside in Gay Street. Who on Earth would be knocking at this hour if not Gerhardt?

Belle rose from bed and lit a candle. Dressed in his nightgown, he made his way down the stairs, to open the door and admonish his lover. But it was not Gerhardt who stood there. It was the coachman from Gaia's household.

'Apologies for waking you so early, Sir,' the young man said.

Belle could see Gaia's carriage. The horses were agitated, their nostrils flared, their hooves scraping the rough surface of the road. His own heart began to race.

'What is it, man? Why have you returned?'

The coachman came straight to the point. Gaia had been concise in her instructions.

'I have news about your cousin, Sir. Herr Kant was arrested close to midnight in Royal Victoria Park.'

Belle took a step back. It was impossible but it was also what he had always feared.

'Arrested? But it cannot be. Magistrate Wood is dead and gone. His times are past.'

'Mrs Champion is informed that Herr Kant is being held by Special Constable Dimm.'

'But he was due to be suspended. Under what charge is Herr Kant being held?'

The coachman hesitated.

'It is not yet known, Sir.'

The candle in Belle's hand flickered as he stared into the night. There was a conspiracy afoot, a conspiracy that threatened the direst of consequences.

'Do you know the circumstances of the arrest?'

The coachman looked awkward.

'Special Constable Dimm and others swept through the new park last night. They found men gathered there, disporting themselves, if you know what I mean, Sir, and they arrested Herr Kant.'

'And the others?'

'Don't know, Sir. I think they was let off with a caution, although it is whispered that Master Lush may also have been apprehended just outside the park.'

'Lucy too? Then we are under attack – but by whom? Decimus Dimm cannot have been acting alone. Does Mrs Champion know who is behind this?'

'Can't say, Sir, but Mrs Champion requests you accompany me back to Somerset Place. Is the news serious, Sir?'

The look on Belle's face said that it was. He leant forward and placed a hand upon the coachman's shoulder.

'My dear young man, it could be a matter of life and death. And the magistrate to whom the case will be brought is none other than your dear mistress. By Zeus, what is she going to do?'

A ND, SO, THE bubble pops, its liquid skin fracturing, shattering in the air – the joyous, fragile sphere that graced the world gone in the blink of an eye.

NOTES

- I have burned the midnight oil and endured sleepless nights trying to find evidence, without success, of my uncle's assertion that Copernicus was an insomniac.

228

- Changes in the *Code Pénal* decriminalised same-sex relations in France in 1791 and were extended to France's dominions by Napoleon Bonaparte in 1810. The Kingdom of Prussia abolished the death penalty for male sexual relations in 1794. In 1811, Holland adopted the French legal code. In 1813, lawmakers in Bavaria followed suit, as did Spain in 1822 and Hanover in 1840. England remained obdurate throughout.
- 'Wicked Henry' is Henry VIII, and the 'vile statute' is the Buggery Act of 1533. Passed in the year that Henry VIII annulled his twenty-four-year marriage to Catherine of Aragon, it was designed to give the sociopathic monarch and future uxoricide a much-needed moral platform. It decreed sexual intercourse between men to be punishable by death. The act was replicated in British dominions and colonies. It remains the basis for the persecution of gay men across the world to this day.

CONCLUSION

An unusually long conclusion in five chapters, in which Belle is sent to Warsaw by royal command, Gaia inherits a field of beehives, Gerhardt loses an arm and Obadiah Wood is found not to have died at all. Or none of the above. And much more besides.

CHAPTER XXV

The hangman's noose

A WEEK EARLIER, when Belle Nash had been summoned to Somerset Place to discuss the arrest of Lady Passmore and Mrs Pomeroy, Gaia Champion had been all purpose and action. She had sent out messages far and wide, inviting whomsoever she knew to attend court and protest her friends' innocence. This time, with Gerhardt Kant and Lucius Lush held in the clink, Gaia was in a position of authority yet she was listless and her quill remained dry.

'I simply have no idea what to do,' she said as Belle entered the study. 'Herr Kant and Master Lush are in Pulteney Gaol, but the charges won't be known until Dimm brings them to court later this morning.'

Belle gratefully accepted a cup of tea offered by Pritchard. Having taken a soothing sip of Darjeeling, he tried to dissect the crisis.

'The new park is closed by city ordinance from sunset. Dare we presume the two of them will be charged with trespass?'

'Trespass, I imagine, will only be the first item on the charge sheet,' Gaia replied. 'You know better than I do what men get up to in public places after dark.'

'And what Dimm might be moved to add.'

They both fell silent, struggling to identify what action could be taken. It was not as if Gerhardt and Lush had been arrested wrongfully; and there were few citizens who would rush to court to clamour for men to be granted the right to cavort with each other at night-time in places of public assembly.

'The fault is mine,' said Gaia. 'I should have established the nature of my authority at once and either stayed silent with Dimm or dismissed him on the spot. Instead, I warned him of his fate and then left him free to retaliate.'

Belle hung his head like a whipped dog, wracked not only by Gaia's despondency over the possible fates of the two young men, but about his own commissioning of an improper ruse: one that Gaia would rightly never have agreed to, and which had now gone badly wrong.

'You are not to blame in the slightest, Gaia. It is all my own dark doings. Decimus Dimm is merely a pawn. Jacob Pollard is our man. He had intended to stand for the role of magistrate himself and I arranged for him to be ... incapacitated. Pollard likes to wander the canal towpath after dark looking for men to commune with, so I arranged for the narrowboat lads to apprehend him and truss him up.'

Gaia looked at her friend, incredulous.

'You had him kidnapped?!'

The response was evasive.

'Only a little. He was not harmed, merely "detained" until the committee meeting was over.'

For Gaia, the time for half-truths was over.

'Detained?! Belle, you have not only broken the law but humiliated a city representative and left him seeking revenge. And who could blame him? What were you thinking? I understand your motives but you have betrayed our friendship. I am astonished.'

Belle could but acknowledge the obvious.

'You are angry, Ma'am, and for good reason. I have been a complete fool, both in what I did and in keeping my stratagems from you. I have left you compromised and our friends vulnerable. I said nothing to you because you would never have agreed to my designs and I was fearful that fate might not smile on you. I did what I did for you – and for social progress.'

'To commit a bad act for a good reason is intolerable,' fumed Gaia. 'There is no bargaining with morality.'

Belle could not meet her gaze.

'I know it now, Ma'am, and am ashamed. If my actions were to divide us, I would be desolate till death. Our companionship is all to me.'

His words calmed her. She and Hercules had agreed to place love and friendship above all else in life, and she was wise enough to understand that misjudgement often lies behind good intentions. She crossed the room to Belle and sat beside him on the chesterfield sofa. They held hands and stared into empty space.

Gaia sighed. 'What do you think Pollard wants? How far is he willing to go?'

'He may not know himself,' mused Belle.

'Then let us consider the options for him, and one cries out more loudly than any other: that I resign ...'

'No!' protested Belle.

'That I resign,' repeated Gaia, 'and clear the way to his own appointment. Were I to do that, would Pollard tell Dimm to release Herr Kant and Master Lush?'

'I think he might, but you must not,' urged Belle.

Gaia maintained her clarity of thought.

'If I stand fast, Pollard can ensure that Herr Kant and Master Lush are charged with an offence for which the penalty is death – and though I can rule on trespass, I cannot rule on a capital charge. For that I am required, without evidence to the contrary, to pass the case on to a higher court. Pollard seeks revenge and holds our friends' lives in his hand.'

Belle now understood that Gaia did not have the authority to rule the charge inadmissible, nor to declare Gerhardt and Lush innocent. If their case went to a higher court, it would not be hers to try. Besides which, she had pledged to fight corruption and apply the law without prejudice or favour. It was inconceivable that she would use her very first appearance on the bench to act otherwise.

Belle, more practically, wanted to explore other recourses, but that would require time, and time was short.

'What hour do you open the court, Ma'am?' he asked.

'Nine o'clock: three hours from now.'

'Can you delay till midday?'

'If needs be, I suppose. On my first day, there will be reasons aplenty to stall. But what are you planning this time?'

He wished he could give her an answer but he had none of substance.

'I cannot say, Ma'am, truly – but clearly, I must go to Guildhall, meet the wretched Pollard and talk to Chairman Camshaft. There must be a solution, and having created this mishap, it falls to me and me alone to find it. I must take my leave. Would you vouchsafe me your carriage?'

He stood to leave and she rose to bid farewell.

'The carriage is yours, Belle. Tell the coachman to return here.'

He started to cross the room, then turned to face her.

'I am distraught, Gaia, and will do everything I can to set things right. But whatever happens, you must not resign. You cannot surrender the progress you have made.'

Gaia watched her closest friend depart. Fine words, she thought, but if the decision were between someone's life and her keeping the job of magistrate, resignation had to be the only choice.

She made her way to her dressing room to find suitable clothes for the day. Climbing the stairs, she considered the actual and irreconcilable conflict that she was presented with. To uphold the law, in this instance, would be to betray her bachelor friends, even to sacrifice their lives. But neither could she dishonour the role of magistrate by ignoring the law of the land.

'I was anticipating tough decisions but none so difficult as this. And never so soon.'

BELLE STEPPED DOWN from the carriage and entered Guild-hall. Although the sun had barely risen, Bullard was already at his post. The usual banter, however, was absent. The best Belle could get was a curt 'good morning' and a shifty expression. He guessed that word of the arrests was already out. It would be a day of snide comments and spiteful wit as Belle's fellow councillors feasted on his misfortune.

'Is Chairman Camshaft here?' Belle asked.

'No, Sir.'

'And Councillor Pollard?'

'He arrived a few moments ago and enquired after you, Sir.'

Belle entered the building, then stood in the lobby deciding on his next step. He could wait for Camshaft in the hope of building an alliance but he had nothing to parlay; he could only appeal to the chairman for his help, and that was unsafe.

It was better to bite the bullet and confront Pollard, he decided. At least by meeting the enemy, he would be made aware of what his demands were. Belle proceeded, therefore, to Pollard's office and was disappointed to find the door locked. He waited a moment, then cursed and walked to his own room, the better to collect his thoughts.

As he approached, he noticed that the door was ajar. He often kept his office unlocked but he would always close the door at the end of the day and, with Lush in gaol, there was no one who had any cause to enter. Unless ...

Belle looked inside and, seated behind his desk, as if taking ownership of it, was Pollard.

'Good morning to you, Councillor,' Belle said, doing his best to sound self-assured.

Pollard looked around, a cold sneer on his face.

237

'I understand from Bullard that you enquired after me,' Belle went on. 'If you would kindly vacate my chair, I would be happy to talk. There is much to discuss.'

But Pollard did not move.

'You are in no position to make demands, Sir, not even for your own chair. If you want to sit, sit elsewhere.'

Pollard indicated a chair on the near side of the desk and Belle did not argue the point.

'Very well. I would offer you tea but, as you know, my clerk is indisposed, as is my dear cousin Herr Kant. My clerk, of course, is Chairman Camshaft's great-grandson. As for Herr Kant, he is the nephew of the esteemed philosopher Immanuel Kant, much admired by Prussian royalty. We would not wish for our chairman to suffer embarrassment on their account, nor for a diplomatic incident to arise.'

It was as strong a case as Belle could muster but it fell far short of what was required. Pollard pressed his advantage.

'I infer that you imagine I was behind last night's events. I had as much involvement in the arrest of your friends as I had in their being in Royal Victoria Park in the first instance. I understand that Special Constable Dimm has several sworn witnesses to indecent acts. Herr Kant was arrested in the arboretum and your clerk, being swift of foot, on the road to Weston.'

Belle interrupted with poorly timed cynicism.

'You seem remarkably well informed for someone with no involvement.'

But Pollard held the upper hand.

'What of it, Sir? Am I not allowed to observe? May I not take pleasure in seeing the wheels of justice grind into action? I wait with bated breath for the accused to stand before Magistrate Champion.'

Belle held back from further criticism. Instead, he changed tack and adopted a conciliatory tone.

'Councillor, you make your point well. What is it you want? Let us agree terms.'

But Pollard had an acid tongue and wished solely for revenge.

'I have no interest in agreement. There is no middle ground to be negotiated. I want to see these men in court, charged with the vile offences they have committed. And when, God willing, they are found guilty, I look forward to the day they hang.'

It was everything that Belle had feared. He felt the blood drain from his face.

'But they are young men, Councillor. Please desist. You and I are politicians and politics is a game we play. They are mere bystanders.'

'No more it seems.'

'Then tell me, what is to be done?!'

Pollard rose from the chair to leave. He had fulfilled his intention.

'Nothing. I came here to tell you that Herr Kant and Master Lush have no defence. My one regret is that the hangman's noose will be around their necks, not yours. But I do not pity them. Such is the cost of befriending Belle Nash. Their blood is on your hands, not mine.'

And with that he was gone.

WHILE DECIMUS DIMM had no regrets about arresting Gerhardt Kant, the warders at the gaol felt otherwise. They could not get the Prussian to keep quiet. Never in the gaol's history had there been such a demanding inmate, a man who treated the prison guards as if they were staff in a hotel.

'Please stop rattling that tin cup against the bars, Mr Kant,' said one of the guards. 'It makes a racket and there's people in the other cells trying to sleep.'

'I refuse the racket to stop until you for me fresh water *und* a mirror provide.'

The guard rolled his eyes.

'You can have water but no mirror. We had a prisoner a few years back who broke a mirror and slashed his wrists with it. We had to wash the whole place down. It was most unpleasant.'

Gerhardt stamped his foot in annoyance.

'That is *lächerlich*. No wonder *du Englisch* are having the bad teeth *und* terrible skin. You never look at yourselves in the glass. *Und* why should I my wrists to slash when they are so beautiful?'

Gerhardt held out his wrists for the prison guard to see.

'Very fine, I'm sure.'

'*Ja*, they are beautiful. *Und mein* nails?' he added, turning his hands over.

'Your nails too … ,' the guard began, before realising he had been drawn into a conversation better suited for a lady's maid. 'Mr Kant! I have no interest in your nails. Go back to your mattress and be quiet. I will bring you water in due course.'

The guard retreated to his post and Gerhardt went and sat down on the mattress. He fidgeted, checking the buttons on his waistcoat and flattening the material of his trousers over his thighs.

'That man, *der Gefängniswärter*, is an imbecile. I cannot without a mirror *mein* wig prepare. *Und* I have *ein* chin pimple.'

Beside him on the mattress, a form turned over. It was Lush, and even in the grey light it was possible to see that he had been crying. His pale cheeks were moist with tears.

'Is that what you're worried about, Gerhardt? A pimple. That's frightfully brave of you in the circumstances.'

The Prussian looked at his English friend.

'*Natürlich*, there is nothing else to worry about. We have nothing wrong done. We had a little fun in the park – but so what? Not even was harmed *ein kleines Eichhörnchen*. It is not as if someone died!'

Gerhardt's final words proved too much for Lush, who tucked himself back into a ball. His body trembled with fear.

'Not yet,' he whispered. 'Help us, Councillor Nash. Save us from the gallows.'

CHAPTER XXVI

The first day in court

UNUSUALLY, CHAIRMAN ERNEST Camshaft arrived late for work and was unaware of all the commotion that had occurred overnight. But then, he had been unaware of most things going on in Guildhall for a very long time. In his early days, Camshaft had prided himself on being the puppet master of the City Corporation. No more, it seemed. The puppets had broken free, and Guildhall had become a riot of competing self-interest that made Punch and Judy look like models of decorum.

'Is there nothing you can do, Sir?' asked Belle Nash, who had demanded an audience as soon as Camshaft had arrived.

The chairman shuffled around his office. He had no desire to get involved in the arrests of Gerhardt Kant and Lucius Lush.

'I can't see how I can help, Sir. I have thirty-seven great-grand-children and this particular one should not have been in the park. There's a reason for city ordinances. Some of the time, anyway.'

Belle considered getting onto his knees to plea, but he worried that Camshaft would wonder where he had gone to.

'Sir, this involves your great-grandson. He's a charming, won-derful young man and his life is in danger.'

But Camshaft was not to be moved.

'I am aware of the nature of the charges, Nash, and I have often made clear my support for the bachelor community in the past. I agree that the law is absurd. If strictly imposed, the city would have to close its theatres, its concert halls and most of its churches. For myself, I care not a hoot for matters of the flesh. At home, General

McCarthy has been tupping my neighbour's spaniel Bob for years. But the fact is my great-grandson and your Prussian second cousin once removed, nice men though they are, should not have been in Royal Victoria Park after dark. This may be a harsh lesson but, in the long run, it's one they'll respect.'

'But that is the point, Sir. There won't be a long run. They'll both be dead.'

'Which sadly is true for us all. I'm sorry that I can't help you. It's an issue you must sort out for yourself.'

Belle did not give up.

'You make your case with the greatest eloquence, as ever, Chairman, but there is a world of difference between the fine for breaking a city ordinance and the hangman's noose. If only you could speak to Councillor Pollard, then ... .'

Camshaft shook his head.

'Pollard, d'you say? The chap who wanted to be magistrate and couldn't be bothered to turn up? Don't you worry about him. I know there's a whole load of hoo-hah going on about the new chap, who turns out not to be a chap at all, but as with my great-grandson and your Prussian second cousin, what's done is done. My wife Audrey told me I had made a fine appointment, and, in my experience, wives should be listened to more often than they typically are. I do with Audrey, twice a day, regular as clockwork. And now, I think, it's time for my morning sleep ... .'

HAVING FAILED TO win Camshaft's support, Belle returned to his office. Sitting at his desk, he racked his brain for an idea to placate Pollard. More tea might have helped him in this process but, without Lush, this morning there was none.

Belle could think of nothing that might reverse the wheels of fate. Eventually, he spent the final thirty minutes of the morning writing a letter that he hoped would never see the light of day for it would change his life — and that of Gay Street — forever.

Having blotted the ink and folded the sheet, he placed the letter in his jacket pocket and departed for the courtroom. He passed by fellow councillors who, as he had anticipated, chuckled and sniggered at his misfortune. He ran a gauntlet of insults, the last of which came from Decimus Dimm, who stood by the door to the courtroom.

'Pederpastry,' sneered the special constable, toying with a new addition to his flawed vocabulary.

Belle noted Dimm's poor command of English and moved on to take a seat. Bachelors, he thought, spend their lives making light of prejudice, declaring that their crowns of thorns are tiaras. On this day, however, all the bile, spite and illiteracy lay heavy on his shoulders.

In the nearby magistrate's office, Gaia was preparing to enter the courtroom. She had held back for as long as possible in the hope of receiving news from Belle, but none had come.

Her clerk, Wallop, had become increasingly impatient.

'Mrs Champion, it is long past the normal opening time. I have provided you details on the workings of the court. There is no reason for further delay, Ma'am.'

She checked the time by the carriage clock on her mantelpiece.

'Mr Wallop, your notion of the court's opening hours seems better suited to a public house. But you are right. I am prepared. We should go.'

At the back of the office, a door led directly onto the courtroom. Wallop opened it and Gaia waited for him to announce her entrance.

'Arise and be upstanding for Magistrate Champion!'

For the first time, she stepped into court as its magistrate. Climbing the dais, she looked out onto her new domain. While dearly wishing for another case to hear, she felt entirely within her element. The command to be upstanding was a reminder that the magistrate's role carries authority. Whatever the length of term of office, whether it be for a day or a decade, this court was hers and she had no reason to be intimidated.

The courtroom was busy. On one side of the central aisle were a dozen councillors, including Pollard. On the other sat the frail-looking figure of Belle. Around them stood a gaggle of townspeople who had come to witness the historic day when a woman first sat in judgement in a public court.

Three, however, had come for a more specific reason. Gaia saw with alarm that Lady Passmore, Mrs Pomeroy and Phyllis Prim had turned up. They knew nothing of Herr Kant's predicament but had come hoping to see Gaia dispatch Hezekiah Porter.

Taking her seat, Bath's new magistrate motioned for everyone else to do the same. It was time for her opening statement.

'I welcome you all. You are here as of right. This court is and always will be open to public scrutiny. And I am here, having been appointed magistrate, to exercise legal scrutiny on the examination of those brought before me.

'Let me outline the rules pertaining to this court. I am required to apply the law fairly and without favour. You are required to show respect to the court, its officers and its procedures. If anyone here is planning a show of disrespect on account of my sex, leave now or you will find yourself in the dock and be sentenced accordingly.'

There was a hushed silence. No one moved.

Gaia continued, 'Let us move on to the first case. Clerk of the court, instruct the special constable to bring in the accused.'

From the back of the court appeared Gerhardt and Lush, the former defiant, the latter broken and sorrowful. Special Constable Dimm accompanied them. The silence in the court did not hold. While there was no explicit calling out, a murmur rose from the public benches. Lady Passmore, Mrs Pomeroy and Miss Prim appeared startled and confused.

The two men were led to the dock and Gaia forced herself to be dispassionate.

'Your names, gentlemen. The addresses where you reside and your occupations.'

'Herr Gerhardt Kant of Königsberg,' said Gerhardt, his wig straight and proud, although in need of a fresh dusting. 'Philosopher.'

Gaia made a note and did not question the address.

'Master Lucius Lush,' replied Lush, 'of Lucklands Road, Weston. I am a clerk in Guildhall.'

His statement triggered an immediate reaction from a member of the public.

'Lucklands Road!' someone shouted to general laughter. 'Your luck's run out today, lad. It's the gallows for you.'

Gaia immediately brought down her gavel.

'Clerk to the court, identify the man who made that comment and bring him before me.'

Several dozen eyes turned to an individual who attempted to shrink from view. He was quickly pulled from the public bench and brought to the front of the court.

'Name?' demanded Gaia.

'Titus Smith.'

'Well, Mr Smith. Perhaps you are deaf and did not catch my opening statement, yet you heard the accused speak well enough. You will spend tonight in a cell and tomorrow I will consider your case.'

Titus Smith was led away.

Gaia continued, 'Let us return to the gentlemen brought before the court. Special Constable Dimm, with what are they charged?'

Dimm had spent time preparing for this moment and was determined not to fluff his lines.

'I have credible evidence of crimes most serious, true and vile, Your Ladyship.'

Gaia held up her hand.

'Two points of order, Special Constable. Kindly refer to me as Your Honour; I have not as yet been elevated to a ladyship. Secondly, as to the alleged crimes being vile, I will judge their nature and their truth, not you. Please continue, one charge at a time.'

The expression on Dimm's face turned sour.

'Your Honour, on receiving reports of persons unknown being in Royal Victoria Park after dark in contravention of a prevailing city ordinance, I proceeded there with two men to investigate.'

'And what time was this?' asked Gaia.

'Approximately thirty minutes after midnight, Ma'am.'

'Identify the two men who went with you.'

'My friends Mr Wellow and Mr Monkton, Your Honour.'

Gaia raised an eyebrow.

'Are they part of the constabulary?'

Dimm hesitated. The questions had come thick and fast.

'No, Your Honour, but they have served well in the past upon request.'

Gaia continued making notes.

'Very well. And you proceeded to Royal Victoria Park taking with you these men. And it was dark, you say.'

'Yes, Your Honour.'

'And where did you apprehend these gentlemen?'

Though not used to such detailed questioning, Dimm had answers to hand. Watching the proceedings, Belle fidgeted with the letter inside his jacket.

'Mr Kant by the arboretum,' Dimm advised. 'And Master Lush, having a turn of speed, outside the park.'

Gaia looked up from writing.

'I see. And who held Master Lush?'

'Mr Monkton did. He caught him.'

'Having recognised him from the park.'

'Yes, Your Honour.'

Gaia paused.

'In the dark.'

Dimm hesitated. Not for the first time with Gaia, he sensed a trap. Belle bit his lip, praying that Dimm would make a mistake. But it was not to be.

Dimm replied in a measured tone.

'His eyesight is good, and I have a sworn statement from Mr Monkton attesting to the fact that he saw Master Lush in the park. What's more that he witnessed the vilest ...'

Gaia raised her hand again.

'I said one charge at a time. That way a picture of the alleged incident can emerge and the part the accused did or did not play within it. Herr Kant, can you please confirm that you were in Royal Victoria Park at the hour described?'

Gerhardt looked thoroughly unengaged with the proceedings.

'*Ja*, of course I was there. It is a park, *nicht wahr*? For public assembly.'

Gaia noted his answer.

'Indeed it is. But it is a feature of public parks in England that they forbid the public's entry after dark. Is it not the case in Königsberg?'

Gerhardt shook his wig.

'*Nein*. In Königsberg, the sun *und* moon, they dictate not when the public the park can be using.'

Gaia recorded his response.

'A reason why you might misunderstand our local ordinance, perhaps.' Then she turned to Lush. 'And now to you, Master Lush. You were apprehended outside the park by a witness by the name of Monkton who attests that he saw you inside the park. One might question the accuracy of that claim given that it was dark. Had you been in the park?'

There was silence in the court. It was clear to Belle that Gaia had provided Lush a lifeline. If his clerk simply denied being in the park, she could rule the evidence against him as unreliable. But Lush, already shaken by the night in gaol, did not have his wits about him. And, as a well-brought-up young man, he had been taught the importance of honesty at all times. Belle yearned to help Lush, to guide him in what to say, but there was nothing he could do.

Broken in spirit, tears welled up in Lush's eyes and he began to sob.

'Yes, Your Honour, I ... .'

But before he could finish, there was a loud shout from the courtroom.

'No!' a voice cried out. 'No!'

It had come from the public benches. More specifically, from the mouth of Belle Nash, who had risen to his feet. All eyes were on him, including those of Gaia, who looked on aghast. Belle made an assertion for all to hear.

'It was I who was in the park with Herr Kant, not Master Lush. This young man, who is my clerk, was merely walking past, on the way to his lodgings. He has been wrongfully arrested. It is I who should be in the dock responding to the charge. Master Lush must be released.'

The announcement had an immediate impact on the courtroom, which descended into disarray. While few dared raise their voices, people muttered loudly and gesticulated this way and that.

Gaia acted swiftly to reassert control and slammed down her gavel.

'Order! I demand order lest you all wish to enjoy the delights of Pulteney Gaol!'

The commotion abated and Gaia got straight to the point. Having done all she could do to assist her friends within the law, she had to be seen to act properly.

'Councillor Nash, you are a respected figure in this city, and,

249

on that basis, I am inclined to accept what you say as being true. Special Constable Dimm, do you concur?'

Dimm, unsure of himself, looked to Pollard for guidance. The councillor, whose greatest wish was to defeat Belle, nodded his assent.

'I suppose Mr Monkton could have got it wrong, and if so, it is Councillor Nash who should be in the dock.'

Gaia closed her eyes for a moment. She had no choice but to say what required saying. Indeed, as a friend, she had to trust that this is what Belle wanted. The best she could offer was a stay in the proceedings, which would have the additional benefit of her lady friends – Miss Prim, in particular, was exhibiting signs of distress – being spared unwholesome evidence.

'Master Lush, you are free to go. But as there is a new defend-ant, we are required to start afresh. It is too late to schedule the hearing for today. I order that Herr Kant be returned to Pulteney Gaol. I further order that he be joined by Councillor Nash. I will consider the charges tomorrow.'

Dimm did not know whether to be triumphant at having Belle arrested or frustrated at the postponement of proceedings. He allowed Lush to descend from the dock and make his way from the court. His path led him past Belle, who took his hand and whispered in the young man's ear.

'Be brave, Mistress Lush, and not ashamed. You have done nothing wrong. Everything will be alright.' At that, he reached into his jacket and handed him the letter he had written earlier. 'Take this letter to Somerset Place this evening. Make certain that Mrs Champion receives it. Promise me, Lucius.'

Lush shook Belle's hand before replying.

'I promise, Sir.'

Then Belle moved towards the dock to be taken to gaol, only to be blocked by Pollard, beaming from ear to ear.

'I was wrong,' he said, grinning jubilantly. 'The hangman will

250

be slipping his noose around your neck after all. You're a fool to take the blame for the ganymede but I won't complain. You deserve to dance.'

Belle leant forward, leaving just an inch between their faces.

'And you'll join Count Ugolino in hell for your treachery, Pollard. In time the world will change, and it will be you in the dock, not me. Now get out of my way. With my pride and honour intact, I've got a gaol to go to.'

NOTES

- Count Ugolino (1220–1289) was an Italian noble of Pisa renowned for his treachery. He met an unhappy end, locked up with two sons and two grandsons in a tower owned by a rival family and starved to death. He is best remembered thanks to Dante's *Inferno,* in which he is placed in the lowest ring of hell, entrapped up to his neck in ice, gnawing at the skull of the Archbishop of Pisa.

CHAPTER XXVII

The last night

GAIA CHAMPION WAS learning fast what it meant to be a magistrate. Not only did she have to justify her decisions to the public in court, she had to do so in private to her friends. Shocked by Gaia's decision to detain Belle Nash and Gerhardt Kant in Pulteney Gaol, Lady Passmore, Mrs Pomeroy and Phyllis Prim descended on the drawing room of Somerset Place.

'Did you really have no choice, Mrs Champion?' said Lady Passmore. 'We were shocked. We were expecting you to put to work our evidence against Hezekiah Porter, as you said you would. That's why we were there! We knew nothing about charges being brought against Councillor Nash and Herr Kant.'

Gaia did her best to provide an explanation.

'In the circumstances, I did not order Mr Porter's arrest, but be assured – we have the evidence to hand. In addition, Mr Cudworth has confessed to supplying animal feed to the store. But I will not have Mr Porter arraigned until this more urgent issue is settled.'

She received welcome support in her stance from Mrs Pomeroy.

'I agree that our greater concern must be for our friends. Both Lady Passmore of Tewkesbury Manor and I have experienced the squalid conditions of that gaol.'

Lady Passmore pursed her lips at the memory. With everyone else having their say, Miss Prim, too, wished to express an opinion, if only she had one.

'I don't understand what happened. I don't understand anything. What I mean to say is, what were Councillor Nash and his Prussian second cousin once removed doing in the park after dark? There would be nothing to see at night apart from owls.'

It made the others pause, for Miss Prim had asked a question that none of them wished to answer. In response, Lady Passmore and Mrs Pomeroy looked out of the window and left it to their hostess to answer. Aware of Miss Prim's sensitivities and her profound ignorance in matters of the flesh, Gaia couched her reply in diplomatic terms.

'The evidence has not been heard, but I rather suspect that that's where bachelors like to meet.'

Unfortunately, Miss Prim was dissatisfied with the answer.

'But they could meet at a restaurant or the Assembly Rooms. There are plenty of lovely places to meet other than a park in the dark. What if it had been raining?'

Lady Passmore stopped looking out the window.

'I expect they could take one of these new umbrellas for men. And sou'westers and waterproof greatcoats. And wet-weather boots.'

Miss Prim thought about this for a moment.

'Even so, it seems most strange. You need daylight to see the flowers. On a cloudy night, they would be trampling over the beds.'

Mrs Pomeroy tried to help.

'That's exactly the problem, Miss Prim. Which is why there's a city ordinance that bars visitors after dark in the first place. To protect the flowerbeds.'

Miss Prim remained unconvinced and, after a moment of silence, Gaia decided the nettle should be grasped. They would never be able to help their friends if they did not speak candidly.

'I appreciate that this is a delicate subject but the truth is that Councillor Nash and Herr Kant are likely to be charged with far worse than entering the park after dark.'

'What could be worse?' queried Miss Prim.

Once again, Lady Passmore and Mrs Pomeroy became distracted by the view from the windows.

'I fear they may be charged with being bachelors because ... ,' Gaia tried, 'because ... oh, for goodness' sake, Lady Passmore of Tewkesbury Manor and Mrs Pomeroy: will you not help?'

'I don't think we can,' replied Lady Passmore. 'Having once been married, Mrs Champion, you are far better qualified than we are to explain the ways of men.'

Gaia's eyes opened wide in disbelief.

'But I am not alone in having been wed, Madam. You have also been married. I'm certain. In fact, you still are.'

'Yes, but Admiral Lord Passmore lives in Jaipur.'

'Then what about you, Mrs Pomeroy?'

Mrs Pomeroy proved similarly reluctant.

'I never really got beyond the wedding cake with my husband. There were ... complications.'

Seeing her friends disagree, Miss Prim emitted a twitter from the couch.

'You all think I'm uneducated. You always do. But I know quite well what's going on.'

The other three looked at her with suspicion. Perhaps Miss Prim was more worldly than they had given her credit for.

'Are you sure?' queried Gaia.

'If you're sure, perhaps you would grace us with your explanation,' added Lady Passmore.

Miss Prim straightened her back in defiance.

'It's because Herr Kant is a foreigner and has been in this country too long. He's outstayed his welcome. That's why he and Councillor Nash are being held.'

Faced with the unknown, Miss Prim's fear of foreigners had come to the fore. Gaia sighed.

'No, Miss Prim. That's not the reason.'

'Then I don't understand the grounds on which either can be charged. Although all will become clear enough when we attend court again tomorrow.'

There was a stunned silence broken by Lady Passmore. None of them could imagine anything more awkward than Miss Prim becoming privy to the carnal intimacies of her bachelor friends. But she was entitled to attend court as much as any citizen.

'That would not be a good idea,' said Lady Passmore.

'Not at all,' agreed Mrs Pomeroy.

'Why not?' demanded Miss Prim. 'I attended court when you were arrested. We all attended court this morning. None of us came to any harm.'

Gaia closed her eyes. This was a conversation, she decided, that should be brought to a close. But how to reach a satisfactory conclusion? She quickly considered her options – of which none were attractive – and chose the least worst among them.

'It would be excellent if all three of you were to attend tomorrow in support of our friends,' she declared, standing up. 'Your presence will also be a great comfort to me in making my rulings, however foolish the law sometimes is. Nevertheless, we must think of dear Miss Prim's wellbeing. She has only just recovered from the assault at the tearoom. We know that bachelors and women are both ill favoured by society, but Miss Prim may be shocked to discover how much more harshly the law treats bachelors than it treats women.'

They all nodded. What Gaia said was true.

'Do you have a solution?' asked Lady Passmore hopefully.

Gaia did, although it required her to make a small fib.

'I do. There is an acceptance in court that ladies of a certain disposition should avail themselves of suitable aids to prevent ... unnecessary incidents of hysteria. I will explain more as I show you out.'

Her friends, however, remained seated. They had not anticipated leaving so soon, and Lady Passmore was unaccustomed to decisions being made on her behalf.

'I wasn't aware that I wanted to depart.'

In response, Gaia replied politely but firmly.

'I would prefer you all to stay, of course, but I have much to prepare. Master Lush delivered a letter from Councillor Nash shortly before you arrived that demands my full attention. I will ring for John to show you to your carriage. While we wait for him, let me explain the following item of headwear you should bring to court tomorrow … .'

W HILE GAIA WAS failing to explain the facts of bachelor life in Somerset Place, Belle and Gerhardt were failing to relish their accommodation in Pulteney Gaol.

'I have stayed in more prepossessing places, certainly,' said Belle, shaking dust and cockroaches from the thin horsehair mattress. 'It is positively Spartan in here.'

Gerhardt could not agree more.

'It is *wilderlich*: the most miserable prison ever I have been in.'

'That's because it's English,' said Belle, laughing weakly, before waking up to what Gerhardt had just said and staring at him in surprise. 'Did I hear you right? You mean that you have been in prison before?'

His Prussian cousin looked at Belle with a coy expression.

'Maybe I have.'

Belle lay down on the mattress to rest and motioned Gerhardt to join him.

'We have lived together for a year but this may be our final night. I'd like to spend it, if I may, sharing memories and understanding a little better what goes on inside that wig of yours.'

Gerhardt did not resist. He lay down and draped himself across Belle's body, resting his head on Belle's chest. It was one of Gerhardt's attributes that, seemingly light as a feather, he could fold himself into another's embrace. Belle gently caressed Gerhardt's cheek.

'So, my dearest,' Belle continued, 'I could ask you what you were doing in Royal Victoria Park but I know the answer. Tell me instead the story of how you previously ended up in gaol.'

'You are wishing to know this, *wirklich*?'

'I'd like nothing better. It seems I have been living with a frightfully dangerous man.'

Gerhardt giggled and Belle hugged him close. It was good to be together, regardless of the location and the circumstance.

'It was in Königsberg.'

'The city of enlightened values.'

'*Ja*, there have many great men from Königsberg been. *Mein* uncle Immanuel Kant, also Herder and Werner, and Reichardt and Hoffmann. But there have also great idiots been in Königsberg. Five years ago, in the month of October, I was at the Albertina studying *und* held a party with *meinen* friends Hänzel *und* Gretel.'

Belle gently pinched his cousin's shoulder.

'You had imaginary, folklore friends?'

Gerhardt shook his head.

'*Nein*, their real names were Siegfried *und* Helmut, but everyone called them Hänzel *und* Gretel. So, we are having a party *und* we are dressing up in the women's clothes ...'

Belle realised he would have to work hard to keep track of this story.

'Isn't Hänzel a boy's name?'

Gerhardt corrected himself.

'But for the party he became Hänzi. Helmut was still Gretel *und* I, *natürlich*, was Brunhilde ...'

Belle laughed.

'The Valkyrie princess.'

Gerhardt responded by poking him in the ribs.

'*Nein*, Belle, this is no joke. I was the witch Queen Brunhilde of Austria, who had for men the most enormous appetite in the *Schlafgemach*.'

257

'Oh, that Brunhilde. I do apologise,' responded Belle. He did not take the story seriously but he was enjoying the telling of it. 'Please carry on.'

'*Also*, we dressed as these ladies *und* then we went to the *Marktplatz* to enjoy the *Oktoberfest* for the excellent *bier*.'

Belle could feel the tale veer dramatically to the right.

'Hang on a minute, Gerhardt. You took part in the city beer festival dressed as Queen Brunhilde and her ladies-in-waiting?'

Gerhardt nodded his head vigorously on Belle's chest.

'*Ja*, it was *fantastisch*. The men, they loved us. We sat on their knees *und* singing the nice drinking songs. *Hier is tzu gutes ok bier. Letzte Nacht betrunken.* So many. But the men, they wanted more. Arnold *und* Lars fancied Hänzi; Gunther *und* Timo wanted Gretel; *und* Steffen, Otto, Ralf *und* Emmerich, they loved me.'

'Good grief. Beer-swilling Prussians on a night out with the girls.'

'I said, "*Herren*, *bitte,* please making a line: then you can all get to play." Let me tell you, Belle, *das Englisch* are at so many things bad. The post-chaises, they never leave on time, your *Kartoffelsalat* is a disgrace, even the excellent Frau Crust would learn from a German apple *strudel*. But *das Englisch* know how to queue. The men in Königsberg, they want everything now now now *und* when filled with the *bier* is worse. There was a tremendous fight. Gretel lost two teeth *und* the soldiers were sent in to arrest everyone. So, we all went to prison for the night. *Und* just in time or else I would have suffered the fate of the real Queen Brunhilde.'

'What happened to her?' asked Belle, unsure as to whether he wanted to know.

'Limb from limb was she torn by her four horses. *Sehr schlecht*.'

'Good God. What a way to go.'

They fell silent with Belle thinking how, at his best, Gerhardt made for the most extraordinary companion. And that in love, as in life, one must accept the hard times to enjoy the good. He gently kneaded Gerhardt's neck as they lay together.

Then Belle decided to face facts and check that Gerhardt understood the reality of their predicament.

'Gerhardt, do you understand the charges we face and what will happen if we are convicted?'

'*Ja*, Belle. We will hang.'

In a strange way, the answer came as a comfort to Belle. It meant that they could talk without misunderstanding.

'I should never have brought you to England. It was selfish of me and a terrible mistake for which I'm sorry.'

For once, Gerhardt relieved Belle of blame.

'*Nein*, Belle, this is *mein* fault. It was I who went to the park with Lucius. What you have done to take his place, it is the act of an honourable man – *die Tat eines ehrenwerten Mannes*.'

Belle again stroked Gerhardt's face with his hand.

'That is most kind, although in truth I had no choice. The law is monstrous, and I could never let Master Lush hang. Nor could I allow you to spend another night in gaol without me.'

They had just fallen silent when a voice called out to them from the neighbouring cell. It was the man whom Gaia had ordered to gaol for making a joke in court.

'Councillor Nash, my apologies to you and your friend for interrupting. This is Titus Smith. I was in court this morning. I'll take whatever punishment Magistrate Champion delivers. I'm not looking to save my skin. But I heard what you and the young foreign fella were saying, and I'd like to apologise to you both for saying what I did. There's nothing funny in killing a man for doing no harm.'

Belle leant forward.

'Your apology is accepted, stranger. Your conscience is clear.'

'Thank you, Sirs,' said Titus Smith. 'Forgive my interruption. I will leave you in peace.'

259

In peace. If only they could, indeed, be at peace, thought Belle, instead of this interminable struggle with a society wedded to prejudice.

They lay on the mattress in the dismal surroundings of the cell and after a few minutes drifted into that space that presages sleep. It is a state of being where one floats, as if carried in the air between life and death itself.

Belle could feel Gerhardt's body meld into his own, their warmth inseparable, two hearts beating in unison. Belle reflected on their past year together and, despite the challenges of living with Gerhardt, had no regrets.

'Belle, do you love me?' Belle's Prussian cousin whispered.

'Yes,' Gerhardt's English cousin replied, for once welcoming the question. 'More than ever.'

'*Und* do you think that I have a beautiful body?'

Tears formed in Belle's eyes at the thought that Gerhardt's need for reassurance would never now be fulfilled.

'Of course I do. And a beautiful mind. Don't ever doubt that I love you, Gerhardt. Fully, wholly, completely. Hold that close, wherever you are, whatever happens to you. Nothing can occur that will ever change that love.'

Gerhardt wrapped his arms around Belle. Fearful for the future, his own tears flowed.

'I love you, Belle. *Du hast mir mehr bedeutet als irgendjemand auf der Welt.* I love you too.'

CHAPTER XXVIII

Sentence is passed

'I have never felt so foolish, Mrs Pomeroy. Must we endure this indignity?' asked Lady Passmore. It was the following morning and the three ladies sat in court awaiting the start of the hearing that would decide whether Belle Nash and Gerhardt Kant should be sent to trial.

Her Ladyship had Mrs Pomeroy to her right and Phyllis Prim to her left. As directed by Gaia Champion the previous evening, each wore a large pair of knitted earmuffs. For their parts, Lady Passmore and Mrs Pomeroy had each lifted a muff from adjacent ears so they could chat.

Mrs Pomeroy was firm in her response.

'Yes, we must, Lady Passmore of Tewkesbury Manor. We cannot possibly risk Miss Prim hearing the details of the evidence against Councillor Nash and Herr Kant. She is a woman of delicate sensitivities. She might never recover from the shock.'

The plan seemed to be working. Miss Prim was in her own silent world, albeit with a determined expression on her face.

Once again, the courtroom was filling up. The bachelor community was well represented, with Arthur Quigley in a group that included Lucius Lush.

Other loyalists included Mrs Crust, who had come to court armed with her rolling pin. She had positioned herself directly behind Councillor Jacob Pollard, who was looking forward to the hearing. He had reviewed the evidence for himself and was content that Gaia had no option but to order a full trial. The scene was set

261

as the door beside the dais opened and Mr Wallop, clerk of the court, appeared.

'All rise and be upstanding for Her Honour, Magistrate Champion.'

The courtroom dutifully rose, the dispatch of Titus Smith still fresh in the memory. Gaia swept in, the magistrate's wig atop her head, a black cape flowing from her shoulders. She climbed the dais, took her chair and motioned for the public to sit. She wasted no time in starting proceedings.

'Instruct the special constable to bring in the accused.'

From the back of the court, Decimus Dimm prodded Belle and Gerhardt forward. The two men ascended the dock as Dimm took a seat on a chair nearby. There was a hum among the public and Gaia fought hard to remain detached. In full view, she had to treat Belle as any other person accused of a crime.

'Councillor Nash, please provide your name, address and occupation for the record.'

Belle responded in similar fashion. In this courtroom, he had to see Gaia not as a friend but as an institution.

'My name, Ma'am, is Bellerophon Nash, known more commonly as Belle. I reside in Gay Street and I am a councillor of this fine city.'

Gaia wrote down the details.

'Thank you. Following yesterday's revelations, please also confirm that you were with Herr Kant in Royal Victoria Park the night before last.'

Belle nodded.

'Indeed, I was in the park with Herr Kant but not, I believe, in contravention of the city ordinance,' he asserted.

Gaia stared at Belle, pleased to note that he was ready to defend himself.

'I note that you were in the park. Please advise the court as to why, in your opinion, your visit was not in contravention.'

Belle took advantage of his height and elevated position in the dock to address the court.

'As the city councillor responsible for the presentation of the park to Her Royal Highness Princess Victoria, I am entitled to unhindered access. Furthermore, I had good reason to be in the park and to be accompanied by Herr Kant.'

The mention of royalty triggered whispering among the public.

'And what was the reason for your visit with Herr Kant?'

Belle paused. On the front bench, Lady Passmore and Mrs Pomeroy listened intently with muffs raised. Miss Prim remained deaf to the surrounding world. Pollard's eyes narrowed.

'The honour of being entrusted as a councillor is great but so is the burden of work that it entails,' said Belle, sparking a few muted guffaws from the benches. 'It has been my intention to establish a Flora & Fauna Society for the park and I sought the advice of my good friend Herr Kant, who knows intimately the great gardens of the Sanssouci Palace in Potsdam. The timing of the visit was dictated by my busy schedule.'

Gaia made notes.

'Herr Kant, is it true that you are something of an expert on gardens?'

'*Ja*, that is correct, Your Honour. I am with the greenhouses of Sanssouci intimately acquainted. They are for the bananas *und* the melons justly famous. *Und* many are *ze* cucumbers that I have admired there.'

Gerhardt's comment led to further tittering in court and a more frustrated expression on Pollard's face. The defence was constructing an unexpectedly robust case and Dimm was yet to speak. His time, however, would come.

Gaia said, 'I have heard sufficient evidence to consider the first charge. I therefore call upon Special Constable Dimm to enquire whether there is any further charge he wishes to make against the accused?'

The question marked a change of atmosphere in the court. The serious business of the day was set to begin.

Dimm rose to his feet and stepped forward to address Gaia.

'Indeed there is a second charge, Your Honour. I have witnesses and sworn statements to the fact that the accused were ...'

He hesitated at first to describe the charge. It would have been easy with the late Magistrate Wood, who would have made a suitably caustic comment and sent the accused to trial in an instant. But with Gaia, it seemed to him almost improper.

She reminded him, 'I can't rule on a charge that isn't made.'

Dimm put his shyness behind him.

'Very well, Your Honour. The accused were seen in a state of undress and engaging in lewd and obscene acts.'

Inevitably, his words caused a sharp reaction from the public. There were competing cries of 'Disgusting' and 'Lies' but a shout of 'Hang the Mollies' was stifled at the sight of Mrs Crust raising her rolling pin. Alarmed, Lady Passmore and Mrs Pomeroy turned to Miss Prim who, cocooned in blissful silence, gave them a wave.

Gaia's gavel swung back into action and three sharp raps brought the court to order.

'I take it, Special Constable Dimm, that the witnesses were yourself and your friends Monkton and Wellow. I have your sworn statements before me.'

'Yes, Your Honour. And with your permission, I will read out excerpts.'

Gaia held up her hand. She was not having her court turned into a laughing house.

'Permission denied. This is not in itself a trial. My job is to consider whether the evidence is sufficient to proceed to one, and I have already read the statements. Be seated, Special Constable Dimm, while I ask the accused to comment on the charge. Councillor Nash?'

Belle filled his lungs. Saving himself and Gerhardt would

264

require all his oratorical skills. The circumstances had to be created to allow Gaia to dismiss the second, more serious charge against them.

'Your Honour, this new charge is vile, repugnant and untrue. It offends against decency. I therefore request the right to study the witness statements before proceeding.'

Gaia gave the request thought before replying.

'That seems reasonable. Clerk to the court, pass the papers to Councillor Nash.'

Wallop passed them over and Belle read them closely. From what was described, Gerhardt and Lush had had an excellent time of it, with the latter's initiation into bachelorhood fully completed. Belle returned the papers, which were in turn taken up by Gerhardt to study.

Belle said, 'These documents contain many sordid details, Your Honour, which I will not repeat before the court today, filled as it is with so many gentlefolk and ladies, but in that detail falsehoods reside. The witnesses by their own admission mistook me for my clerk in the dark. It follows that their descriptions of unwholesome acts cannot be trusted. If they could not recognise my face, how could they provide such an intimate description of my appendage?'

There was much laughter among the public. Dimm's face turned puce and Pollard, for the first time, questioned the wisdom of having allowed Belle to replace Lush in the dock.

'Your appendage?' asked Gaia, suppressing the urge to grin.

'Yes, Your Honour. My appendage.'

'It is a reasonable point you make,' she said.

Belle continued, 'Moreover, the witnesses state that there were other men in the park but who and where were these men? And what were they doing? None is identified in the witnesses' statements; none was arrested. To be charged with unseemly crimes when one is merely measuring the flowerbeds in preparation for the introduction of new cultivars, assisted by an international expert in the horticultural arts, is an outrage.

'I have long harboured the wish to introduce to Bath the auricula and polyanthus, and the ranunculus with its hermaphrodite flowers, especially the ranunculus of Herr Kant's friend and colleague Johann Friedrich von Eschscholtz, the Imperial Russian botanist. And who is not charmed by the sight of native pansies, which so well withstand the challenges of our unwelcoming English climate?

'Moreover, to assess the likely drainage of the soil in order to encourage succulents, which do not tolerate West Country rain, a man is required to bend over; sadly, my arms are not of sufficient length to touch the ground while standing up. Your Honour, I can and do refute these charges absolutely.'

Belle took a half-step back. He had done his best to counter the accusations, but would it suffice?

Dimm now rose to his feet, but Gaia again held up her hand.

'I will pre-empt you, Special Constable. I do not doubt that the statements were written in good faith. You can speak later, but now is the time for the accused to make their comments. Herr Kant?'

In Pulteney Gaol the previous night, Belle had asked Gerhardt to mind his tongue in court, knowing that an attack on England's illiberalism would not aid their cause. Having read the witness statements, however, Gerhardt had something to say.

'*Ja*, these papers are most interesting. Like *mein* uncle, Immanuel Kant, I am on the workings of the mind an expert, as well as on the workings of plant *Biologik*. It is possible to make in good faith a statement but for it to be completely false, especially in the dark *und* in conditions that encourage the imagination. In such a situation, *die Individuen* – in this case Constable Dimm *und* others – do not see what actually happening is, but what they *wish* to be happening. These statements record only the witnesses' desires, in this case Constable Dimm's desire to have sexual connection with a young man. I, too, refute these charges *und* suggest that Constable Dimm receive immediate medical assistance for his condition. If the court requires it, I can recommend *meinen guten* friend, the psychiatrist Carl Wilhelm Ideler in Berlin, who can Constable Dimm's mental drives to a forensic analysis submit, *und* his proximity to insanity calculate. Regarding my organs, unnatural interest has he shown, perhaps because of disharmony in his own mental organ.'

The special constable leapt to his feet, amid a dual outbreak of hilarity and outrage.

'How dare you accuse me of such filth, Prussian scum!'

Gaia cast an eye over to Miss Prim and was glad to see that she remained engrossed in her knitting. She also caught Belle giving her an imploring look. He, like her, scented an opportunity. Down came the gavel again, repeated thrice more until order was restored.

'Herr Kant, your insight and recommendation are noted. It is now the occasion for the special constable. I suspect he may have something to add before I rule. You should feel free to speak your mind in my court, Special Constable Dimm.'

Incandescent with anger, Dimm jumped at the opportunity.

'I will speak, Your Honour. That man Herr Kant has labelled my good name!'

Gaia replied calmly, '"Libelled", Special Constable. Or perhaps I am wrong. In your opinion, what have you been labelled?'

'It is Councillor Nash, not I, who is the peddler,' he declared, trying desperately to recall the expressive word that Councillor Pollard had used to describe Belle.

Further laughter in court indicated that he had formed the word wrongly. He cursed as he tried to correct himself. 'A ped ... ped ...'

Belle leant forward and seized the moment.

267

'A pedagogue, perhaps?' he suggested. 'Or a pedicurist.'

Dimm looked around for help. Pollard attempted to mouth the word 'pederast' but to no avail.

'Neither of those,' Dimm said. 'You know what I mean, damn you.'

Belle's eyes widened as if in a moment of illumination.

'A *pedologist*, perchance. I think you mean that Herr Kant and I are both pedologists, Sir, which I openly acknowledge.'

Dimm fell headlong into the trap.

'That's exactly what I mean, Councillor Nash, and thank you for sealing your own fate. You're a pedologist. And what you were doing in the park with Herr Kant proves it. It was disgusting. I rest my case!'

There might have been a wider response in the courtroom if more of the public had known what pedology entailed. Instead, a silence descended as the public looked to Gaia to define the word. She made a point of taking her time and reached across her table to consult several large books, one of which was a dictionary. She made more notes and only after several minutes had passed did she put down her quill.

'I have made a decision,' she announced to a full but silent courtroom. 'On the second charge of engaging in pedology, namely the study of soil samples ...' – her words were met with raucous cries of celebration from the supporters of Belle and Gerhardt as the meaning of the word was revealed for them – '... which corresponds wholly with Councillor Nash's account of visiting the park for the purpose of establishing a Flora & Fauna Society. Do you plead innocent or guilty to the charge, Councillor Nash?'

Belle smiled. On the public benches, Pollard gritted his teeth and clenched his fists.

'Guilty, Your Honour,' said Belle happily, before Dimm could utter a word.

'And you, Herr Kant?'

268

'*Gleich*! Total guilty.'

'Very well,' said Gaia. 'Your pleas are accepted.'

She made some final notes before using her gavel.

'Silence in court,' shouted Wallop.

What noise there was abated as Gaia readied herself to announce her first judgement.

'This has been a contentious, some might say peculiar, case. The identity of one of the two accused has changed, bringing into doubt the integrity of the special constable's evidence. Nevertheless, some facts are certain. Councillor Nash and Herr Kant freely admit to being in Royal Victoria Park at an hour prohibited by city ordinance.

'Councillor Nash, however, says he is not bound by the ordinance given his duties relating to the park and his intention of establishing a Flora & Fauna Society. In this regard, Herr Kant, an international specialist in royal parks, was his guest and adviser.

'I have studied the ordinance and its language is unclear. Where doubt arises, reasonableness should take its place. On the first charge, therefore, of improperly entering the park at a proscribed hour, I find that the two accused have no case to answer. I recommend the ordinance be redrafted to provide greater clarity.'

On the benches, Lady Passmore and Mrs Pomeroy clapped. Miss Prim, with her earmuffs firmly in place, waved with both hands.

Gaia continued, 'There is a second charge, of course; one that changed in nature during the course of proceedings. Special Constable Dimm finally set the charge as being one of pedology without proper authorisation or, in layman's terms, the illicit collection of soil samples. Both Councillor Nash and Herr Kant pled guilty to this charge. It is on this charge that I shall now, as I am able to as magistrate, pass sentence.'

The silence in the court became ever more complete. It had suddenly dawned on those present that the accused were far from

269

in the clear. They had, after all, pled guilty to a misdemeanour and their fate was uncertain.

Gaia said, 'I understand that members of a prospective Flora & Fauna Society are likely to engage in pedology, but such activity must be regulated. One might think that there is plenty of soil in Royal Victoria Park but if every visitor helped themselves, there would shortly be none left. Moreover, this is a royal park with royal soil. This deepens the gravity of the offence.

'Some might argue for leniency but the people of Bath should know that I will not tolerate corruption and I will not abide transgression. The improper collection of soil samples is against the law and must be punished.

'I hereby order Herr Gerhardt Kant to pay a fine of three pounds. The court further demands that he return forthwith to his home city of Königsberg. I similarly order Councillor Nash to pay a fine of three pounds. In addition, the court orders that he depart these shores for a period of four years in exile to the island of Grenada in the Caribbean, there to reflect on his indiscretion.

'There is no need for Herr Kant and Councillor Nash to return to gaol, so long as the terms of this judgement are met in full and within a week. That is my ruling. The case is closed.'

Gaia slammed down her gavel and stood up.

'All rise and be upstanding for Magistrate Champion,' declared Wallop as Gaia exited.

She left behind a courtroom stunned by the severity of her sentence, with no one bar Dimm and Pollard noting that Belle and Gerhardt had escaped on a far lesser charge than that intended.

'Does this new magistrate of ours have the power to deport?' asked one councillor.

'I don't know,' said another, 'but would you want to risk deportation by challenging her on it?'

'I thought Mrs Champion and Councillor Nash were friends,' said Mrs Crust to a neighbour.

'If they are, I wouldn't want to be her enemy,' came the reply.

The public benches emptied as people filed out of the building. They left behind Lush – who, with Mr Quigley, was waiting to give Belle his thanks – and the three sirens: Lady Passmore, Mrs Pomeroy and Miss Prim.

'You can take your earmuffs off now, Miss Prim,' shouted Mrs Pomeroy.

'I'm so sorry, Mrs Pomeroy,' replied Miss Prim, 'but I can't hear you.'

Finally, Belle and Gerhardt appeared. Normally they would have embraced the others, but their sentence seemed more of a defeat than a triumph.

Lady Passmore summed it up for them all.

'I wonder, Councillor Nash, what Mrs Champion thought she was doing? She could have dismissed the case in its entirety.'

Belle shrugged and said nothing. Had he won – or lost?

The answer lay with Gaia, who had walked back to her office with her head hung low. The effort of overseeing the proceedings in a neutral manner had taken its toll. In her office, she ordered Wallop from the room.

'Go. And don't return. I no longer require your services as clerk.'

She leant on her desk, breathing heavily. Then, unable to hold back her emotions any longer, she swept her arms across the desk, sending papers, quills and inkpots flying through the air.

She shouted in anger at the sentence she had handed down.

'Why did you make me do it?!'

Pulling open a drawer from the desk, she retrieved the letter that Lush had delivered from Belle the previous evening. She placed it on the desk and slammed a fist repeatedly upon it.

'Dammit, Belle, this is *your* doing!' she cried, weeping. 'I would have set you free. Now we face years without you. What have you made me do?!'

271

CHAPTER XXIX

To distant climes

THERE ARE OCCASIONS when the good of the many and the good of the few come into conflict. It had not been Belle Nash's intention to part with Gerhardt Kant but, when presented with the choice, he had chosen to put progress before personal comfort. It had caused him pain, but forgoing a life with his Prussian bachelor was, he decided, a necessary sacrifice in ensuring that Gaia Champion remained Bath's magistrate.

The terms of Gaia's ruling, that the accused pay their fines and depart British shores within a week, left little time. Gerhardt was initially distressed and interpreted the judgement, ridiculous in its severity, as further proof of the meanness of the English *Geist*. But Belle consoled him with the thought that he had the instinct of a survivor and would soon adapt to his new circumstances – that Prussia would even welcome the experience he had gained overseas.

'Gerhardt,' he said, 'this has been a year that neither of us will ever forget. We find ourselves in the hands of the Fates – and very possibly the Furies too (let their name remain unspoken). Our ships now sail on opposite courses, I into the realms of Oceanus, you beyond those of Poseidon. Lest we broach the waves and end up tossed on the spray-beaten reefs, let us join hands and place our trust in Leukothea and Palaemon: "αλλ᾽ επιθεις λίθων εματου επί την καρδίαν, καθησυχάσομαι υμείς δ᾽υγιαίνετε, φίλοι."

'Write to me often from Königsberg. Post letters to Gaia and she will forward them to Grenada. Let her know your address, so I can write back to you. And when I return in four years' time, I will endeavour to visit Königsberg. This need not be the end of our friendship.'

Gerhardt, who had only taken Greek until the age of eleven, promised that he would.

'In four years will I the science of *Regression* have perfected, *und* the world a happier place will be. *Ja*, we each have great challenges to overcome.'

The immediate challenge was how to fit Gerhardt's wardrobe, with his enormous wigs, onto a single stagecoach. Belle planned to have Gerhardt packed and on his way in four days, leaving a further three days to arrange his own journey to Bristol and thence by merchant ship to the British West Indies.

On the morning of Gerhardt's departure, Lucius Lush arrived at Gay Street to assist with the luggage and to say goodbye.

'You honour us with your presence, Lucy,' said Belle. 'Gerhardt will as always be gratified to see you. As am I.'

'Are you sure, Sir? I will understand if you wish to share these final moments with Herr Kant privately.'

'Tears have been shed,' acknowledged Belle, 'but now it is time to move on. Let us grasp hands and swear on Uranus to eternal friendship.'

And so it was. The three men, whose lives had become so inextricably entwined in the previous two weeks, embraced. Then luggage was loaded, boxes of wigs hauled and Gerhardt prepared to climb up into the carriage.

He gave Belle a final hug.

'*Mach's gut, mein Schatz.* Is everything loaded? The twelve wigs … ?'

'All twelve,' said Belle.

'And the Cyprus powder to dust them?'

'And the Cyprus powder.'

Gerhardt nodded.

273

He began, '*Und du – mein Cousin zweiten Grades*, who has on one occasion been removed – do you ... ?'

There was no need to finish the sentence.

'You know I do. Forever.'

They held hands until, with reluctance, they agreed to part.

'*Mein Herz weint*,' whispered Gerhardt, clutching at his heart.

Belle closed the door and, for a final time, their fingers touched through the open window. Then, with the crack of a horsewhip, the carriage moved off, Gerhardt's head through the window looking back. The movement of air caused a fog of powder to blow out of his wig, wispy as clouds of cirrus that slowly, like the man himself, disappeared from view.

Belle and Lush turned and walked back into the house. Gay Street would never be the same again.

'Sir, I would be happy to stay and help prepare for your own departure,' said the clerk.

Belle accepted gratefully.

'That would be kind. Word comes to me from Mrs Champion that the three Graeae – Dread, Horror and Alarm – intend to visit and say their farewells. Tea and cake will be required, and that will leave little time to complete my packing, so let us get started.'

'And Mrs Champion, Sir?'

Belle closed the front door.

'She cannot visit without injury to herself. A judge cannot be also a friend, so I must part without the tenderness of her adieu. It is unbearably hard – she is the closest of friends – but so the gods have willed it.

'ὁπότε οι θεοί το θέλησαν,' translated Lush.

'Good man!' said Belle, delighted. Lush would be missed too.

O VER THE NEXT three days, Gaia consolidated her position further as magistrate. Wallop was replaced by a temporary clerk, Decimus Dimm was removed as special constable and the brother of her husband's former clerk was appointed in his stead. Gaia received support from Chairman Camshaft who, after the court hearing, expressed delight that his great-grandson had been saved from the gallows.

'Dreadful waste of rope, hanging bachelors,' he told her. 'You can count on my backing until the day I die. Although that might be quite soon.'

Belle's request that they not meet was painful and impossible to explain to Lady Passmore, Mrs Pomeroy and Phyllis Prim. It was no surprise that their final tea party with Belle was a melancholic affair, made worse by Gaia's absence.

Miss Prim handed over a new tea cosy and a pair of woollen gloves for Belle to take with him to Grenada.

'In case it is cold,' she said.

'Thank you, Miss Prim. They will be most useful, I am sure.'

Mrs Pomeroy advised, 'Remember to consume plenty of fruit while sailing.'

'And take quantities of liquorice,' Lady Passmore added. 'It helps, I hear, on interminable sea voyages when accompanied only by rum-soaked sailors. Alternatively, eat nuts.'

A S FOR GAIA, there was no opportunity to share feelings and regrets. All she could do was to read and re-read the letter from Belle that Lush had delivered to her the evening after she had sent him to Pulteney Gaol. Seated in the magistrate's office ahead of the day's proceedings, she opened her desk drawer and took it out once more.

Dear Gaia,

Who would have thought that so much could arise from the failure of a soufflé to rise? But we live in modern times and our world is beset by such reminders of its fragility.

Pollard and Dimm are weak – the one, arrogant; the other, a fool.

275

By the time you have received this, I will have replaced dear Lush as the one accused. I have some hopes that proceedings in court will provide the opportunity for Gerhardt and me to escape the charges that they are framing against us, but I cannot allow you, Ma'am, to conspire with us or in any way assist our cause.

If you dismiss all charges against us, you risk your neutrality – the very cornerstone of the career you have chosen. There will be murmurings and mutterings, noises and agitations, and before long factions will call for you to be removed. You cannot risk that.

It is often said that ours is the Age of Enlightenment, but we would be worse fools than Dimm to believe it. If enlightened values can be won, they can more easily be lost.

Your selection as magistrate is a mighty advance. Never before has England appointed a member of the fair sex to wield authority over brutes. From such a start, a broader campaign can be advanced: female rights of suffrage and rights independent of men. Then, of course, rights for bachelors too. To achieve all that, we must first secure your victory.

In this context, I fear my time with Gerhardt may have run its course, regardless of this evil prosecution. He has too much to accomplish in life to remain in Bath and is at odds with our petty English ways.

I, too, have other work to do. As you are now aware, my aunt has come into possession of a plantation on the island of Grenada. What I did not tell you is that she has asked me to oversee its administration.

Neither my aunt nor I could countenance the good name of our family being besmirched by the slavery currently practised on that isle. If I were there, I could end it.

But I could do more than that. Human kindness demands that I free the families that have been lately and cruelly enslaved and grant them the land on which they labour. Every day I linger is another day of unimaginable misery for them.

Emancipating the slaves can only be done by my travelling to the British West Indies. But I am committed to my work at Guildhall. The dilemma has preyed on me, Ma'am, since I became aware of it two weeks ago. Last week I came to a decision: I must give up my council-lorship and cross the seas. Then this business with Pollard and Dimm came up and their framing of charges.

Madam: if Pollard's charges bring me down, my mission in the Indies is also brought down. I implore you, then: when you find us guilty, as you must, find us guilty on a lesser charge. Do so with delib-eration: be hard, be firm. Find us guilty – and banish us. You will win the admiration of the courtroom and its fear. Both will strengthen your position enormously thereby.

Do so and I will vacate Bath for some years. With this in mind – with the deepest regret – I must sell Gay Street to secure me against an uncertain future. I merely beg that my beloved porcelain and other possessions are packed and placed in safe storage to await my return.

Finally, Mistress Lush: he is an excellent and diligent clerk but, on my departure, will no longer have employment. Knowing that the days of Mr Wallop are numbered, I recommend Lucy to you. Take him as your clerk and he will repay you with loyalty and intelligence a hundredfold.

These are momentous times. Knowing that we act aright must hearten us. Feel no sadness, therefore, in passing sentence upon us tomorrow, but be strong! One day I will return and pray, on that day, to be restored to the bounteous friendship that we have always en-joyed hitherto.

Your ever devoted friend,
Belle

Gaia put down the letter. Although it caused her much distress, she agreed with the logic of its argument. The next four years would be lonely without Belle and she expected many a battle in her role as magistrate. She would not only have to overcome opposition to her womanhood but to the measures she took to confront corruption. She would become the prey of two factions.

It was shortly before nine o'clock when there was a knock on her door and her new special constable entered.

277

'Good morning, Magistrate Champion. As instructed, I have drawn up a list of those who were taken into custody overnight. Just two. A drunk who threw a stone through a haberdasher's window and a petty thief who stole some candles from the abbey.'

'Very good,' she replied. 'I will dispatch them briefly. After that, I have two tasks for you.'

The constable, Hugh Littleton by name, was eager and attentive. He was proud of his appointment and respectful of Gaia.

'What tasks, Madam?'

'The first is a favour. I would ask you to go to Councillor Nash's home in Gay Street. He is due to leave for Bristol by midday. At his house, you will find Master Lucius Lush. Please ask him to come to this office once Councillor Nash has departed.

'And second, you did fine work last week in taking a statement from Mr Cudworth about selling old cattle-feed to Porter's store. I delayed the arrest of Hezekiah Porter until Herr Kant and Councillor Nash had met the terms of their sentences. With those terms now assured, I wish you to arrest Mr Porter this afternoon and arraign him before me tomorrow morning. Understood?'

Littleton nodded.

'Entirely, Your Honour.'

'Very well. Let us proceed and tackle the matters to hand.'

BY THE EVENING, Belle was in Bristol and on board the merchant ship *Dochfour*, a two-deck three-master built in 1810, with his luggage loaded and his personal effects unpacked in the small cabin that would be his home for the next twelve weeks. Although the ship was not due to sail until the morning, Belle went up the gangway early to fulfil the deadline of Gaia's sentence.

He then had a night of fitful sleep and it was with some relief when the ropes were cast off next day and the sails raised, leaving the *Dochfour* to drift into the Bristol Channel.

Belle did not make his way to the prow – this was not the moment for melodrama – but to the starboard deck, where he could watch his past recede, even while the winds blew him steadily towards his future.

He imagined where Gerhardt would be. Having arrived in London, he would now be on board a coaster heading east to Rotterdam. He thought of Gaia, who might at this moment have Hezekiah Porter in the dock. He smiled at the thought that Lush would be her new clerk.

And then he thought of himself: of the weeks aboard this ship and of the distant shores that awaited him, shores to which he was travelling in freedom, but to which so many before him had journeyed in chains, stolen from their homes and families in Africa, traded like raw goods for profit. Life, he concluded, was not easy but his – even as a bachelor in England – was gentler than most.

Then, unexpectedly, he found himself sobbing for all he was leaving behind, for the failure of his time with Gerhardt and, as he looked forward to the next four years, for the state of a world that enslaved and belittled and demeaned – and did not care.

He wiped his tears away. He told himself that Gaia would not wish him to cry. And though with each passing second the distance between them grew, he took courage in knowing that he and Gaia were kindred spirits. No ocean could keep them apart. When bonded by friendship and honoured by love, adversities could be overcome.

The time apart, he acknowledged, would change them in ways yet unknown. But he would be back for new tales to be told. And for the wondrous, comic, tragic experience of life in Royal Bath to unfold.

END OF PART ONE

279

ACKNOWLEDGEMENTS

A collective enterprise

MY THANKS GO first to my insomniac editor, Dr Stephen Games, who burned gallons of midnight oil working on the text and context of this novel. Given that *The Gay Street Chronicles* is a series, I fear there will be plenty more sleepless nights to come. Also, to Michael Holman, the peerless former Africa Editor of the *Financial Times*, to whom I reported in the early 1990s and who introduced me to Stephen. Thank you, both.

There have been many others who have advised and supported me on the series and whose feedback I am deeply grateful for: Christopher Rodriguez, Alasdair McWhirter, Rosanna McWhirter, Daphne Wright, William Teasdale (and his mother and her dog), Sanjeev Bhopal, Jane Kingdom (and her mother), Louise Hobhouse, Robert Hobhouse, Gary Griffith, Elena Hill, Orwi Manny Ameh, Michael Lashley, Jessica Oura, Biyama Kadafu, Munuela Saragosa and my Number One Fan, Adrian Finch, among others.

My heartfelt thanks to my siblings Mark, Nick and John, who taught me how to laugh and from whom I have received unconditional love and support. Finally, to my English teachers: Miss Harnett, Mr Venning, Mr Wood and Mr Bennett.

Writing is often considered a solitary occupation. For me, in truth, it has been a collective enterprise and I have been reliant along the creative path on the professionalism, friendship and wit of others. I hope that, on publication, this collective will include a bevy of readers; I welcome each one of you on the journey ahead.

Other titles from EnvelopeBooks

www.envelopebooks.co.uk

Spy Artist Prisoner

GEORGE TOMAZIU

Artist George Tomaziu expected to be imprisoned for monitoring Nazi troop movements during the war but thought that his heroism would be recognised when Socialism came to Romania. He was terribly mistaken.

EB10

Postmark Africa

MICHAEL HOLMAN

Made an Amnesty Prisoner of Conscience while he was under house arrest as a student in Southern Rhodesia, the author went on to document Africa's emergence from colonialism as Africa Editor of the *Financial Times*.

EB1

Why My Wife Had To Die

BRIAN VERITY

Huntington's disease is a terrible wasting condition that sufferers acquire from a parent and that wrecks lives. In this angry memoir, the author vents his rage at society, lawmakers, health services and the Church for not grasping the need, as he sees it, to legalise compulsory sterilisation and assisted dying.

EB9

Non-fiction from EnvelopeBooks

www.envelopebooks.co.uk

My Modern Movement

ROBERT BEST

London's Festival of Britain in 1951 marked the belief that Modern design was visually, morally and commercially superior. Robert Best, the UK's leading lighting manufacturer of the period, thinks the dice were loaded. This is his memoir.

EB8

A Road to Extinction

JONATHAN LAWLEY

When Britain colonised the Andamans in 1857, the welfare of its African pygmy inhabitants was of no concern. Nine tribes died out. Dr Lawley now assesses the three remaining tribes' prospects and the legacy of his grandfather, who ran the colony in the early 1900s.

EB2

From Bedales to the Boche

ROBERT BEST

Bedales, the progressive boarding school founded by J.H. Badley in 1893, instilled values that sustained many of its pupils through the rest of their lives. Robert Best recalls its influence on him as an enthusiastic army recruit in 1914 and, from 1916, in the Royal Flying Corps.

EB3

Novels from EnvelopeBooks

www.envelopebooks.co.uk

A Sin of Omission

MARGUERITE POLAND

Emotionally intense tragedy, set in South Africa in the 1870s. A gifted black preacher, hand-picked for training in England as a missionary, is then neglected by the Church he loves. Based on a true story. *Winner of the 2021 Sunday Times CNA 'Book of the Year' Award in South Africa.*
EB6

Mustard Seed Itinerary

ROBERT MULLEN

When Po Cheng falls into a dream, he finds himself on the road to the imperial Chinese capital. Once there he rises to the heights of the civil service before discovering that there are snakes as well as ladders. Carrollian satire at its best.
EB5

Frances Creighton: Found and Lost

KIRBY PORTER

Love demands trust but trust is a lot to ask for victims of abuse. Having been bullied by two teachers in Belfast as a boy, Michael Roberts suppresses his childhood pains until the death of a girlfriend years later forces him to revisit lost memories.
EB7